MW01146173

KILLER *IN* PARADISE

MilaBooks.com™

FICTION

DANGEROUS WATERS
A young woman's perilous journey of adventure and romance,
from the California Pacific to the Mexican Caribbean

WHALES' ANGELS
A husband and wife battle whalers in a
seagoing adventure of international intrigue and murder

FIREWORKS
Terrorists plan an explosive Fourth of July for New York.
Can two divers and a dolphin foil their deadly plot?

NEAR MISS
Spies, treasure hunters, and Cozumel divers
collide in a Caribbean thriller

NONFICTION

BUBBLES UP!
Buoyant Adventures in Planet Ocean

BASIC UNDERWATER PHOTOGRAPHY

CHILDREN

HARRY HAWKSBILL HELPS HIS FRIENDS
(Best Publishing Company)

"This terrific little book has everything. The story is fantasy, but the underwater color photos showing the interaction of reef characters are real. The information about turtles is easy to understand, and the fish learn a great lesson about befriending those who are not always just like you. It even has easy, fun questions at the end to enhance the learning."

—Cathy Church
award-winning underwater photographer, teacher, author

KILLER *IN* PARADISE

A NOVEL

Paul J. Mila

MilaBooks.com™

Copyright ©2017 Paul J. Mila

Milabooks.com
75 Titus Avenue
Carle Place, NY 11514

Edited by Magnifico Manuscripts, LLC
www.magnificomanuscripts.com

Interior Layout/Design by MINDtheMARGINS, LLC
www.mindthemargins.com

Cover Design by Naomi Blinick

Front and back cover photos:
Blood Photo © jamenpercy - stock.adobe.com
Palm on Island Photo ©Iakov Kalinin - stock.adobe.com
Divers Underwater Photo ©Jag_cz - stock.adobe.com

Interior photos used with permission.
"Blue-ringed octopus Hapalochlaena fasciata"
by OpenCage.info is licensed under CC BY 2.0

Library of Congress Control Number: 2017914700

ISBN-13: 978-1-9765-6575-5

Printed in the United States of America

DEDICATION

To the many friends and dive buddies
I have had the pleasure to meet.

Of course, to my grandchildren
Ava, Max, Emma, Sophie, and Luke.
May you enjoy a lifetime of adventures,
above and below the waves.

PREFACE

While researching material for a new adventure, I came across a story about a unique archeological artifact in *The Portolan*, the quarterly journal of the Washington Map Society. I also visited the New York City Public Library, which houses a replica of the artifact. The history and details about this unique and valuable object astounded me, especially the possibility of a connection with the ancient Mayans.

Australian native Layle Stanton, the real-life inspiration for my fictional character Dayle Standish, owns an art gallery (LaLa [Latin American Lifestyle and Art] Art Gallery and Garden Café) in Roatan, Honduras, and makes regular trips through Mexico and Central America to acquire various art objects for her gallery. Two powerful words "What" and "If" had stimulated my imagination when I wrote *Near Miss,* my previous Cozumel-based dive adventure/thriller, several years ago. Those two words resurfaced in my brain, and creative thoughts percolated again. I thought, *What if,* while Dayle was hunting for this valuable object in a part of the world that many people consider paradise, her path intersected that of a vicious killer seeking the same object?

In *Killer in Paradise,* the characters I introduced in *Near Miss* (Dale Standish, Jeff Becker, and Fulvio Cuccurullo) return, joining longtime regulars Terry Hunter-Manetta and Joe Manetta. In this story, I added new characters named after friends I have met over the years while diving and traveling throughout the Caribbean (Greg Dietrich, Mike Handy, and Jeff and Jamie Margolies).

People say fiction writers steal from real life. I enthusiastically plead guilty as charged, and hope you enjoy reading this tropical thriller as much as I enjoyed writing the story.

Sincerely,
Paul J. Mila
Carle Place, New York
Cozumel, Mexico

CHAPTER 1

Xcaret, the Mexican Yucatan
1535

Eighteen-year-old Tepeu walked quickly through the thick, green underbrush to the clearing where he and his lover always met. He padded along quietly, listening, alert for any sound. He stopped when the leaves rustled a short distance away. He heard a voice whisper.

"Tepeu. Over here."

He spun toward the sound and saw two dark eyes peering out from a bush. As he ran toward her, she stood. Seventeen-year-old Akna rushed into his waiting arms and they grasped each other tightly in a breathless embrace. Tepeu wore only a simple loincloth, and Akna wore a traditional Mayan huipil, a long skirt decorated with embroidered flowers. They spoke no words as they clung together. Tepeu felt Akna's firm breasts press against his muscular chest. His fingers stroked her long, silky, braided hair. He pulled her head back and kissed her hard on the lips. "Akna, my Akna, I love you."

She moaned softly as she felt his body react to her, and her knees buckled.

"Not here. Come with me," Tepeu gasped. He took her hand and they stumbled through the trees and bushes until they reached the small clearing, their special, secret place. He threw a blanket to the ground and they immediately sank to their knees as their hands eagerly explored each other's bodies in a surge of teenage passion.

The two were so consumed in making love that they never heard a branch snap in the distance. Nor did they detect the sound of leather sandals shuffling closer, following their trail. The unseen presence lurked close, hidden by the thick jungle, watching their every move, listening to their every sound. Their hidden observer grew angrier by the moment.

Tepeu had been careful, making sure no one had trailed him from the village. Akna was not as careful. Her powerful father's most trusted friend, Balam, had followed her at her father's request. Named after the Mayan jaguar god who protected the community, he remained quiet and still, hiding in the tree line. His coal-black eyes burned with fury as he watched Akna and Tepeu consummate their love. He squeezed the handle of his sacrificial knife tightly in his rage, turning his knuckles white. He drew the knife from its scabbard. But then, Balam remembered that Akna's father ordered him only to report what he discovered, not to act. He slid his knife back into its resting place and left so silently that the two young lovers never knew he was there.

Balam reached the village and went directly to the grand home of the chief, Coyopa, named after the Mayan god of thunder. The chief greeted his friend expectantly, querying him silently with his eyes. Balam drew a breath before he spoke. "I wish you had been wrong, but your suspicions were correct. Your daughter, who you betrothed to another man, is no longer a virgin."

Coyopa squeezed his eyes shut and gritted his teeth. "Who violated my Akna?"

"Tepeu, the son of—"

"Yes, yes, I know who he is," Coyopa replied, spitting the words bitterly. "He is not worthy to stand in my daughter's shadow. This explains all the recent problems in our village. The babies born dead, the women dying in labor. Our crops wither for lack of rain. It all makes sense now. The gods are angry. My own daughter, who I have promised in marriage to the son of another chief, has betrayed our family and our people."

"But there is hope," Balam said. "Next month we make the crossing to Chankanaab, where you can make a significant sacrifice to Ixchel. The goddess will expect blood, and she will make all things better."

"Yes, Balam. I trust you to protect our people with your silence. Thank you for your loyalty. I will need you again."

"You know I remain always at your service," Balam said, bowing as he left his king.

Coyopa knew whose blood Ixchel, the primary goddess of the moon, fertility and childbirth, would require. But angry as he was, he could not bear to sacrifice his only child, which is what his people would demand if they knew the truth about Akna's indiscretion. Tepeu would die instead. Coyopa knew the blood from a common defiler would not appease Ixchel sufficiently for her to lift the curse afflicting his people. Ixchel would also demand that he give her his most precious possession. His eyes fell on the strange round object he had guarded for over twenty years. He stepped over to the small altar he had erected in his private chamber, where he prayed, asked the Mayan gods for guidance, and contemplated the universe as he knew it.

This mysterious object provided insight into that universe and the creation of the earth, far beyond what his religion revealed. Coyopa lifted a thin white veil and stared at the object. He picked it up and his fingers caressed it, almost reverently, as gently as if he were stroking a newborn baby's head. He looked at the strange markings and his thoughts drifted back in time.

Twenty-three years earlier, Coyopa was a young warrior chief, standing on the shore supervising the preparation of his tribe's battle canoes. Several young men came running, gesturing toward the sea, a channel which ran between the mainland and an island they called Kùutsmil, Mayan for Land of the Swallows. He ran back with them and looked where they pointed. What he saw mystified him. Far in the distance, a boat was coming in their direction. The fact they could see it at such a great distance, almost to the horizon, meant it was a very large boat. He was astounded when he saw puffy white clouds pulling the boat.

Are the gods themselves sending this strange boat to us? he wondered.

When the strange vessel neared shore, he realized the clouds were actually large white cloths that captured the wind. Coyopa and his warriors watched the boat stop as the men aboard pulled in the white cloths, then lowered small boats and began rowing to shore.

The two groups eyed each other warily on the beach, but then the strange visitors opened trunks containing beads, trinkets, and other items the Mayans found appealing. Through sign language, the visitors made it clear they wanted to trade their items for food and fresh water. Eventually they invited the natives aboard their ship.

The captain realized Coyopa was his counterpart and welcomed him into his cabin. Inside, his eyes fell upon a round object decorated with strange markings. The captain noticed his interest in the object and let him hold it. Coyopa turned it around in his hands, examined the markings, and tried to figure out what they meant. Using sign language and the strange round object, the captain made him understand where the ship had come from and where they were located now.

Coyopa was dumbfounded. This challenged his understanding of his world and the universe. *But if this object brought these strange visitors here, their story must be true,* he thought. He decided he must possess this representation of the earth, with the knowledge and power it represented. When the captain refused the chief's offer to trade for the object, Coyopa drew his battle-ax and smashed the captain's skull with one swing. Grabbing the object, he ran outside and shouted his tribe's war cry. In the ensuing battle, the European visitors fought off the natives using their superior weapons. They weighed anchor and escaped when the Mayans finally retreated.

Coyopa's thoughts returned to the present. His fingers traced unknown land masses labeled with strange markings, separated by unfamiliar oceans, places he dreamed of visiting, perhaps even conquering. He sighed as he realized an ordinary blood sacrifice would not appease the goddess, but he would not give up his daughter. He knew he must also give his most treasured object to Ixchel as an offering.

In the days leading up to the ceremonial crossing from the mainland to Chankanaab on the island of Kùutsmil, he and Balam made plans to carry out the offering and sacrifice.

Balam informed Tepeu he would have the honor of carrying the offering to Ixchel. A strong young man who could swim underwater was required to reach the goddess, who resided in a cave partially underwater. The Mayans called these natural formations a ts'onot (cenote).

When preparations were completed, the entire village assembled on the shore of the mainland and boarded dozens of canoes for a ten-mile journey across the channel to Kùutsmil. Tepeu sat in the front of the largest craft with Coyopa's family, holding a sealed golden urn containing the representation of the earth. Behind him sat Akna, who beamed with pride. Behind them in the stern sat her father, glaring with hatred toward Tepeu.

Upon reaching the island, the group assembled on the beach, waiting for Ixchel to signal she was ready to receive their sacrifice. They waited for an entire day until finally they heard a low moaning sound emanating from the sacred lagoon several hundred yards inland, like the sound of a woman in agony.

"Ixchel calls. She is ready to receive us," Coyopa announced. He turned to Tepeu. "Bring our offerings to the goddess. Balam will accompany you with the blood sacrifice."

The two men set off for the sacred lagoon. Balam led a goat he would slaughter and Tepeu followed, carrying the urn. The assembled group waited on the beach for their return. When the two men reached the lagoon, Balam stopped.

"Hold the rope tightly," he said. As Tepeu held the goat on a short leash, Balam stepped behind the animal and slit its throat. They dragged the dead goat to the lagoon edge and he pointed to a rock painted with the image of the goddess Ixchel. "There, beneath the rock is the opening to her cave. Bring the sacrifice and leave it on her altar."

Tepeu pulled the goat into the lagoon, swam to the rock, took a deep breath, and submerged. He swam forward and then surfaced, finding himself inside a large cavern. Several narrow shafts of light beamed down through limestone holes, providing just enough light to see a flat stone slab. He saw dozens of bones and several human skulls on the slab. He hauled the goat onto the slab and then returned to Balam.

"Now leave this offering for the goddess," he said, handing the urn to Tepeu.

Tepeu took the urn and dived back inside the cave. He deposited the urn in the middle of the stone slab as the moaning sound grew louder. He did not hear someone surface just behind him. Tepeu turned, his eyes wide open, startled to see Balam holding his raised knife.

"You are the real blood sacrifice for Ixchel!" Balam shouted, as he plunged the knife into Tepeu's chest. Then, with a quick twist of his wrist he excised Tepeu's still-beating heart as blood poured over his hand.

The last thing Tepeu saw before he lost consciousness and sank into the red-stained water was his organ pulsing in Balam's palm. Balam placed the quivering, bloody heart onto the stone slab next to the urn, said a prayer to the goddess, and swam out of the cave.

When Balam returned alone, Akna looked for her lover. "Where is Tepeu?"

"The goddess has claimed him for herself!" he said, staring at her. She fainted in her father's arms. Just then, the moaning from the lagoon intensified and turned into a loud shriek as the crowd shuddered in fear.

"It is Tepeu's angry spirit!" someone cried out, as the natives ran back to their boats.

And the legend of The Ghost of Chankanaab was born.

CHAPTER 2

New York City
PRESENT DAY

Artist Matthew Jaslow and his fiancée, Elaine Weatherly, left Christie's Auction House at 20 Rockefeller Plaza arm in arm. Only several hours earlier, all the art world knew about Matthew was what *The New York Times* had written about him in the advance reviews.

> Tomorrow's auction at Christie's will include work by Matthew Jaslow, a promising young artist, whose paintings have garnered serious acclaim and have already proven a sound investment for collectors searching for upside potential.

Matthew and Elaine were thrilled that Christie's had invited him to submit six paintings as part of a wider auction. Neither expected all six would have sold, and they never dreamed anyone would have kept bidding until the paintings eventually sold for more than twice their estimated value. They stopped at the crosswalk waiting for the light to turn.

Matthew brushed Elaine's windswept, blond hair from her face. He looked into her blue eyes, pulled her close, and kissed her lightly on her lips. She leaned forward and kissed him back. He was about to kiss her again but the light turned green, and a typically impatient New York crowd swept them along.

"Let's go, buddy," he heard a pedestrian comment, bumping his shoulder as he brushed past.

"I'm going to stop at the liquor store on our corner and pick up a bottle of Champagne to celebrate!" Matt said.

The enthusiasm in his voice was contagious, and Elaine nodded, flashing a smile. "I know where the candles are. I always wanted a famous artist to seduce me."

"And tonight one shall," Matthew replied, with a devilish grin.

"Hey, if your *New York Times* advance review was so complimentary, I can't wait to read tomorrow's story about tonight's auction." Their pace quickened, as they both anticipated a night of torrid lovemaking, heightened by the aphrodisiac of success. When they arrived at their West Side apartment building, Matthew ran into the lobby and pushed the elevator button. The light above the door indicated the elevator was still on the way up, at the seventh floor.

Matthew grabbed Elaine's hand and winked. "Let's take the stairs. I'm a man on a mission!"

Elaine laughed and followed him. Three floors later, Matthew fumbled with his key, repeatedly missing the lock. "Sorry, babe. I think my blood's already going to the wrong place," he said, glancing down at the bulge in his pants.

Elaine followed his eyes and smiled, anticipating an exciting night ahead. "Let me, Mister Mission Man," she said, easily inserting the key and pushing the door open. Matthew stepped inside and Elaine looked at him as she closed the door. "What's wrong? You don't look good. You sound out of breath, and we haven't even started having fun."

"Yeah, I feel weird. Only three floors and I'm winded. I do more climbing on the stairmaster at our gym without skipping a beat."

"You look a little pale. Sit down and let me do the honors," Elaine said, taking the bottle of Champagne from Matthew. She twisted the metal retainer holding the cork. "What's wrong with your hand?" she asked, watching him flex his fingers and rubbing a strange bruise on the back of his right hand.

"Maybe it's just worn out from all that handshaking after the auction. That one guy who did most of the bidding and bought most of my paintings was really enthusiastic, pumping me with two hands."

"Stick to painting, dear. If you can't shake a lot of hands without complaining, you'll never make it in politics," Elaine said, smiling. She popped the cork and ducked when it rebounded off the ceiling and flew past her head. Then she filled two Champagne flutes with expensive Piper-Heidsieck Brut, their favorite. They intertwined arms and sipped, their eyes inches apart, drinking in each other's essence. They kissed, and just as Matthew's tongue darted toward Elaine's lips she pulled back.

"Hey, that's not—"

"I'll be right back. I want to slip into something more appropriate." She winked. "Something you can properly seduce me out of."

"Let's drink to that," Matthew said.

Elaine was trying to decide which of several sheer and revealing outfits she would wear. "Hmm, Matt enjoys stripping me out of this one," she said, softly to herself. She heard a thump in the kitchen. "Matt? Did you drop something?" She ignored the silence and continued dressing. She anticipated

Matt embracing her as he pulled down her back zipper. She closed her eyes, knowing he would slip the top of the suit off her shoulders, run his lips down her throat, and kiss her nipples. The thought sent a tingle through her, and she sighed.

Wearing a skintight, low-cut leopard jumpsuit, she slinked out of the bedroom like a cat, holding her empty glass. "I'll have another . . ." Elaine's mind could not comprehend the tableau in front of her. Matthew was on his back, his face ashen. Half-open eyes stared up, focusing on nothing. His mouth was open as if about to speak, his lips a pale shade of blue.

Elaine dropped her Champagne glass, which shattered on the tile floor. She ran through the shards and knelt next to his body. "Matt! Matt! Are you okay?" she shouted, shaking him, even though her heart knew the answer.

Two nights later, Elaine, dressed in a conservative black dress, sat alone in her apartment, in a stupor. Absentmindedly, she flipped the pages of *The New York Times*, but not to the story about Matthew's successful art auction in the arts section. Instead, she turned to the obituary section. She still could not believe the words she read:

> Jaslow - Matthew, aged 31, of Manhattan, New York, died unexpectedly. Beloved son of Bernard and Ethel of New London, Connecticut, engaged to Ms. Elaine Weatherly. Mr. Jaslow was a rising young artist who . . .

Elaine checked her watch, just as her phone beeped. The limousine service she had called for transportation to the first night of Matthew's wake in Connecticut messaged her phone that the car would arrive in fifteen minutes. She glanced at two baskets on the coffee table in front of her. One basket contained stamped, addressed envelopes. The other held invitations she had planned to insert into the envelopes tonight. She picked up one of the expensive, ivory-white invitations and stared at the page.

Mr. and Mrs. Adam Weatherly
invite you to share in the joy
of the marriage uniting their daughter,
Elaine Marie, to Mr. Matthew Jaslow.
Their celebration of love
will be held on Sunday, the sixth of . . .

Elaine's eyes teared. Unable to continue reading, she stared at the invitation no one would send. She shook her head slowly, still not comprehending how much her life had changed in a few seconds.

CHAPTER 3

Roatan, Honduras

"Okay, for our first dive today we're diving the wreck of the *Aguila*," said Jeff Becker, co-owner of Roatan Adventures dive operation with his wife. He stood near the bow of their thirty-eight-foot boat, *Pirata,* while his wife, Dayle Standish-Becker, perched her athletic 5'8" frame on the stern and watched him begin his dive briefing.

"Our first dive will be down to about 110 feet, where the ship sits. It's about 230 feet long, and a hurricane broke it into three pieces, so there are plenty of nooks and crannies where you can find critters hiding. You can see garden eels, large groupers, and a pretty good-sized resident green moray eel. The moray is curious but not dangerous as long as you don't do something stupid like trying to pet him."

The group laughed while Dayle eyeballed the group of four couples. She had made this dive many times and had also given the briefing. Instead of concentrating on Jeff, she focused on the divers, watching for signs of anxiety, nervousness, or any other clues to potential trouble. She was very thorough and safety conscious. But then, she had been trained in Cozumel, Mexico, by her friend, Terry Hunter-Manetta, considered one of the best dive operators on the island. Satisfied the group was prepared, she watched the reaction of the four women in the group to Jeff as he continued his dive briefing, punctuated with jokes and personal patter.

Dayle overheard one of the ladies refer to Jeff as "that blue-eyed hunk" during yesterday's surface interval. Dayle was used to it. Only three years since he left the Navy SEALS, Jeff was still in good shape. He stood a shade over six-feet tall, with no fat hiding his well-toned muscles, which were accentuated by a Caribbean tan and a sheen of perspiration. Dayle laughed to herself, knowing when she gave tomorrow's dive briefing, the men's eyes would be glued to her, and Jeff would shift uneasily at the stern knowing exactly what they were thinking about his wife. She knew their dive customers envied them for living and working in paradise.

"Okay, any questions?" Jeff asked, looking at each diver for the same warning signs as Dayle.

No one answered.

"Then let's suit up and we'll give you a safety inspection before you roll in."

After all divers had donned their wetsuits, buoyancy compensator vests (BCs), fins, tanks, and regulators, Dayle and Jeff checked each person individually, making sure everyone had turned on their air, inflated BCs, buckled straps and weights properly, and secured any other equipment. Dayle noticed Jeff's quick check was more cursory than usual. She wondered why he seemed so distracted lately. She dismissed the thought, as she and Jeff back-rolled into the blue Caribbean, followed by the group. They splashed in, descended a few feet, and then popped to the surface as their inflated BCs brought them back up.

"Everyone okay?" Dayle shouted.

She and Jeff watched each diver respond, either by making the OK sign with three fingers extended with thumb and forefinger touching or by touching the top of their head with one fist. "Let's go down. Group one with Jeff, group two with me."

The divers pressed the deflator valves on their BCs and descended slowly, clearing their ears every few feet. However, one of the divers in Jeff's group could not descend. He jackknifed his body and kicked toward the bottom to no avail. He kept floating back to the surface. He drifted just above Dayle, so she surfaced to check his equipment. Jeff popped up a moment later.

"Hey, your weight pouches are missing! Jeff! Didn't you check that Bob's weights were in his BC?"

"Sorry Dayle, guess I missed that," Jeff said. He swam to the boat and asked the mate, a Brit named Quigley, to hand him the weight pouches. Then he swam over to Bob and slipped the two pouches, each containing five pounds of lead, into his BC. He pressed them in until he felt the plastic buckles click. "Okay Bob, you're good to go. Sorry about that."

Bob nodded, gave Jeff the OK sign and slipped beneath the surface. Before Jeff descended, he caught Dayle's eyes. Even through her mask he saw her penetrating blue-gray eyes glaring at him.

The water was so clear that even from just below the surface, the wreck of the *Aguila* was visible 110 feet below. They separated as pre-arranged, two couples following Jeff toward the wreck's stern and the other two couples shadowing Dayle as she headed for the *Aguila*'s bow.

Dayle's group encountered several large groupers swimming around the bow. One of her divers had a camera and two groupers posed for some nice photo ops near the divers. She let her divers examine the bow for several minutes, and then signaled them with her hand to follow her along the ship's raggedly torn hull toward the stern.

Along the way her divers peeked into holes and cracks, hoping to see interesting creatures inhabiting the wreck. Occasionally they stopped to shine a dive light on a brown encrusting sponge growing on the hull, which turned bright red in the light, or a small coral formation, which had attached itself to a bulkhead and was starting to grow. Dayle guided the divers toward the stern, where she knew they would enjoy taking photos of each other posed around the large propeller blades.

Their usual plan on this dive was that when Dayle's group reached the back of the ship, Jeff would lead his divers toward the bow to avoid congestion. But when she reached his group Dayle was shocked when she saw one of Jeff's divers in danger.

CHAPTER 4

Two of Jeff's divers were benignly peeking into an empty porthole, shining their dive lights inside. But Eric and Jan, two other divers, hovered over several pieces of twisted metal, which the green moray had adopted as his current residence. Eric was trying to pose next to the eel while his wife, Jan, focused her camera to capture the photo op.

Eric enticed the eel out of his lair by waving his fingers inches in front of the eel's needle-sharp teeth. Dayle knew divers were not moray eels' favorite food, but she also knew morays have notoriously bad eyesight and Eric's fingers might resemble tiny fish, a tempting morsel for any eel. Jeff, positioned between both pairs of divers, was oblivious to the danger.

Too far away to reach Jeff or Eric, Dayle quickly slid her dive knife from its leg sheath and rapped the metal butt handle against her tank. The sharp metallic noise jarred Jeff from his inattention and he whirled around, just as Eric looked up, away from the eel. At that moment, the moray lunged toward what seemed like an easy meal and sunk its teeth into Eric's fingers. As Eric struggled to free himself, the eel began a twisting motion.

Dayle knew the powerful jaws would snap off Eric's fingers in a few more seconds. She quickly finned toward the stricken diver and plunged her knife into the thick-bodied eel, just behind its jaws. The startled eel released its vice-like grip slightly, just enough for Eric to pull his fingers out, as the moray's teeth shredded his skin. Jeff reached Eric just as he tried to shoot for the surface in a wild panic, which would have resulted in serious, perhaps fatal, damage to his lungs. Jeff wrapped his arms around Eric's body, stopping his ascent. Then he guided Eric slowly toward the surface, a stream of blood trailing behind them, which, at 100 feet deep, looked eerily green instead of red.

The wounded eel pulled itself free from Dayle's knife and retreated into the safety of its lair. She pointed to the other seven divers and indicated they should all slowly ascend as a group. Then, she held them at fifteen feet for a three-minute safety stop before heading for the surface.

Dayle and the seven divers broke the surface and heard Eric's screams. Climbing aboard, they found him crouched in a fetal position. He held a bloody towel around his mangled hand as Jeff tended to him. Jeff looked up. "Everyone on board?"

When Dayle nodded, he shouted, "Okay, Quigley, head for shore as fast as you can!" Then he jumped up and ran to the cabin to call in a medical emergency and request an ambulance to meet them at the dock. Quigley opened the throttle and ran the boat at full speed back to the pier. Jeff and Dayle lifted a moaning Eric to his feet, helped him disembark, and then walked him unsteadily to a waiting ambulance. Jan stumbled into the ambulance next to her husband.

"You go with them," Dayle said sharply to Jeff.

He jumped inside, slammed the door and shouted, "Go! Go!" The ambulance spun its wheels in the dusty gravel and disappeared in a cloud.

She turned back to the remaining six divers. Dayle was about to wipe a tear from her eye and noticed her hand tremble. "I'm probably having a damn adrenaline rush," she said, breathing deeply to calm herself.

"You okay, Dayle?" Quigley asked.

"Sure, mate. I'll be fine in a bit."

"Relax, Dayle, Eric'll be all right," said another diver in her group, trying to reassure her.

"I'm not worried about that bloody fool," Dayle snapped back, more angrily than she intended. She explained the source of her anger to the startled diver. "Eric was lucky. I watched a YouTube video last year showing a moray eel snapping off a diver's thumb. He'll have a bad time of it, but I think they'll save his fingers. I'm more concerned about that poor eel. I've seen it down there for over five years. We invaded its home. It's never shown a bit of aggressiveness toward divers. When Eric wiggled his fingers in front of the eel's nose, the poor thing reacted to an impulse interpreting that as food. You all heard Jeff warn everyone not to touch or harass the sea life during his briefing, did you not?"

She saw the group nod affirmatively.

"That's what can happen when you disturb wildlife in the ocean. I didn't kill the moray, so I hope it heals and survives. They're pretty tough." She closed her eyes and composed herself. "Okay, let's gather our dive gear. Sorry we won't be doing our second dive today. You can either have a refund or a credit for another dive. I'll meet you in the dive shack to do the paperwork."

After the divers left, Dayle still felt unsettled. She had a headache. Her brain was muddled with conflicting thoughts. First, she was concerned for Eric. As dive operators, they were responsible for their customers' safety. She was also concerned for the reputation of Roatan Adventures, a business she and Jeff had worked hard to build up. But what about Jeff's role in the accident?

Blimey, what the hell was Jeff thinking about down there? she wondered. *Certainly not about his responsibility for our divers.* She planned to discuss the issue with him as soon as he returned from the hospital. Dayle shook her head. *I need a drink.* She glanced at a wall clock, a turtle whose front flippers rotated like the hands of a Mickey Mouse watch. It was only 11:30, too early to drink most days. But this wasn't like most days, and she wasn't diving anymore today. *Fuck it. I'm ready for a stiff one,* she decided.

She closed up the dive shack and walked down West End's main street, passing hole-in-the-wall dive shops and a familiar assortment of casual cafés, toward one of her favorite haunts, Sundowners Beach Bar. When Dayle arrived, Sundowners was almost empty, except for a couple of regulars whose drinking patterns were not ruled by the sun or stars. She hauled herself onto a stool, rested her elbows on the teak bar, and said to Andre, her friend, "Two Barenas, nice and cold."

"Two ya be havin'?" Andre replied in his Caribbean lilt.

"Right, mate. Serve 'em up now, pronto."

Andre knew Dayle preferred the local brew to anything else. "Ah yes, we heard ya be havin' a rough mornin'."

"You heard right, Andre. Shit, bad news sure travels fast," she said.

Three hours later, the ambulance dropped Jeff off at the dive shack, on its way to make another pickup. A tourist had stepped on a stingray in shallow water off a sandy beach. Jeff's boat mate was busy working on one of the two Yamaha engines.

"Quigley, is Dayle around?"

"Yes, you can find her at Sundowners."

"Okay, thanks." He got into his Jeep and headed off toward the popular watering hole. As Jeff approached Sundowners, he glanced at his dive watch. He was surprised Dayle would be drinking at the bar so early. He spotted Dayle, leaning on one arm, the other tipping a bottle back. The sea breeze blew through her shoulder-length blond hair. "Hey, babe! How ya doin'?" Her narrowed gaze told him she wasn't doing well.

"Fine, Jeff. How was your trip to the hospital? You didn't lose anyone on the way, did you?"

"Look hon, I'm—"

"Skip it. I won't argue with you in public. We can discuss it at home." She slid off the barstool, agile as a cat, and Jeff followed her. Dayle slipped into the passenger seat and pulled the door shut as Jeff walked around to the driver's side and climbed into the Jeep.

He knew it would be a quiet, tense ride home. He turned the key and pulled away from the curb. Occasionally, Jeff shot a sideways glance at Dayle, but she kept her head turned away, looking out the passenger-side window. The silence made the short drive home seem longer than usual. No sooner had the tires crunched to a stop on the gravel driveway than Dayle jumped out and had her key in the door before Jeff had gotten out of the Jeep. He found her in the living room, hands on her hips, back to the door. He heard her breathing heavy. "Dayle, everything happened so—"

She wheeled around before Jeff finished his explanation.

"So fast?" she completed his sentence. "I watched you, Jeff. You were somewhere else. In your own little dream world, fantasy land, I don't know where. But wherever the bloody hell you were today it wasn't 110 feet underwater keeping track of your divers!"

Dayle waited for a reply but Jeff remained silent, watching her. "And even before the dive, you forgot to check that Bob had put his weights in his BC! That's not like you, blowing a predive safety check." She watched him, expecting a rebuttal, a reply, or argument but he remained mute. Dayle pressed on. "And it hasn't been just today. I've seen a change in you over the past month. You've been detached and preoccupied. What's wrong, Jeff? Are you worried or concerned about something ..." Jeff's piercing blue eyes shimmered with tears, and Dayle feared the worst ". . . or someone else?" She held her breath, suddenly thrown off-balance by her own thoughts.

When Jeff finally answered, Dayle's knees sagged as if she had been punched in the gut, and she sank into the nearest chair.

CHAPTER 5

"The Agency? The bloody CIA?" Dayle whispered, dumbfounded by Jeff's reply. Her mind raced, trying to assess the threat to their marriage. "Crikey, another woman I could fight. But how do I fight a legendary institution?"

"I'm sorry, Dayle," Jeff said, almost apologetically. "I do love you, and I love our life here. I really do. But—"

Dayle interrupted him. "Remember one night at dinner in Cozumel, you said you had left the SEALS and joined the CIA because your body couldn't take getting shot up anymore? And then three years ago when you joined me here you told me you were through running around the world putting out fires for the U.S. Government." Dayle's eyes brimmed with tears as her fingers traced a line along a thin scar on the side of Jeff's head, a souvenir from a Taliban bullet.

"I know. I thought I was finished with the Agency, too." He walked into the study and pulled a letter from a desk drawer. "But last month they sent me this."

He handed Dayle the letter. She took it but didn't read it.

"No specific details, but they're planning a special mission, top secret, extremely classified and also dangerous. They feel there are only a handful of people qualified to pull it off."

"And you're part of the handful?"

Jeff didn't reply to her question. "The Agency believes this operation is vital to the success of our overall mission over there, and it could shorten our involvement in the war. So, when they contacted me I felt . . ."

"Jeff, we've worked hard, built a successful dive operation and a wonderful life for us here in paradise. And the art gallery is almost turning a profit. I thought the next step for us was children. You told me you wanted kids. I'm sorry that it hasn't happened for us yet, but I'm sure it will. We just need to keep trying." Jeff paused before speaking and she feared the worst.

"I know. I should be totally satisfied. I'm married to a beautiful woman, we have everything that you said, and I do want children, too, but, but . . . I feel something's missing."

"Missing? Missing?" Dayle spread her arms and looked around, finally letting her emotions explode. "Blimey! If all this isn't enough, if *I'm* not enough, if our future as a family is not enough . . . then perhaps you should leave! When are you telling your spook buddies you're going to rejoin them?"

Jeff pursed his lips, and then replied. "I already did. Two weeks ago."

"Two weeks ago? Two bloody fucking weeks ago?" Dayle shouted. "Without even discussing it with me first?"

Jeff stammered, unable to formulate a reply. "Well . . . I . . ."

"When, definitively, are you planning to leave, if it's not too much trouble to inform me?"

"Actually, in five days. This coming Thursday. But if you need a hand getting things settled here, I can . . ." He stopped talking when Dayle brushed away the tears and he saw the fire in her blue-gray eyes.

"This Thursday? Only five days from now? Even some poor bloke getting sacked gets at least two weeks' notice from his employer. Thank you, but I can settle things very well without you. I've survived corporate backstabbers ruining my international consulting career and dodged an assassin chasing me around the world, so I can certainly survive this little bump in the road." She turned toward the bedroom and Jeff stepped forward.

"Hon, let's go to bed and figure this out in the morning, okay?"

Dayle spun around and halted him with a stiff-arm palm against his chest. "Not so fast, mate. Evidently, you've already figured out your plans, so you can take the sofa out here. I'm sleeping in what used to be *our* bed." She turned, walked into the bedroom, threw out a pillow that landed at Jeff's feet, and slammed the door.

Jeff stood still, as if riveted to the floor. Then he heard the lock click.

Dayle threw herself onto the bed and buried her face in the pillow. She didn't want to give Jeff the satisfaction of hearing her cry. "Damn, damn, damn!" She pounded her fist into the bedding as her tears stained the pillowcase, angry and frustrated that she was losing the man she still loved so dearly. She shook her head, searching for answers. She closed her eyes, feeling emotionally, mentally, and physically exhausted.

After an hour of twisting and turning, Dayle fell into a restless, fitful sleep. She felt herself falling into a dark tunnel. The walls spun faster and faster as she dropped into the black void. She awoke in Switzerland, dressed in a gray business suit, sitting across the desk from her boss. She expected him to congratulate her for completing a major consulting project for their firm's client, a large bank. Instead, a door opened and the human resources director entered. Dayle knew something bad was going to happen. She frowned. The dream was turning bad. Her boss handed her a large envelope. The HR director explained it contained her severance package. She stormed out of the office in a rage, realizing her company had sacrificed her for political reasons, to appease a senior executive from their client bank whom she had crossed. Dayle rolled onto her back, flailing her arms. "Bloody bastards!" she shouted, loud enough to wake Jeff, dozing on the sofa.

Jeff stared at the closed bedroom door and listened. He hoped her dream would end better this time.

Then, Dayle smiled as the warm Caribbean enveloped her in a weightless realm. Soon, she watched herself swim out of an underwater cave in Cozumel, Mexico, holding her camera after she had snapped a picture. An unknown diver appeared from the cave and pointed a speargun at her. She bolted toward the divemaster, Terry Manetta, who was swimming in the distance. Suddenly she found herself inside her Manhattan condo. Her cell phone rang. She answered and heard Terry's voice.

"Get out, Dayle! Someone's coming to kill you!"

Dayle's legs kicked off the bed sheets as she tried to run from her apartment. In her dream, her legs felt heavy as lead. Next, she was pounding her fist against the door of her friend Janet Millard's apartment. The door opened, but instead of Janet's face she saw only a black void. She stared into the blackness and soon two eyes formed, staring back at her. At first, she thought she was looking at her own eyes but she realized they were Janet's eyes. They became clearer, and she heard her friend's accusing voice.

"I died because of you. He killed me instead of you. He thought I was you."

"No, no! I'm sorry, Janet. I'm sorry!"

Dayle moaned, loudly enough for Jeff to get up and quietly pad toward the door, listening. She remained quiet for several moments so Jeff retreated back to the sofa.

Next, she found herself sitting in a plane leaving the United States, accompanied by a CIA officer. She looked into his friendly blue eyes and smiled in her dream. He spoke.

"Hello, Ms. Standish, my name is Jeff Becker, and I've been assigned to protect you."

Dayle curled into a fetal position, frightened again. She was at her friend Terry's house in Cozumel. She stood next to Terry, cornered by the Cuban secret service assassin, Juan Ortega. He pointed his gun at Terry, and then at her. He smiled as he started to pull the trigger.

"Pirata! Pirata, where are you?" Dayle cried out. She waited for Pirata, a black-and-white lab mix to leap from the shadows and tear Ortega's arm apart before he could shoot.

Sometimes the dream ended that way, just as it had actually happened. But this time Pirata did not materialize.

Dayle saw only Ortega's wicked smile. She heard a loud bang, saw a muzzle flash, and watched the bullet head for her eyes, spiraling in slow motion, coming closer, and closer, and . . .

She screamed and bolted upright.

"Shit!" Jeff exclaimed. He leapt off the sofa and crashed through the flimsy door. He found Dayle drenched in sweat, sitting up, trembling in the middle of bed. He wrapped his arms around her as she sobbed.

"Jeff, stay with me. Don't leave."

"I won't," he said, lying down with her. He stroked her damp hair and pulled her against his chest. Soon, he felt her relax. Her breathing slowed, and she fell asleep again. Jeff saw her smile and wondered what she was dreaming about now.

Dayle felt the setting sun warm her face as she leaned against a palm tree on a Roatan beach. She squinted and shaded her eyes with her hand as she watched a dolphin pod play in the surf. She heard footsteps behind her, and a muscled arm wrapped around her waist. A man's deep voice spoke.

"Happy, Mrs. Becker?"

She looked over her shoulder and reached up. Her fingers gently brushed a scar on the side of the man's head, a souvenir from a near miss with a sniper's bullet on his last mission. "Yes, Mr. Becker, very much so." She closed her eyes and felt Jeff's lips meet her lips.

Jeff looked at his wife as she snuggled closer, curled up in his arms. "Man, I must be crazy for leaving her," he whispered, just before he finally dozed off.

CHAPTER 6

The next morning, Dayle woke to the aroma of strong coffee. She shivered, feeling cold after sweating through her nightmare. *Where was Jeff?* She recalled the warm sensation of his muscled arms enveloping her, making her feel safe. She stepped into the kitchen and watched him prepare breakfast.

"Morning, hon. How about eggs, toast, and bacon?"

"Nah, I'm not really hungry. Just toast and coffee if you don't mind."

"Sure thing."

"I had the dream again last night, didn't I?" she said, hugging herself with her arms, biting her lip.

"Yes, you did. Worse than usual. You know I think you really are dealing with posttraumatic stress after all you went through. I think you should see a doctor who—"

"Don't worry about me, Jeff. I'll be fine. What time are you leaving Thursday?"

"I take a ten o'clock plane from here to Atlanta, and then I fly to Reston, Virginia. Our SEAL team leaves from Dulles

Airport later that night."

"Ah, the spooks fly by night. Is that the plan?"

Jeff ignored her sarcastic comment. "According to the schedule you're not diving Thursday, so I was wondering if you could give me a lift to the airport?"

"Sorry, mate, you're on your own. I planned to give Felix a hand at the gallery that morning," she said, turning her back to Jeff so he would not see the tears filling her eyes.

"Okay, then I'll call for a cab."

Thursday morning, while Jeff finished packing his bags, he heard their Jeep start up. He ran outside before Dayle could drive away. "Hey, are you leaving now?"

"Yes. I need to keep busy," she said. Her voice caught in her throat.

"You know I'll miss you."

"I'll miss you, too. Be safe, Jeff," she replied, staring at his face, drinking in a last look of the man she loved.

"I will. I'll be back." He moved closer to the Jeep to kiss her goodbye.

"Will you?" Dayle asked, leaning back. He stopped in his tracks. She gunned the engine and spun the tires, covering Jeff's shoes with dusty gravel. He looked down at his shoes, and then saw her turn a sharp corner on two wheels.

"You stay safe, too," he whispered.

After a short ride through town, Dayle pulled up in front of a multicolored, hand-painted wooden sign: *LaLa Art Gallery & Garden Café.* Two years ago, she had opened the Latin American Lifestyle & Art Gallery, which she stocked with indigenous art from artists throughout Latin America.

Dayle traveled throughout Mexico and Central America to find unique original art for her gallery. Six months later, she had added a café so guests could enjoy local dining fare from Roatan and surrounding areas.

LaLa had turned into a popular eating and meeting location for locals as well as tourists who wanted to return home from their Caribbean vacation with a souvenir that did not say *Made in China*. She was also beginning to find success shipping art to the United States through her new online catalog.

"Good morning, Felix," she said to her manager, sounding jauntier than her mood.

"Morning, pretty lady," Felix said in his distinctive Caribbean lilt. "What can I get for you today?"

"Ah, you know how to make a girl feel special," she laughed. "I'll have a spot of tea and a muffin."

"Okay, coming right up."

"How's business been this week?"

"Not bad, but slower than we'd like. The café has kept busy. But the gallery has slowed down a bit. When people come, they like what they see and they usually purchase something. Especially when you're in the gallery. You sure know how to charm the tourists into parting with their money."

Dayle smiled. "Yes, you're right. I do enjoy chatting with the visitors and telling them about the art I've purchased for the gallery. The sale is the easy part."

"The problem is getting the volume. We need a steady flow of customers. If we had something to draw them, we could sell a lot more. We need publicity, something really unique to make them come and look."

"Yes, I know what you mean," Dayle said. "I'll give it some thought while I'm away."

"Ah, where you be goin'?"

"I need a break. A temporary change of scenery. Maybe a little expedition to acquire some new art. The dive operation has been slow and I've referred my customers to Blue Seas Divers. You can hold down the fort here for a couple of weeks, can't you, Felix?"

"You bet, pretty lady. We be fine 'til you return. Maybe you bring us back somthin' to wow the customers," he said, smiling, as the light glinted off a silver-capped tooth.

"I'll see what I can do."

Felix turned serious. "You be careful, ya hear?"

"Don't worry. I'll keep out of trouble. I promise." She leaned across the counter and kissed her manager. "Good luck while I'm gone." She slid off the stool and waved over her shoulder as she left.

"Wait a minute, pretty lady!"

Dayle turned around.

"I forgot. This came in the mail for you yesterday. I don't know why it was delivered here instead of to your house, but it is addressed to you." Felix handed her a magazine.

"Ah, *The Portolan*, one of my favorite magazines. Thanks." She noticed Felix's puzzled expression. "It's published every quarter by the Washington Map Society. Lots of interesting articles about maps, historical artifacts, and archeological history. You'd be surprised what you can learn from reading old maps." She glanced at the cover and saw a photo of an ancient globe. "Newly Discovered Early Sixteenth-Century Globe Engraved on an Ostrich Egg: The Earliest Surviving Globe Showing the New World."

"Wow, this looks fascinating. Thanks, Felix. Bye."

"Bye, pretty lady. Be careful."

"I will," she said.

Back home, Dayle stared at the empty spaces where Jeff had kept his personal possessions. The rooms looked and felt lifeless. "Blimey, he took more stuff than I thought he would. Jeff, are you ever coming back?" she asked the empty room. Dayle sat at her desk, answered emails, and took several orders from customers buying LaLa artwork. She rubbed her eyes, taking a break from the screen and glanced at the globe on the cover of *The Portolan*. "Let's see what Google says about you."

Dayle never noticed the time pass as she Googled story after story about the globe, flitting from link to link, jotting down notes.

> Certain details predate Magellan's voyages in 1520 . . . Globe likely made around 1504, possibly 1490s . . . evidence of Leonardo da Vinci's influence . . . possible use as navigation aid by Columbus in later voyages to the Yucatan . . . interaction with Mayan traders . . .

Two hours later, Dayle wrote an email to her friend Terry. She clicked *Send* and packed, even before she received a reply. She knew her friend would not let her down. She was exhausted but not too tired to begin reading *The Portolan* as she eased into bed. As she flipped the pages she forgot about sleep and started to formulate a plan for putting LaLa on the map.

CHAPTER 7

New York City

"I don't know how I can ever repay your generosity," William Bennet gushed.

His dinner companion smiled and waved his hand, as if brushing away an annoying fly.

"Paying fifty-percent more than the estimated value of my paintings was a wonderful gesture of faith in my ability. I hope I can justify your confidence in my future work."

"Don't worry, William, I consider your work outstanding, as do many other collectors."

"Still, I will do my best to make sure your investment in my work appreciates in value."

"I'm sure it will grow in value faster than you could ever imagine. I don't know where our waiter is," he said, craning his neck. He stood and grabbed both empty glasses. "I'll get us another glass of wine."

Before William could object, his new friend was standing at the bar ordering two Kendall Jackson cabernets. He took the two glasses from the bartender, and two fingers positioned over William's glass parted. A small capsule dropped into the red wine. Then, he stopped momentarily to speak with two young ladies, swirling the wine as they talked for several minutes. The intentional delay allowed the capsule to dissolve completely.

William watched him and shook his head with a smile, hoping the women would join them for dinner and perhaps entertainment afterward. His friend returned to his table alone.

"Here you are, William. Cheers!" he said, clinking glasses. His heart pounded with anticipation as he brought the glass to his lips, expecting William to do the same. But William just placed his glass on the table. "Something wrong?"

"No. But I'd like to get your opinion on something."

"Yes, yes, of course."

"I've been invited to two exhibitions only three days apart. I'd love to appear at both but the folks at the second one, which will be much larger, have asked me not to appear at the other. It's a strange request. They mentioned something about overexposure. Do you think I should honor it and blow off the smaller exhibit?"

"In my opinion, I think you should . . ." When William finally sipped his wine, his companion watched him like a lion focused on a gazelle that didn't have long to live.

"Hmm, this wine has a strange taste. Seems slightly off somehow." He took another, longer sip. Then he resumed eating. After a few bites, he tasted the wine again. "It's not bad exactly, but . . ." His eyes opened wide, in panic. "I . . . can't breathe," he wheezed. William's chest heaved, and he clutched his throat. His pallor turned blue as his body hungered for oxygen. He grabbed his chest, feeling that his lungs had ceased to function. The glass slipped from his grasp, shattering on the floor as he lost consciousness.

William's companion leapt from his chair, making sure he stepped in the spilled wine, spreading it across the floor while he appeared to help William. "What's wrong? William! Speak to me!" he implored, shaking the limp body as it sagged in the chair like a rag doll. William's head rolled and only the whites of his eyes showed.

"Call 911! Get a doctor! Help!" someone shouted, as other dinner patrons surrounded the table. A waiter pulled William to the floor and administered CPR. Seconds later they heard sirens. Two EMS personnel rushed in wheeling a stretcher. The waiter performing CPR stepped aside as they attached an oxygen mask to William's face and lifted him onto the gurney.

"What happened?" one of the EMS techs asked, facing the crowd.

"We were having dinner, and then he just suddenly collapsed. Can I ride in the ambulance with him?"

"Sure. Jump in. We're heading straight to the hospital."

During the fifteen-minute ride to New York's Bellevue Hospital, he studied William's body while the EMS tech continued to administer CPR. He saw no sign of life and was positive William was dead. He calculated that his $125,000 investment in purchasing eight of William's paintings would more than double in value now that the well-known artist could paint no more.

Not a bad couple of days' work, he thought. *This New York trip was much more profitable than a grinding week at my law firm.*

CHAPTER 8

Cozumel, Mexico

Terry Manetta paced impatiently outside the den. "Peter, Jackie, you guys done using your computer yet?"

"I'm already off," Peter said. "I'm watching TV."

"Almost done, Mom! Please give me another few minutes," Jackie said. "I'm emailing the turtle conservation people about our volunteer application."

"Okay, please hurry. I have to send over a dozen replies to my dive customers and check my bookings. My computer sure picked a great time to crash," Terry fumed.

"It's all yours. I'm done," Jackie said, logging out. Terry shot an annoyed glance at Jackie, as she passed her mother and headed upstairs to her bedroom.

"Gee, sorry Mom," Jackie said, with an intentional sarcastic note at what she perceived as her mother's unreasonableness.

"What a brat," her brother said.

Terry was surprised that Peter uncharacteristically took her side in a family spat for a change and attributed it to just a normal brother and sister give-and-take. "Okay, I probably shouldn't have been so impatient with you guys. After all, it is your computer, and I know how important your sea turtle application is."

Terry went online, reviewed her bookings, and accepted most. But she referred a couple of her more difficult customers to other dive operators. She had lost patience with divers who always went too deep beyond safe limits, or never followed the group and got lost, or committed several other mortal sins on her list. "I sure don't need that aggravation," she rationalized, as she typed, "Sorry, but I'm booked for that week." She perked up when she saw an email from her friend, Dayle.

The subject header read: "Got room for one more?"

She opened the email.

Hey Terry & Joe,

How's life treating you? Do you have room on the boat next week? I'm single for a while. Long story. I could use some company and some laughs. How 'bout it, mate?

Love, Dayle

Terry typed back as fast as she could, hoping Dayle was still online.

Sure. I just had a cancellation. And we have plenty of room at our place. Is Jeff away or is he minding the store?

Next Friday, a week from now, works for us.

Terry waited impatiently for Dayle's reply, curious about her temporarily single comment.

Just me, mate. Closing down the dive op for a while, and my manager's running the LaLa. Jeff took a leave of absence from me. Plus, I'm on a mission. Tell you all about it when I see you. Appreciate the offer of staying with you & the family, but I've rented a small condo where I've stayed before, on San Francisco Beach. I love the owner's description of the place: "Your Own Slice of Paradise." Some time alone in paradise is just what I need right now, to think and sort out my life. Hope we can meet and catch up over dinner.

Dayle

"Damn!" Terry said. "That doesn't sound good."

"What doesn't sound good, hon?" her husband Joe asked, walking into the den.

"Looks like Dayle and Jeff are having problems. She didn't give any details, but Jeff left and she wants to visit us and go diving. Plus, she wrote something cryptic about being on some kind of a mission."

"That's too bad about her and Jeff. Hope it's nothing serious. It'll be great to see Dayle again, but I wish the circumstances were better." Joe stepped behind Terry and placed his hands on her shoulders. He felt her relax, and then bent down and nibbled her ear.

The sensation hit Terry like a lightning bolt. She felt a familiar flutter in her stomach. Joe nuzzled her cheek and kissed her neck. Terry arched her back and sucked in a quick breath.

"Coming upstairs soon?"

"I'll race you for the stairs," she whispered, signing off. She took Joe's hand and led him up to their bedroom.

The next morning, Terry prepared a ham and eggs breakfast for Peter and Jackie. "Where's Dad?" Jackie asked.

"Dad ate early and drove my truck to the marina to prepare the boat. We have a large group today," Terry explained. She noticed Peter staring at her, pursing his lips as he suppressed a grin. "What's up with you this morning, Peter?"

"Oh, nothing, Mom."

Terry realized Peter had probably noticed her and Joe holding hands as they went upstairs last night. She narrowed her eyes, and her expression told Peter, *Okay, buster, I got it.* Peter held her stare and did not look away, piquing Jackie's curiosity.

"Hey, am I missing something?" his sister asked.

"Nothing, dear," Terry said quickly, wondering what Peter thought about his parents' expression of intimacy. She felt relieved when a car horn blared outside. "I think I just heard Mrs. Hernandez pull up. She's waiting for you two. Get going or you'll be late for school. I have to get down to the marina and help Dad."

Everyone left the table and raced in separate directions, but Peter glanced over his shoulder with a final grin as he left. Terry smiled and shook her head. "Oh Peter, you're just like your irrepressible father."

"What's repressible mean, Mom?"

"Get going!"

CHAPTER 9

New York City

The well-dressed man strolled through the main area of the New York Public Library. Sotheby's, the international art auction firm, had rented space for a major auction event at the library. He stopped and glanced at his watch. His flight had landed on time and traffic from JFK Airport to Manhattan was uncharacteristically light, so he arrived early. The auction was not scheduled to begin for another forty-five minutes, so he wandered the halls and browsed the exhibits. He noticed a small globe, about the size of a grapefruit, in a glass case. An armed guard stood next to the globe. He stepped closer and casually rapped his knuckles against the case.

The guard turned toward him. "Please don't touch that," he said in a stern manner.

"Sorry, I was just curious about what it was made of." He realized it was the same bulletproof material banks used to protect tellers, which meant the globe was a valuable artifact. He wanted to inquire about the object but decided the unfriendly guard was not a good choice to engage in conversation. He spotted a young woman wearing a name tag giving directions to an elderly couple. He waited patiently until the young lady had pointed the couple in the right direction. "Excuse me . . . Kelly," he said, reading her name tag. "I was wondering about that little globe in the case."

"Oh yes, that's a very interesting exhibit," she said, leading him back to the case. "It's the famous Hunt-Lenox Globe. At one time it was believed to be the oldest known representation of a globe to portray the Americas, the New World."

"How old is it?"

"It's been dated to around 1510, but more recent estimates put it between 1504 and 1506."

"What is it made of?"

"It's a copper sphere, perfectly round, approximately five inches in diameter."

"Would you happen to know where it came from?"

"It was named after the architect Richard Morris Hunt, who discovered the globe in France and brought it to America in 1855. He gave it to his patron, James Lenox. In 1937, the library mounted the globe in a bronze armillary sphere."

"A bronze what?"

"Armillary sphere. That's what you call those intersecting bronze rings holding the globe in place."

"That's fascinating." The man immediately wondered how he could steal it for his private collection. "I think you said 'At one time it was believed to be the oldest'? In the past tense?"

"Yes, we now believe it was copied from an even older globe."

"Well, since Columbus discovered the New World in 1492, and this globe was made between 1504 and 1506, there wasn't too much time to produce an older globe, was there?"

"No, but an even older globe was recently discovered. The unknown artist used an ostrich eggshell, of all things. Some experts who have examined both have determined that the copper globe was actually copied from the older ostrich egg globe."

"How did they arrive at that conclusion?"

"I don't know all the details. However, I've read that the contours of the land masses and names of the oceans and even the script on the eggshell match those on the copper globe. Also, certain key phrases of an older origin appear on the eggshell globe but not on the copper globe. Consequently, they believe the metal globe was copied from the eggshell globe and not the other way around."

"And where is the ostrich egg globe now?" the man asked, his curiosity piqued.

"A private collector purchased it several years ago."

"Do you know who?" His mind rapidly switched targets, from the library's copper sphere to an unknown private individual who owned the oldest, most valuable representation of the New World in existence.

"Yes, a collector in Europe purchased it. But I'm afraid it's a moot point. That eggshell globe was destroyed in a house fire several months ago. However, there is also a rumor that the same unknown artist actually made two ostrich egg globes at about the same time. Supposedly, the other one still exists somewhere in the western Caribbean. Historical research indicates that explorers around the time of Columbus might have used that globe as a navigational aid on one of their voyages, when they explored South America between 1502 and 1504. There was a reference to it recorded in the log from one of the ships that returned from the voyage."

"And the ship's log has survived all these years?"

"Yes. It's in a museum in Cadiz, Spain, which was a major port at that time. In fact, Christopher Columbus sailed from

Cadiz on his second and fourth voyages to the New World. That's where most of the transatlantic voyages started and where they returned. Eventually, Cadiz became the home port of the Spanish treasure fleet, which brought back gold and silver. According to the ship's log, the Mayans attacked one of the ships and stole the globe. It was last seen somewhere in Mexico's Yucatan." Kelly's phone buzzed and she answered it while the man studied the small copper sphere. "Thank you. Goodbye," she replied to the caller. She looked over. "Are you here for the auction?"

"As a matter of fact, yes I am."

"My boss just informed me the auction will begin in five minutes. I'll be happy to walk you over there."

"That's very kind, Kelly, thank you," he said, glancing at the tiny globe one last time.

The well-dressed man followed Kelly into the auction room. He took an end seat six rows from the front, where he knew the auctioneer could see him. As an experienced art buyer, he preferred to remain as inconspicuous as possible, so he had prearranged a signal with the Sotheby's auctioneer. To signal he was bidding, he would tap his chin with the rolled-up program listing the items up for sale. To a casual observer, he would appear as someone thoughtfully assessing a bid.

He perused the auction list but was only interested in several wood carvings crafted by a Mexican artist he had read about named Arturo Bavarro. He knew nothing about the carvings and had no appreciation for the art itself. He was only interested because he had read that Bavarro's work was becoming very popular and increasing in value. He also read that the artist planned to attend the auction. This information presented him with a convenient opportunity.

By the conclusion of the evening, he had acquired all of Bavarro's carvings except one. Another persistent bidder had caused him to spend most of his budget during the auction, and he was out of funds when his competitor outbid him for the last piece.

At a cocktail reception following the auction, Bavarro was sipping a glass of Spanish port when he spotted the man who had purchased most of his artwork. The auctioneer had discreetly informed Bavarro about the identity of the wealthy patron who had run up the bidding, far exceeding their estimates, and had purchased seven of his eight carvings. The man noticed Bavarro approaching but glanced away, simply letting the fly approach the spider's web.

"Excuse me, but I've been informed that you were the aggressive bidder who bought almost all of my work."

"Yes, I am," he replied in a conspiratorially low voice, looking over the top of his glasses.

"Very pleased to meet you. What do you plan to do with my carvings?"

"I have an extensive private art collection. Besides enjoying your work, I believe it will prove to be a sound investment," he said.

"I hope so, and I appreciate your confidence in my work," said Bavarro, extending his hand.

He smiled and shook Bavarro's hand, then clasped the artist's hand in both of his, squeezing so tightly that Bavarro never felt a ring scratch the back of his hand.

"Congratulations on your success tonight, Arturo. I'm sorry but I must leave now. I have an appointment uptown. Good evening and good luck."

"And to you also, my friend."

He left the library and hailed a taxi for the ride back to his hotel. Relaxing in the back of the cab, he wondered how much his investment in Bavarro's artwork would appreciate over the coming months. When he arrived at his hotel, he packed for his flight home tomorrow. Then he drifted off to sleep think-ing about a vacation.

Business has been slow. My paralegals can handle the light caseload for the next few weeks. Seems like a good time to get out of town. I'll ask my wife if she wants to come.

The next morning as his flight lifted off from JFK Airport, he stretched out in first class. A flight attendant walked down the aisle, offering complimentary newspapers. He selected *The New York Times.* He knew it was too soon for anything to show up in the obituary notices, but he found the headline he was hoping for in the main section.

ARTIST DIES AFTER SUCCESSFUL AUCTION

Last night, artist Arturo Bavarro suddenly collapsed at a reception following an art auction held at the New York Public Library. He was pronounced dead at Bellevue Hospi-tal. Today, the local art community is grieving the loss of . . .

He smiled and ordered a mimosa from the flight attendant to celebrate while he read the rest of the story.

He was back in his office by early afternoon, catching up on his snail mail, emails, and telephone calls. He looked up from his desk, glanced at a painting on the wall, and remi-nisced about how a simple piece of art had changed his life. It was a still life—a dusty, crushed, cowboy hat resting against a cactus. The painting was his favorite among his growing col-lection. The artist, a local rancher, had died after he fell from his horse and broke his neck. One day, a wealthy client offered to purchase the painting for several times what he had paid for it because the popular artist could paint no more.

The idea struck him like a lightning bolt. His law firm, a partnership at the time, was not as successful as he had hoped, especially since the business had to support two partners. Supplementing his income by tapping into the escrow and investment accounts of wealthy clients and widows helped somewhat. But the mounting credit card bills that his free-spending wife ran up at various boutiques more than offset his illegal, risky, cash flow. He had suddenly discovered a better plan, but not the method.

Then came that fateful scuba diving trip to the Pacific. During one of the dives, they had just descended to the bottom, about seventy feet down, when one of the divers stupidly picked up a small creature hiding under a ledge and showed it to him. The diver was dead by the time he reached the surface. Returning home, he did some research and visited a local aquarium shop specializing in rare and unusual tropical fish. Now, he had the method and the means. Shortly after purchasing what he needed, his law firm partner died. The local coroner stated "cardiac event" in his autopsy report.

The law firm was now all his. Over the coming months, several artists in various parts of the country mysteriously died. The money rolled in.

CHAPTER 10

Cozumel

Terry cleaned the kitchen quickly and jumped into her car. Knowing she would see Dayle in a few minutes gave her a rush, and she could feel her adrenaline pumping. In addition, she wanted to get to the boat before her next dive group arrived. She liked to be fully prepared for a new dive group, especially divers she had never met. She glanced at the email she had printed from her computer:

Group Name: Diversified Divers
How many in group: 2
Group leader: Scooby Margolies

Ten minutes later, Terry pulled into the Caleta Marina and parked near where the *Dorado* was moored. The boat appeared empty. "Anyone home?" She noticed movement in the boat's front cabin. Then Joe and Manuel, her longtime skipper, materialized in the doorway.

"Yes, we're home, dear. And now that you've arrived conveniently after we finished the heavy lifting, perhaps you could organize a few things."

"Very funny, Joe," she said, stepping aboard and delivering a sharp elbow to his ribs. "Hi, Manuel. Everything all shipshape?"

"Si, Terry. All is in order."

Terry had hired Manuel when she started her dive operation. After working together for almost twenty years, she trusted him with her life and the lives of her customers. "Thanks, good job."

They heard a noisy engine and turned to see a van approaching. The van pulled up next to Terry's car.

"This the *Dorado*?" asked the driver.

"Sure is," replied Joe. "Are you the Diversified Diver group?"

"That's us," said the driver, stepping out of the van. "I'm Jeff Margolies," he said, extending his hand. "And this is my wife, Jamie."

"Nice to meet you," Jamie said. "We usually dive with another operator, but we've read so many great reviews about you guys on TripAdvisor that we decided to dive with you while we're still here."

"I hope Terry and I live up to our advanced billing," Joe said with a confident smile. He looked around. "I see there's a Scooby Margolies on the reservation. Is he here?" Joe asked.

"That's me, too," Jeff said, grinning.

Joe laughed. "Scooby? For real?"

"When my husband is diving or riding his motorcycle that's what we call him," Jamie explained, rolling her eyes.

"So, you're just a two-person group?"

"Not all the time," Scooby replied. "There's usually at least six of us, but the rest of the group went home already. Jamie and I extended our trip for a couple of extra days. As Jamie said, we heard a lot of good things about your operation, so we decided to book with you."

"Hi. I'm Terry, Joe's boss," she said, nodding to her husband.

"Okay, I get it. Jamie's my boss, too." Scooby laughed.

"Great meeting you. Grab your gear, step aboard, and you can start filling out some paperwork," Terry said, pulling out a clipboard with forms for them to sign.

Once everyone was settled, Manuel flipped a switch and the *Dorado's* twin 200-horsepower Yamahas rumbled to life. Terry cast off the mooring lines and Manuel eased the boat from between two adjacent boats. He slowly threaded his way through the marina, past the El Presidenté Hotel into the open channel toward their next pickup point.

⌣

Dayle walked through the sand toward the pier where the *Dorado* would soon pick her up. It was a short distance from the beachfront condo she had rented, only about a hundred yards, but even at eight o'clock the early morning sun already pierced through the palm trees. She perspired as she carried her dive gear in a mesh bag slung over her shoulder.

"This feels delightful," she said, strolling the last few yards through the surf to cool her toes. She climbed several stairs up to the pier and walked toward the end. Looking down through the crystal-clear water, she spotted schools of Bermuda chubs swimming around the pilings. Several needlenose fish skimmed along, darting beneath the pier every time a hunting pelican's shadow flitted across the surface. A palapa roof covered the end of the pier, providing shade to about twenty divers waiting for their morning pickups. They looked like commuters at a train station, waiting for the morning express.

Dayle dropped her gear bag with a heavy thud and sat on a short piling. She faced north, the direction the *Dorado* would be coming from. She watched the morning dive-boat parade pass the pier toward the southern reefs, Palancar, Colombia, Paso del Cedral, among others. Occasionally, a boat would peel off and race toward the pier to pick up customers, and then speed off toward their dive destination.

Dayle was still waiting at 8:20 and glanced at her watch. She spoke to another diver, also waiting for his dive boat. "I don't know where my ride is. My dive operator told me she would pick me up at 8:15 Mexican time. I guess that means I should add about ten minutes."

At 8:30 Dayle spotted three dive boats racing in her direction from the north. One was clearly outpacing the other two, bow riding high in the water, exposing the aqua blue color of the hull. She recognized the *Dorado*. Manuel expertly swerved the boat toward the pier as the other two boats sped past.

"Buenas dias, Dayle!" Terry shouted, recognizing her friend.

"G'morning, mate," Dayle said with her characteristic Aussie pluck.

Manuel steered the *Dorado* next to the pier as Joe lassoed a piling with the bowline. "Pass me your gear and hop aboard," Terry said. Dayle swung her gear bag over the side of the boat and Terry caught it. She grabbed a railing, swung onto a seat and jumped to the deck, almost in one motion. Terry embraced her with a long hug. "It's so good to see you!"

"Same here, mate."

"Hey what about me?" a male voice asked.

"Hi, Joe. Great to see you as always," Dayle said, hugging him with teary eyes. "And you too, Manuel."

After Terry wiped her own eyes, she introduced Dayle to Scooby and Jamie.

"Sorry we were late, Dayle. Scooby overslept," Jamie said.

"Hey, cut me some slack, Jamie." He turned toward Dayle

and grinned. "I guess I had one too many margaritas last night."

"No problem, mate. Oh, excuse me, I mean Scooby," Dayle said, teasing.

Jamie broke in. "My husband's real name is Jeffrey. But when we're scuba diving, he's Scooby. But none of the clients at his law firm know that. To them he's strictly Jeffrey Margolies, Esquire."

"Ah yes, I can relate. I'm married to a Jeff. He's a challenge, too. Must be something about the name," Dayle said with a forced smile. She noticed Terry looking at her watch. "What's up? Are we waiting for anyone else?"

"Yeah, some guy who just contacted me. I never met him before . . . I think I see him coming now."

They glanced toward the end of the pier and saw a tall man running toward them, carrying a dive bag loaded with his equipment.

"Hey, sorry I'm late. Are you Terry?"

"That's me. Are you Mike?"

"Sure am." He handed his bag down to Joe, then grabbed a metal rail and swung himself onto the boat. He landed with a thud. "Mike Handy," he said, extending a beefy hand. "Sorry I'm a bit late. Had a flight delay last night and I guess I overslept."

"Hi, Mike, I'm Joe. You've been emailing my wife Terry about your arrangements. And this is Jamie and Scooby. Terry'll take care of your paperwork and I'll set up your gear. How much weight do you need?"

"I'm wearing a 3-mil suit, so I'll take sixteen pounds. Four fours if you have 'em."

Joe assessed Mike's physical build. "Let's see. I'd say you're about six-one, maybe 190, pretty muscular, and you look pretty fit for a guy in your, what, I'd say mid-fifties?"

Mike laughed, listening to Joe's estimate. "Close enough, Joe."

"Okay, then. Sixteen pounds should do it. You using a weight integrated BC or a weight belt?"

"Got a belt in my bag, thanks. I'm traveling light this trip so I told Terry I'd rent a BC and regulator."

"Okay, fine. How about you, Dayle?"

"Brought my own BC and reg, but I'll take six pounds. I'm not wearing a wetsuit."

"Ah yes, I remember from last time. No wetsuit, just a bikini," Joe said, smiling.

Dayle caught Mike's scrutinizing glance, as he listened to her exchange with Joe. "Don't need a wetsuit on this trip, mate. The water's warm and my buoyancy is spot on, so I won't be scraping my arse on the coral."

Mike smiled, as he contemplated her paisley-print bikini. "I sure hope not. Not that I'm worried about the coral, but I'd sure hate to see you scar up those beautiful legs. By the way, where're you from? I haven't heard 'ass' pronounced 'arse' in a long time. Isn't that British?"

"I'm originally from Australia but been living on Roatan for the past three years . . . with my husband." Dayle emphasized the last piece of information when she noticed Mike's friendly smile turn into a leer.

"Ah, I see," Mike replied, catching Dayle's curve ball. "Excuse me for a minute. I have some paperwork to fill out."

Dayle nodded with a smile as he walked toward the front of the boat where Terry waited with several forms he needed to sign. Joe cast off the line and Manuel steered the *Dorado* into the open channel and turned north.

"Hey, where're we diving today?" Scooby asked, knowing most of the reefs were located south of the pier.

Terry was still working on Mike's paperwork but replied, "In your email you mentioned that you're tired of just seeing coral and fish, so I thought for our deep dive we'd dive on a wreck. I noticed on your paperwork you have a master diver certification, and Jamie's a divemaster. Mike's an advanced diver, so I think you'll all be able to handle it. Then on our second dive, we can explore the sea life on Chankanaab Reef."

"Sounds good" said Scooby. "What wreck are we diving?"

"It's called the *C-53*, an old converted minesweeper. Joe'll give you the briefing."

"Okay, Ter," Joe said, on cue. "The wreck sits upright in about eighty feet of water. She's about . . ."

Terry tuned out Joe's dive briefing. She knew all too well about the *C-53*. It was a shipwreck that had changed her life sixteen years ago.

CHAPTER 11

Terry's mind wandered back to a time when she was single, and her last name was Hunter. She had left California after her fiancé, Mark, died in the jaws of a great white shark. She selected Cozumel as the place to start her life anew and worked for a hotel's dive operation for several years.

After an altercation with her boss, which left him with sore, bruised testicles, she left and started her own dive operation, *Dive with Terry*. One day while diving with her customers on this wreck, Terry spotted dead fish on the bottom. Other fish swam around, some upside down, others in a spasmodic motion, obviously sick and disoriented. Drug smugglers had stored boxes of contaminated cocaine inside the wreck for later retrieval. One box had split open, poisoning nearby sea life.

She also remembered the near-fatal attempt on her life by the head of the drug cartel and meeting a New York City detective named Joe Manetta when she woke up in the hospital. She recalled teaching Joe how to dive and how she had helped his task force crack the drug ring.

Terry's mind returned to the present. She smiled thinking about her life now, as Mrs. Manetta with their two teenagers, Jackie and Peter.

"For our descent," Joe continued, "we'll use a downline tied to a mooring buoy. The line is attached to the bow of the wreck. Although divers aren't permitted to wear gloves while diving in the marine park area, use them if you brought them. The line is usually covered with hydroids and you don't want your hands getting stung. And there are also some sharp, rusty edges on certain parts of the ship. Terry'll be waiting at the bottom and I'll pick up the rear. Follow her along the hull, down near the sand. The current will be weaker there. You'll end up by the prop. If anyone has a camera that's a great photo op. Use your flash and you'll get nice shots of red encrusting sponges on the prop blades. Then we'll . . ."

While Joe spoke, Terry observed that the divers appeared relaxed and confident. Even though they were all experienced divers, she preferred to follow the normal protocol of everyone diving with a partner. She decided to pair up Dayle and Mike. At the conclusion of Joe's dive briefing, Terry pulled them aside. "If you two don't mind buddying up, I'd appreciate it."

"Sure Terry, no problem," Dayle said.

Mike just nodded with a Cheshire-cat grin. Dayle jumped in first and descended along the mooring line. After the other divers jumped in, Joe followed. They looked below and saw the bow of the *C-53*. One by one they descended using the line, while Terry waited on the sandy bottom, eighty feet below. A moderate current tugged at them, and they held the line to avoid being swept off the wreck. Reaching the ship's bow, they let go of the line and descended quickly to the sand, where the hull blocked the current.

They swam single file with Terry leading them toward the stern. Along the way they peeked beneath the bottom of the hull, spotting an occasional lobster or eel hiding. At the stern, Scooby took shots of the group posing next to the propellers. Every time his strobe fired, the prop blades, which appeared a blotchy brownish-green underwater in natural light, exploded into colorful shades of reds and orange for a split second.

The divers followed Terry around the stern to the port side and ascended to the deck. Mike Handy was just behind Dayle with Joe trailing. Joe noticed Mike seemed more interested in watching Dayle's legs than the shipwreck.

On the ship's rear deck, they swam around the corroding structures and beams, playing tag with French angels, butterfly-fish, and a school of curious horse-eye jacks. A large resident grouper, easily weighing over a hundred pounds, watched them while several tiny cleaner fish nibbled dead skin and ectoparasites from its gills. They all stayed clear of a four-foot barracuda that eyed the intruders entering his domain.

Terry continued to the starboard side of the hull, where a large hole had been intentionally cut, allowing the divers easy access below deck. The group followed Terry through passage-ways, dimly lit by ambient light. They stopped to peek into large rooms, some inhabited by schools of tiny silversides and glassy sweepers. When Scooby's strobe fired, the rooms illu-minated from the reflections of their silvery scales.

Along one passageway, Terry spotted a line tied to the top of a stair rail, descending to a lower deck housing the ship's latrine. She knew some dive operators let their customers follow the line down for a toilet bowl photo op. She never thought the possibil-ity of someone getting lost or trapped below deck was worth the risk for a photograph, so she kept going, swimming out through the opposite side of the hull and up to the ship's wheelhouse.

Scooby directed his wife and the group inside the wheelhouse while he remained outside with his camera, in front of a row of portholes. They stuck their heads through the portholes for a group shot. Since they had been underwater for forty-five minutes, Terry motioned the divers to check their air. Mike and Scooby were down to 700 pounds of pressure, less than one-quarter of a tank, Terry's safe minimum. She signaled everyone to ascend to fifteen feet for their three-minute safety stop, and they swam single file toward the bowline. The current had picked up and they looked like flags in the wind, holding tightly to the line to avoid being swept away.

At only two minutes into the safety stop, Scooby saw Jamie resume her hand-over-hand ascent. He tugged her fin trying to keep her down longer, but she kicked him off and continued slowly to the surface as he held onto the line. When all the other divers completed their safety stops, surfaced, and clambered aboard the *Dorado*, Scooby lost no time getting in Jamie's face.

"Hey, Jamie, you blew your safety stop! Don't you know—"

"Whoa big guy! I know what I'm doing. My arms were tired from holding onto the line and I was afraid I'd lose my grip in the current and—"

"No excuse, babe! You could have . . ."

After the two argued, Jamie went to the other side of the boat and sat next to Dayle. Dayle leaned over and whispered to Jamie, "He's a pretty intense bloke, isn't he?"

"Oh, not really. Scooby's just very safety conscious. Our group that we usually dive with has always had a perfect safety record and he wants to keep it that way," Jamie explained in her husband's defense. "And we've dived all over the world, even to some exotic locations in the Pacific, where we've experienced some amazing adventures and seen some pretty strange creatures." Jamie looked out over the multihued, blue water and smiled. "But the Caribbean, especially Cozumel, is my favorite place to dive."

Dayle smiled back. "I agree. It is a beautiful part of the world. What kind of work do you do?"

"I'm a mortician."

"Really? Handling dead bodies would creep me out. How do you stand it?"

"It's not so bad. You get used to it. Besides, the job has its exciting moments."

"Such as?"

"Oh, you'd be surprised how many details coroners and detectives miss when they examine bodies at crime scenes. I've actually proved that some suspicious deaths they were going to write off as natural causes were really murders."

"No way!"

"Yeah. I've actually been called to testify in court several times. And based on my testimony, two suspects were convicted of murder."

"Pretty impressive," Dayle said. "I think you mentioned Scooby's a lawyer?"

"Yes, he owns his own law firm."

"Sounds like you're living the good life."

"It was pretty rocky for a while. We struggled for the first several years. But then the business became more profitable. A couple of years ago, Scooby's partner passed away suddenly. That was unfortunate, of course, but financially it worked out for us since the law firm didn't have to support two partners anymore. And the extra money enabled Scooby to follow one of his passions, which is art collecting. He's gotten pretty good at selecting art that he believes will appreciate in value, and it usually does."

Scooby heard Jamie talking about his investment prowess in art and sat next to her. "Yeah, it helps me support Jamie's expensive taste in clothes."

"Oh, I don't spend that much," she said, playfully slapping his thigh.

Dayle started to ask Jamie another question when Mike moved closer to her.

"Where are you staying, Dayle?" he asked.

She turned and saw that Terry and Mike had been eavesdropping on her conversation with Jamie.

"I saw you getting on at our pier."

"I rented a studio condo at the Residencias Reef. I stayed here last time I was in Cozumel several years ago. I really like the location. It's a small unit but beachfront with a fantastic second-floor view of the water. And it's just like the owner advertised, my own little slice of paradise. I had saved his email address so I contacted him directly, and the condo was available. I heard he's a writer or something."

"I know the guy," Terry said. "He writes pretty good adventure novels. Dives with me when he comes down. Dayle, you know you could have stayed with us. We have plenty of room."

"Thanks. I thought about asking you, but I really need some peace and solitude on this trip. I need to do some serious thinking about my future. I'll tell you all about it later."

"Now that's a coincidence," Mike interjected. "I recently bought a place at the Residencias Reef. You'll have to stop in for a drink sometime and I'll show you around," he said, with a purposeful grin.

"Thanks for the invite, Mike. But like I told Terry, I'm just looking for peace and solitude on this trip," she said, shutting him down.

Terry checked her dive computer while Dayle was busy dodging Mike's invitation. "Hey gang, we've been up about twenty minutes." She turned to Mike. "For our surface intervals, I like to stay out of the water for about an hour. You okay with that?"

"Fine by me," he said, nodding his head.

"Okay. Since we're this far north, I figured we'd dive on Chankanaab Reef since it's close. There's no pier around here, so we'll just float around and Joe will tell you about our next dive. I think you'll find it interesting."

CHAPTER 12

During the surface interval, the group snacked on light refreshments that Terry and Joe had brought aboard. Joe began his dive briefing.

"Okay, this is a flat reef with some nice coral formations and plenty of sea life. Maximum depth will be sixty feet, and when someone gets down to 700 pounds of air, we'll move into a shallower area for our safety stop. Good chance that you'll see turtles, stingrays, some groupers, lobsters, and a wide variety of fish. We'll encounter some current, but nothing you can't handle. Just a typical Cozumel drift dive. I'll take Jamie and Scooby. Dayle and Mike, you go with Terry. Just try to keep together. No stragglers. Any questions?"

"Do they still keep captive dolphins over there?" Scooby asked, pointing to the dolphin pens at Chankanaab Park.

"Yes, they still do. For a hefty fee, you can swim with a dolphin. It's a big moneymaker for the park."

Just then a wild dolphin leapt into the air near the boat, somersaulting before falling back in a huge splash.

"Whoa!" one of the group shouted as another dolphin breached.

"Of course, you might get lucky and swim with a dolphin out here for free," Terry said, laughing, as everyone craned their necks waiting for the dolphins to surface again.

"That last one looked like Gemini," Joe said.

"Who?" asked Scooby.

"Yeah, I think you're right, Joe. Hey Scooby, did you notice that distinctive saddle-patch mark on her back? That's Gemini. She's a wild dolphin, but Joe and I have a long history with her," Terry explained. "We see dolphins in this immediate area pretty frequently. They're probably visiting their captive cousins. They can see each other through a chain-link fence. It's also quite possible some of those dolphins were captured from Gemini's pod. Dolphins do have a strong social bond with each other." Terry checked her wrist computer again and saw they had been on the surface for over an hour. "Okay, let's go diving!"

The divers donned their gear faster than usual, hoping to see the dolphins underwater if they were still in the vicinity. They descended and scanned the area but the dolphins had left. Scooby followed Joe, drifting along the top of the reef. Immediately, they spotted a large hawksbill turtle, as big as a coffee table, snacking on a sponge. The turtle was surrounded by French and queen angelfish snapping up the floating crumbs. Scooby snapped photos with his underwater camera.

Dayle smiled broadly, which allowed some water to leak into her mask. She blew air into the mask from her nose to clear it so she could enjoy watching the action. The interaction between the turtle and the angelfish reminded her of the photos in the children's book, *Harry Hawksbill Helps His Friends,* that Dayle had bought from the author who owned the condo she rented.

Terry took Dayle and Mike slightly deeper and focused on Mike to assess his dive skills, since she had never dived with him before. She already knew from past experience that Dayle was a good diver and had become a divemaster in Roatan. She noticed Mike's buoyancy and ear clearing were good, and he swam in a relaxed manner, in a perfectly horizontal body position with his arms folded. He descended easily and maintained whatever depth he chose. Terry decided this would be an uneventful dive.

Mike tapped his tank with a brass snap hook strapped to his BC to catch Dayle and Terry's attention. They joined him and he pointed out two large lobsters hiding under a rocky outcropping. While they observed the lobsters whipping their long antennas back and forth, they heard his distinctive metal tapping again. He found a green moral eel poking its head out of a hole in the coral. They assembled around the eel as it opened and closed its mouth, pumping water over its gills.

Terry and Dayle swam away to explore on their own and soon saw Mike's legs extending from a small cave. He backed out holding his hand over his head like a fin, diver sign language indicating he had spotted a shark. They finned over and looked into the cave and saw a large nurse shark sleeping. Dayle was impressed at his skill in spotting creatures and decided he was a good diver.

They continued their dive and toward the end of the reef met up with Joe, Jamie, and Scooby, already ascending for their three-minute safety stop. Terry, Dayle, and Mike waited below until Joe boarded the boat with Jamie and Scooby, and then ascended for their safety stop. Back on board they discussed their impressions about the dive, exchanging comments about the creatures they had encountered. Their drift had taken them closer to Chankanaab Park, where they observed divers entering the water from the beach.

"I didn't know you could do any shore diving around here," Dayle said to Terry.

"There's not much shore diving in Cozumel, but Chanka-naab's beach is an easy dive for new divers or for people trying a dive for the first time. There are some coral and sponge formations, a good variety of fish, and they even sunk a few statues. Plus, there's a couple of underwater caves that divers can explore. I think one of them leads into a lagoon in the interior of the island."

"Interesting. Perhaps I'll give it a go one of these days."

"You might get a chance this week. Remember Fulvio from your last visit?"

"I sure do," Dayle said, enthusiastically.

"He'll be diving with us this week, and he knows where a huge school of glassy sweepers hangs out inside one of the caves there. He likes to commune with them or something. It's a riot to watch him." Terry turned. "Okay, everyone onboard?" she asked, making sure no one was in the water. After a quick head count she turned to Manuel. "Let's head back to the dock and drop off our customers."

During the trip back to the dock, Mike deliberately picked a spot next to Dayle. "What brings you to Cozumel?"

"Back on Roatan my husband and I run a dive operation. I also own an art gallery. That's strictly my baby, though. He doesn't want to get involved with it. I'm taking a break from the business to look for some new original art. Some of the local artists are pretty good."

"That's interesting. I dabble in art collecting a bit. I have a pretty extensive collection."

"What kind of art do you collect?"

"Oh, nothing in particular. I just buy what I like at the time. But I'm in Mexico to do some collecting, also. Where do you obtain most of your art?"

"All through Latin America, but in Mexico I go to Oaxaca. The artists there produce some very unique pieces."

Terry was listening to the conversation and offered a suggestion. "Have either of you ever been to Galeria Azul, the art gallery downtown?"

"Been past it several times but never stopped in," Dayle said.

"It's owned by an American, Greg Dietrich. He produces some of the most amazing glass art you've ever seen. Some of his pieces are expensive but really nice."

"I'll definitely check it out."

"Me, too," Mike said. "Sounds interesting. Listen Dayle." He moved closer, invading her personal space as she leaned back. "Perhaps with our common interest in art we could check out Galeria Azul sometime."

"Possibly, mate," she replied with some reservation, concerned about Mike's intentions. "I wouldn't mind some company if you're knowledgeable about art. You might even come in handy," she said, as they both laughed about her pun.

Terry watched their exchange with interest, visualizing what Jeff would do to Mike if he saw him flirting with his wife. She also noticed that the mention of the art gallery had piqued Scooby's attention, and he was trying to listen to the details of their conversation without appearing conspicuous.

The dive site was a short distance from the Residencias condos. Terry expertly lassoed a piling as Manuel maneuvered the *Dorado* next to the dock. Mike consciously let Dayle climb onto the dock ahead of him. He enjoyed watching the way she moved and decided catching up with her was a less conspicuous way to continue the conversation than getting off first and waiting for her to disembark. He swung his gear bag onto the dock and climbed off the boat. "Good diving, people!" he said to the rest of the divers as the *Dorado* pulled away and headed toward the marina. He watched Dayle walk away.

"Hey, Dayle, wait up," he said. "How about dinner and then maybe we check out the art gallery that Terry mentioned?"

"Not tonight, Mike. I'm having dinner with Terry and Joe. They invited me over to their house this evening."

"Okay, perhaps another night or maybe lunch downtown?"

"Lunch sounds better," she said, concerned about where dinner with Mike might lead.

CHAPTER 13

New York City

D
r. Stephen Atcheson stepped toward the gurney, checked the white tag tied to the body's big toe, and compared it to his examination order and the attached death certificate. "Arturo Bavarro," he said aloud, confirming his next case. "Well, Arturo, let's take a look and see what circumstances brought you to us," he said to the corpse that could not hear his voice.

Atcheson enjoyed working in the office of the Chief Medical Examiner, also known as The City Morgue, because he was attracted to forensic medicine. Solving the puzzle of why someone died unexpectedly appealed to his inquisitive nature, and he also preferred patients who could not talk back. "The live ones are such a pain in the ass," he said to Bavarro's body, reminiscing about his unsatisfying days as a more conventional doctor of internal medicine. "And no more dealing with those fucking insurance companies," he said, continuing his monologue. He smiled. "Glad those goddamned, never-ending billing disputes are over. Now I can play golf whenever I want to."

The Office of Chief Medical Examiner of New York City investigated cases of people who died within New York's city limits due to criminal violence, accident, and suicide, or suddenly when in apparent good health. When Arturo Bavarro collapsed while hailing a taxi and was pronounced dead, he was brought to the city morgue, located at New York's renowned Bellevue Hospital.

Atcheson started with a cursory examination of the body, looking for obvious signs of apparent injury. Finding none, he proceeded with the autopsy, performing the classic Y-shaped incision in Bavarro's chest and examining the internal organs. One by one, he recorded each organ's size, weight, and description. Because of Bavarro's sudden death, Atcheson expected to see classic signs of a heart attack, such as an obstructed artery or an aneurism in the brain or other major artery. But he found no apparent cause of death. He was writing his autopsy notes when another doctor walked past.

"Hi Steve, how's it going?" Dr. Phillip Caruso asked.

"This one's a puzzle, Phil. Young guy, no apparent cause of death. I hate it when I can't find out why, especially with someone so young."

"I hear you. I had one like that the other day that was real weird. The guy died having lunch with a friend, just after holding a successful art exhibition. Since they were already on the East Side, we were the closest hospital so they rushed him down here, but he was DOA. Poor guy had a lot of success ahead of him. Shame. And I couldn't find any reason for him to collapse and die. Well, see you 'round. I have a pretty full schedule ahead of me today."

"Good luck. Hope you have better luck today."

"Hey, at least my luck's a lot better than my patients' luck," Caruso said, laughing. "See you later."

Back in his office, Atcheson was completing his report when he read what Bavarro did for a living. The notes said *Occupation: Artist/Painter/Sculptor.* He sat back in his chair, a niggling detail in his head making him tap his pen repeatedly on his desk. He tried to finish his report, but the nagging thought kept interrupting his concentration.

"Damn, what the hell am I missing? What am I trying to recall?" he muttered as he searched through the database of cases for the month.

The new operating system the city had recently installed enabled him to sort and browse cases by various criteria. He tried the obvious first: *Unexplained Cause of Death.* Several names came up. He selected various age brackets. There were many names due to the heavy caseload of a major city, and more names in the younger brackets than in the older age ranges, as he expected. Crime victims, accidental deaths, and drug overdoses were more prevalent in the young than the old. Then he selected *Occupation,* and scrolled through the list. Three *Artist/Painters* appeared.

"Hmm, that's odd," Atcheson murmured. He expected to find higher risk occupations, like truck drivers and construction workers. "What the hell is risky about being an artist?" he wondered aloud. He scrolled the three names. His most recent case, Arturo Bavarro, appeared first. Next, Caruso's case, William Bennet, appeared. Finally, a case he had worked on earlier in the month: Matthew Jaslow.

"Holy shit!" he exclaimed. "He was an artist too. That's what I was trying to remember." Atcheson read the case details, then made a call. "Helen, on the Bavarro case, please delay releasing the body. Something's come up. I need to take another look at him."

He took the elevator downstairs to the autopsy rooms and

found Bavarro's body in the fridge, awaiting transport to the funeral home. He slid the body out of the compartment and found an assistant to help him transfer it to a gurney and then to an autopsy examination table. He strapped on powerful magnifying glasses and examined the exterior of the body meticulously, like a paleontologist sifting through gravel for tiny fossils.

To begin the examination, he held Bavarro's right hand under the strong magnifier. He turned it over and examined a faint, innocent-looking bruise on the back of the hand that he had noticed the first time but dismissed. Thanks to the magnifier, he saw an almost imperceptible mark that appeared as a pinprick. "I wonder if that could be a needle puncture," he said softly. Using a scalpel, he confirmed the needle puncture.

"I'll be damned." He drew more blood and ordered additional tests. Then he snipped the "Y" incision sutures and re-opened the body cavity, looking for evidence his investigative instincts told him he would find. When he was finished re-examining the body, he called Caruso.

"Hi, Steve. What's up?"

"Phil, I did some additional investigating and examined Bavarro's body again. I ordered some additional toxicology tests to confirm my suspicions. I'm pretty sure his death was not an accident or from natural causes. What happened to your unsolved case, William Bennet? Can you redo the autopsy?"

"I think the family scheduled a cremation, but I'll check."

"Okay, let me know. In the meantime, I'm calling the chief. I think we have a problem."

CHAPTER 14

Cozumel

Dayle kept blow drying her shoulder-length, sandy-colored hair until she was satisfied. Then, she pulled her hair back in a loose ponytail. Next, she applied a bit of mascara to her already long lashes, a thin line of eyeliner, and a splash of eye shadow to accentuate her blue-gray eyes. She assessed the results in the mirror and decided she was satisfied. "Okay, got my keys, wallet, and I'm off."

Twenty minutes later, she pulled her rented car off the main road when she saw a wooden sign in the shape of a dolphin and followed a trail of beaten-down grass and brush through the mangrove. Several hundred yards later, she broke through the dense vegetation. A familiar, two-story, white stucco building stood in a clearing, with a view of the blue Caribbean behind the house. Just as she pulled up, the front door swung open and two teenagers emerged.

"Hi, Dayle!" the young boy said, waving. His sister ran a step behind him.

"Peter and Jackie! Oh, you've grown so much!" Dayle tousled

Peter's thick hair. "You're an inch taller than I am! And you're a young lady now," she said hugging Jackie.

"Welcome back," said Terry, as they walked inside.

"Ah, I smell Joe's famous paella."

"It's almost ready. How about a nice margarita? I recall on the rocks with salt?"

"Good memory," Dayle laughed. "So, where's your hunk?"

"I'm right here," Joe said, appearing from the kitchen holding a wooden spoon. "Why don't you all have a drink on the deck and the chef will join you in a few minutes."

"Sounds good," Dayle said, stepping out on a large deck that wrapped around three sides of the house. She sat with Peter and Jackie, waiting for Terry to bring drinks. "How old are you two now?"

"We're fifteen," Jackie said.

"Don't forget, I'm three minutes older," her twin brother said proudly.

"And you're still holding that over your sister. My goodness, last time I saw you, I guess about four years ago now, you already looked like carbon copies of your parents and now even more so. Jackie, with your long auburn hair and green eyes. And Peter, with your dad's athletic physique and wavy brown hair. Are you beating off the girls yet?" Dayle grinned as he blushed.

"Drinks are up," Terry announced, carrying a tray with three margaritas and two soft drinks. "Let's toast another amazing Cozumel sunset."

"Good idea," Dayle said, squinting through her sunglasses as a blazing pinwheel of colors shot out from behind the clouds. Seconds later, an orange ball slipped below the clouds and hung just above the water, creating a golden path that shimmered from the horizon to the beach. They sipped their drinks as the glowing orb oozed into the ocean and disappeared. "Bloody fantastic sight, isn't it?" said Dayle, clinking glasses with her hosts. "Here's to the sunset!"

"Here, here!" Joe said.

Peter and Jackie departed for the sixty-inch wide-screen television in the family room, letting the adults catch up. "Good diving today, eh Dayle?"

"Sure was. Scooby and Jamie were fun to dive with. And the fact that she's a mortician really blew me away."

"Yeah, me too. I can't picture a pretty little thing like her embalming bodies. And I noticed you have a secret admirer."

"Oh, you mean that guy Mike? Not so secret. I mean, he's so obvious. Kinda creeped me out at first. But he's a good diver, and when I talked to him later, he turned out to be an interesting bloke, what with his interest in art and all."

"Is that the mission you referred to in your email?" Terry asked.

"Yeah, I'm looking for something special to display or perhaps sell for the gallery. Something that will put LaLa on the map. Create some publicity, draw crowds. That sort of thing. Thought I'd start here and search on the mainland. I've had pretty good luck finding good Alebrijes art in the Oaxaca area over on the west coast."

"Excuse me, alebri-who?" Joe asked.

"Al-e-bree-hes," Dayle pronounced. "It's a form of brightly colored sculptures of fantastical, imaginary creatures. The genre started in the 1930s, when an artist fell ill and started to hallucinate. Maybe he ate too many mushrooms. He dreamt about a forest, where the trees, rocks, clouds, and animals turned into unknown animals. He saw donkeys with wings, chickens with horns, lions with bird heads, really weird stuff. Later, the artist recreated the animals he saw in his dreams using cardboard and paper mache. He called them Alebrijes, whatever the word means. Now it's very collectible art. A four-inch piece might go for several hundred dollars. Larger sculptures sell for thousands of dollars. We sell quite a bit at the gallery. But I'm very selective. I only buy from exceptional artists. A good piece might take almost a year to make."

"Oh yes, Joe, I forgot to tell you," Terry said. "I had never heard of it until recently either, but last week driving out from town, I saw a sign along the highway at the Discover Mexico Museum. It advertised that a renowned artist was visiting Cozumel and exhibiting his Alebrijes work. He was also going to teach an Alebrijes workshop for anyone who wanted to try their hand at making their own art. I think his name was Ramon Valdez or something like that."

"Yes, I know Ramon. His large pieces sell for thousands of dollars. In my gallery I've sold some of his small pieces, about the size of a coffee cup, for several hundred dollars. Since I'm here, I'll check out that gallery you mentioned, Galeria Azul, and then head over to the mainland. What I'm looking for on this trip has a connection to the ocean, so I'll stay along the coast. I'll check out the Playa del Carmen area, and then head south to Xel-Há and Chetumal, places like that." She reached into her shoulder bag. "Take a look at this." She handed Terry her copy of *The Portolan*.

Joe leaned over and read, "The earliest known globe to show the New World drawn on an ostrich egg?"

"Yep. I know finding something like that is a long shot, but the globe seems to have some connections to the Yucatan and the Mayans. It would make a fantastic addition to the LaLa collection. That diver Mike Handy mentioned he's an art collector, too. Maybe he's heard about it. Perhaps I'll pick his brain and get some ideas." Several seconds of silence followed Dayle's explanation, until Joe spoke.

"I don't know if involving Handy in your art expedition is a good idea, Dayle. Something about the guy just doesn't feel right. I can't put my finger on it. Maybe it's my old NYPD detective instinct rearing its ugly head, but I don't trust him. Why don't you ask Scooby to go with you? I heard he's an avid art collector."

Dayle nodded, considering Joe's advice. "I doubt Jamie would let him just take off with me, and I don't want to turn my expedition into a caravan. Mike's alone, and I don't even know if he's married. I haven't heard him mention anything about a wife."

"Okay. In any case, let's go inside and eat before my delicious paella gets cold."

After dinner, Jackie and Peter went to their rooms. They came back a few minutes later, wearing long sleeves and long pants.

"Where are you two going?" Joe asked.

Peter started to explain but Jackie answered first. "Did you forget we're going to watch the turtles nesting tonight, Dad? We just changed to longer clothes in case the mosquitos are out tonight."

"Oh yeah, I did forget. Sorry. Who's picking you up?"

"Lemuel and some of the other volunteers. They have this cool beach truck that can go off-road and—"

"Okay, okay. Have fun and don't get back too late."

"Don't worry, we won't." Just then they heard a horn beep. "Bye, guys."

"What was that all about?" Dayle asked.

"Peter and Jackie are involved with the sea turtle conservation society on the island. They applied to join the volunteer program, and they're attending as many events as they can to show their interest," Terry explained.

"And you can actually watch turtles making nests and laying eggs?"

"Yep. Greens and loggerheads. And you can also attend turtle nest releases, when they open a nest that's due to hatch, and you can watch the baby turtles race to the sea. It's one of the few places in the world where you can see that."

"That's amazing. I'd love to do that someday."

"Okay, I'll ask the kids to arrange it for you. But for now, let's have coffee out on the deck." Terry opened the screen door and looked up at the sky. "Oh my, look at that full moon. It's so bright you could almost read a book out here." She poured coffee and then there was an awkward lull in the conversation. The only noise was the tinkling of spoons against china, while they stirred and sipped.

Dayle finally broke the silence. "So, I guess you want to talk about the 500-pound gorilla in the room."

"Only if you're comfortable discussing what's going on with you and Jeff. You know we love you both. We're not going to take sides or judge anyone."

"It's pretty simple, I guess. We've kept pretty busy getting on with our lives in Roatan. Our dive business was successful, I got the art gallery off the ground, and I thought everything was wonderful. In my mind, starting a family was the next stop for us. We even started trying for a while but no success yet. But then Jeff started acting different. He became distant, distracted, making stupid mistakes with customers during dives. Finally, I confronted him." Dayle stopped speaking and took a deep breath.

"Don't tell me there was someone else," Terry said. "I can't bel—"

"Oh yes, there certainly was. Several thousand someone elses." Dayle saw Terry and Joe just stare, not comprehending her meaning. "A call from his CIA buddies woke up some yearning for action that he had suppressed. I guess once a SEAL always a SEAL? I don't know. Anyway, he said he had to leave on some top-secret mission. He couldn't talk about it. Some highly classified, top-secret shit. Said he still loved me, and he would return. I asked him when, but he didn't know. I—"

"Have you heard from him since he left? Do you know where he is?"

Terry glanced at Joe, which he knew meant stop interrupting.

"I heard from Jeff when he reached Europe. Just a short email to say he was okay. He said no more communication was permitted until the mission was completed. He told me some bullshit about going dark. I guess that's what's called going off the grid or some nonsense like that. Anyway, even though he couldn't say exactly where he was going, he said a few things that hinted he might be going to Iraq. So that's all I know." Dayle shrugged her shoulders.

"Jeff said he'll be back. Do I still love the big jerk? Yeah. But honestly, I don't know if I want him back. Maybe I won't know until I see him again, whenever the hell that'll be. I mean, if you really love someone, want to share a life together after all we've been through, how the hell do you just decide to leave? And if he does come back, will he wake up one day and want to take off again? Are his SEAL buddies more important to him than I am?" She drained her coffee. "So now you know as much as I do."

Terry paused before she spoke. "Wow, that's quite a story. I never expected to hear ..." She looked at Joe and knew he was concentrating, trying to make sense of what Dayle had revealed.

"We really hope things work out between you two," he said.

Dayle's eyes teared up. "I don't know, Joe. Sometimes it seems that my life is a roller coaster of unplanned misadventures."

"Oh Dayle, that's an overly dramatic assessment, don't you think?"

Before she could reply, Terry jumped up and gave Dayle a tissue to dab her eyes. Her own eyes flashed at Joe. "Overly dramatic assessment? I don't think so. Think about it. First, Dayle's successful career as an international business consultant comes to a crashing end because of some corrupt, politically connected idiot. Then, diving with us four years ago, because she accidentally photographs a couple of divers hiding gold inside a cave, an assassin working for the Cuban secret service chases her halfway around the world. And he almost kills us both—in case you forgot the details of that misadventure! And now the love of her life, who helped save her life back then, just ups and leaves her to go play soldier of fortune!"

Joe stared at Terry, speechless at her angry outburst. "Well, I didn't mean to—"

"Hey guys, I didn't mean to start a fight between you two." Dayle stood up. "I understand that Joe was just trying to put things in a different perspective to make me feel better." She hugged Terry, then Joe. "I really do feel better just talking about it with good friends. Thanks."

"We're glad if we helped," Terry said.

"We're diving tomorrow so I should leave and get some sleep. See you on the pier."

CHAPTER 15

New York City

Alexander Watkins, New York's Chief Medical Examiner, walked into the conference room and found doctors Stephen Atcheson and Phillip Caruso drinking coffee and slathering their bagels with cream cheese. "I'll take cinnamon raisin if you have one," he said, sitting down and pouring coffee into a travel mug he usually carried with him. Caruso passed him a platter and Watkins selected the last cinnamon raisin bagel. "I love these the best," he said spreading butter on his bagel instead of cream cheese. His informal manner temporarily concealed his no-nonsense managerial style. He got right down to business. "What's so important that I had to reschedule my meeting with the police commissioner this morning?"

Caruso deferred to Atcheson with a nod. "First of all, thanks for rearranging your schedule, Chief. But we either have a weird string of coincidences or a potentially serious problem."

"What kind of serious problem?"

"Serious as in a possible serial killer targeting the artist community."

Watkins stopped buttering his bagel and looked at both men. "Okay, gentlemen. You now have my undivided attention. Tell me more."

"A couple of weeks ago, I filed my first unknown cause of death in over a year. I'm not used to not determining the cause of death in my cases. Young guy just keels over in his apartment after a successful art auction. Girlfriend comes out of the bedroom dressed for a big night and finds him dead on the floor. I couldn't find anything wrong with him. Phil?"

"I had a similar case last week. Young painter having dinner with a friend, perhaps a patron, after selling a lot of his work at auction. He collapsed at the table. Some Good Samaritan gave him CPR until EMS arrived, but he died on the way to the hospital. I examined him and he seemed to be in perfect health."

"Except he was dead," Watkins deadpanned.

"Yeah. Looked like his heart just stopped. Steve?"

"A couple of days ago I had another young DOA, a guy named Arturo Bavarro. Same deal. No signs of arteriosclerosis, no aneurisms in the brain or other major arteries, nothing. When I was filing the case, something kept bothering me so I did some checking using our new wiz-bang system you just installed. That's where I found the occupational link. All three were already successful or up-and-coming young artists. Two painters and a carver. They all died within hours after successful auctions, where they had sold a lot of their work. I went back and re-examined the Bavarro case, more thoroughly . . ."

"You mean like you should have done in the first place?"

"Okay, Chief, you can bust my balls later. I've had a pretty heavy caseload lately. I just didn't . . ."

When Watkins raised his eyebrows, Atcheson realized he should just proceed with his report without making excuses. "Anyway, I found a bruise on the back of Bavarro's hand. I had noticed it the first time, but it just seemed like a minor thing, a slight discoloration, so I dismissed it. This time I examined it with those new high-power specs you bought for us—"

"You're welcome."

"... and I saw what might be a puncture mark. I did a little cutting and discovered a tiny, almost microscopic, needle puncture. I saved some skin particles around the margins of the wound and I redid the autopsy, this time looking for signs of poison, something that could cause heart stoppage or nerve damage, like neurotoxins. I also ordered some additional toxicology."

"And?"

"The tox report hasn't come back yet, but I found evidence that his diaphragm had been paralyzed."

"Respiratory arrest?"

"Yes. That's probably what caused heart failure."

"And did you determine what caused the respiratory arrest?"

"A lot of things can cause respiratory arrest, as you know. But I'm not sure yet. A fast-acting neurotoxin could certainly do it. That's why I scraped the skin cells around the wound. I should have the results back later today or tomorrow morning."

Watkins turned toward Caruso. "What about you?'

"Well, Chief, my case, William Bennet, exhibited some of the same characteristics, but his appearance suggested he was in more distress before he died than in Steve's cases. If they were all poisoned, perhaps the killer used something different."

"Now you're jumping to conclusions. Did you redo your autopsy yet?"

"Unfortunately, I just learned the family cremated the body, so we're out of luck on that."

"Whaddya mean 'we,' Sherlock? You're the one who performed the half-ass autopsy." Caruso blinked nervously but said nothing, hoping he would still have a job after the conclusion of the investigation.

Watkins turned back to Atcheson. "What about the first case you mentioned?"

"With your official 'okay,' I can get an exhumation order and re-examine the body, now that I know what to look for."

"All right, I'll sign the order. I'll lay some groundwork with the commissioner when I see him later, but I'm not ready to tell him we have a serial killer on the loose in our fair city until we have more evidence. Let me know what you find out as soon as possible. Like yesterday."

"Sure thing, Chief, I'll get right on it."

Watkins stood up, left his half-eaten bagel but took his coffee, and went back to his office. Atcheson looked at Caruso, who was perspiring from nerves. "We better get moving."

"Yeah, I'll give you a hand, Steve. If we missed something big, we're in hot water together."

CHAPTER 16

Cozumel

Dayle slung her dive bag over her shoulder as she walked to the end of the pier and checked her watch. She estimated Terry would arrive in about ten minutes. She shook her head, trying to clear the cobwebs.

Blimey, what a headache. Those margaritas were strong last night. Joe must have doubled up on the tequila.

"Good morning, Dayle."

She turned and saw Mike Handy walking toward her.

"Looks like a good day to dive, don't you think?"

"Yeah, I'd say so, mate. Sunny, no breeze, and a flat sea."

"Hey, isn't that Terry's boat?" he said, pointing at a small craft riding high in the water, running at high speed.

Dayle looked where Mike indicated. "Yep, that's the *Dorado*. But what the hell is that on the bow?"

The boat was less than a hundred yards out, and the figurehead stood up and waved. "Hi Fulvio!" Dayle shouted, recognizing her old friend.

"Hi Dayle, so good to see you again!"

"Who's that?" Mike asked.

"You mean you've never heard of FOTD, otherwise known as Fulvio of the Deep?"

Mike shook his head. "Can't say that I have."

"He's an interesting character, almost a Cozumel legend. I've heard he has over 2,000 dives here now. When Fulvio's not diving, he spends his time managing condos for clients. But since he prefers diving to managing, I almost feel sorry for them," she joked.

Manuel docked the *Dorado* next to the pier. Dayle and Mike handed their gear to Terry and Joe, and they jumped aboard.

"Here's to another good day of diving!" Dayle said to Jamie and Scooby. She hugged Fulvio. "Great to see you again! What's it been, four years since our last adventure?"

Fulvio thought for a minute. "Yes, at least that long."

"I notice you're wearing your summer whites instead of your wetsuit," she joked, looking at Fulvio's thin, white, almost see-through shorts.

"Gee, I hope I don't scare the fish away," he said, as everyone laughed. Joe watched Mike, who stayed apart from the group as he quietly arranged his dive gear.

"Where are you from, Fulvio?" Scooby asked. "I can't quite place your accent."

"Well, I've lived in Egypt, Kenya, Italy, and Canada, so perhaps my accent is a blend of all those locations."

"And he's got stories about every place he's lived," Dayle said. While she chatted with Scooby, Terry arranged the dive gear, filling weight pockets with lead as Manuel maneuvered the *Dorado* away from the pier and headed south. "Where are we diving today?"

"Scooby requested Palancar Caves. You know the site, right?"

"Sure, I remember it from last time I was here. Great dive site."

"Good. And during our surface interval we can decide the location for our second dive. Sit back and enjoy the ride."

She whispered in Manuel's ear and he nodded. Seconds later, the twin 200-horsepower outboards roared to life and the boat accelerated. Terry gave the dive plan. "Okay, in a few minutes we'll arrive at Palancar Caves, part of the Palancar Reef system. We'll start off at about forty feet, and once we're all at the bottom and comfortable, we'll head deeper. Maximum depth about eighty feet. Everyone okay with that?"

They all nodded and she continued with her briefing. "As some of you know, these aren't actually caves, but swim-throughs. You'll always see daylight. But swimming through the tunnel-like formations should be interesting and something different. Of course, lots of coral and sponges but less sea life than we see at some of the flatter reefs and walls. However, we could see almost anything—turtles, eagle rays—you just never know. Sometimes we've even seen a school of baby blacktip sharks."

Ten minutes later, Manuel cut the engines. "We're here, Terry."

"Thanks, Manuel. Okay. Everyone suit up. Scooby, Jamie, Dayle, and Mike, let's try to stay together. Fulvio will be on his own, as usual. Between his experience and all the extra safety equipment he carries, I know he can take care of himself. Fulvio, do you have your spare air and super-sized safety sausage?"

"Of course," Fulvio said, as he attached his safety equipment to his BC vest.

"He likes to head deeper and meet us in the shallows at the end of our dive. Everyone can do either a roll-back entry off the side of the boat or a giant stride off the stern. Dayle and Mike, are you guys okay doing a giant stride entry?"

They both nodded.

"Okay, you all know the drill by now. Take your positions and I'll come around and give everyone a predive safety check."

Once they were in the water and signaled Terry with the OK sign or fist touching the top of the head, they pushed the deflator button on their buoyancy vests and slipped below the surface, descending to a sandy bottom at forty feet. When the group was settled, Terry pointed toward the reef and everyone followed her. After they passed over the top of the reef, Terry and the group descended further.

They saw tall, seventy-foot cathedral-like columns of coral, hundreds of years old, rising from the sea floor to within a few feet of the surface. They followed Terry past coral walls, decorated with yellow tube sponges, five-foot-tall barrel sponges, and small pink vase sponges growing out of the coral. As Terry mentioned, there were not many fish, but Jamie pointed out a small hawksbill turtle in the distance. Terry swam toward a hole in the coral wall and they followed her into the first of several tunnels through the coral. Dayle and Mike trailed, preferring to take their time and enjoy the scenery.

Dayle followed the group into yet another swim-through, this one even more narrow than the others. A movement below caught her eye. She saw a striped fish, more than a foot long and very fat, sporting beautiful, long fins and spines. She knew it was a lionfish and immediately realized the danger. Dayle recalled seeing what happened to divers who brushed against those venomous spines. They all experienced excruciating pain, and occasionally the encounter proved fatal for the diver.

You probably filled your belly with a lot of reef fish last night, you bloody bastard, Dayle thought, watching the fish closely.

The normally shy lionfish moved toward Dayle, its long fins flowing and dorsal spines extended. She wondered if the fish was being aggressive or just curious. Not wearing a wetsuit, which would have provided a measure of protection, Dayle tried to maneuver away, but she was limited by the confines of the tunnel. The lionfish was now directly below her and began to ascend. Just as the fish was about to brush its spines against her exposed thigh, she rolled and kicked her fins, propelling herself as far from the fish as possible.

Damn, that was close!

She kicked again, to move farther away from danger, when her tank bumped against the ceiling of the tunnel. She heard a metallic scraping noise, and then, a mass of bubbles enveloped her. She attempted to breathe but received no air from the regulator. She froze.

What the . . . don't panic. Think your way out of this mess.

Dayle's training kicked in, preventing her from experiencing a diver's worst enemy—panic. She knew panic attacks underwater had killed more divers than all the shark attacks combined.

Okay, no air from my reg, and bubbles shooting everywhere. I probably tore a hose. Gotta switch to my backup reg.

She pulled out her alternate regulator from her BC pocket and pushed the purge button to clear out the water. She worried when no bubbles emerged from the regulator. Her worst fears were confirmed when she attempted to breathe slowly but received a mouthful of water instead of air.

Fuck! I need to kick out of here and get to the surface.

She surged forward with a strong kick, but her forward momentum abruptly jerked to a halt.

Shit! My damn hose is snagged.

She flailed her arms over her head, trying to free the hose as her lungs burned for air. Suddenly she felt the hose move.

A pair of hands gripped her waist and pushed her forward. When she neared the wide exit of the swim-through, Mike moved in front of her, holding his spare regulator in front of her mask. She grabbed it, spit out her mouthpiece, inserted Mike's regulator, and pushed the purge button to vent water from the regulator. Then she sucked in several deep breaths.

God, a breath of air never felt so good.

After several seconds, Mike gave the OK sign, asking if she was all right. Dayle replied with the identical sign and nodded her head for emphasis. They exited the tunnel opening, joined together by Mike's spare regulator hose, and saw Terry searching for her two missing divers.

Terry knew that Dayle sharing Mike's air supply meant something bad must have happened. She inquired with the OK sign, which both divers confirmed back. Then she pointed to Mike and held up her air gauge, asking how much air he had. Mike checked his air supply and held up five fingers, followed by three, indicating he had 800 pounds of air left, about one-quarter of a tank. Terry gave a thumbs-up sign, telling him she wanted them to surface now. Dayle immediately replied with the same sign. But Mike held up three fingers and a flat, palms-down hand sign, requesting that since they had sufficient air remaining, they should perform their three-minute safety stop. He looked at Dayle. She shrugged, and then nodded her agreement.

Terry immediately purged a strong bubble flow from her regulator, then inflated her yellow safety sausage and sent it to the surface, a signal to Manuel, who was following their bubble trail, that divers would be surfacing soon.

After completing their safety stop, Dayle and Mike surfaced. When Terry saw the *Dorado* pull alongside Dayle and Mike, she waited until they climbed aboard, and then she returned to Jamie and Scooby, who were still below, and continued their dive. They finned toward Joe, but Terry was distracted, wondering what had happened to Dayle and Mike.

CHAPTER 17

Aboard the *Dorado*, Dayle recounted her misadventure for the group. Terry stepped over to the tank rack and examined Dayle's equipment. "Holy shit, look at this!" she exclaimed. "Your tank valve cracked when you hit the top of the swim-through. And I bet I know why. Manuel, give me that light, please."

Terry unscrewed the damaged valve and shined a light into the exposed interior of Dayle's scuba tank. "See that corrosion?" she said, calling everyone over one-by-one for a peek inside the aluminum cylinder. After they had all taken a look, Terry explained what caused Dayle's near-fatal accident.

"These tanks are supposed to be visually inspected annually. We call it getting the tank VIP'd. Unscrewing the valve and looking inside like we just did will show whoever is inspecting the tank if there's any corrosion. If it's not in too bad a shape, the tank can be cleaned and put back in service." Before Terry could finish, Scooby interjected his thoughts.

"Yeah, and in addition to that, tanks are supposed to be

pressure tested every five years to make sure they don't explode when they're filled with three thousand pounds of compressed air. Otherwise . . ." He stopped when Jamie poked him in the ribs.

Terry smiled and continued.

"You can see here that besides corrosion inside the tank, the threads where the tank valve screws into the cylinder are also corroded. So, when Dayle bumped into the rock above her, the valve just tore out. I think I'll have a heart-to-heart conversation with our tank supplier when we get back this afternoon. You're lucky you had a pretty cool-headed dive buddy with you today. He saved your life." She looked at Mike, who just grinned, casually accepting the hero accolades from the group.

Mike glanced over at Dayle. She remained quiet, staring down at her feet, still visibly shaken after her near-death experience. Fulvio moved over and sat next to Dayle. He put his arm around her shoulder.

"Are you okay? That must have been a frightful experience."

Dayle took a deep breath. "You can say that again, mate."

"You feel like doing another dive today or would you rather sit the next one out?" Terry asked.

Dayle pushed her wet bangs back from her eyes and took a deep breath. "I think I'll take a pass on a second dive today if you don't mind."

"No problem," Terry said. "We have to drop Fulvio off at the Residencias Reef pier anyway. He has to meet the owners of some condos he's managing. He likes to check if they need anything repaired, if the maids are cleaning properly, details like that. We can hang out there for our surface interval since we'll be diving in that vicinity for our second dive."

On the way back to the pier, Terry engaged Jamie and

Scooby in some light conversation. "Besides diving, what else are you guys doing for the rest of the trip?"

"We're heading into town," Jamie said. "Dinner and some souvenir shopping."

"You know, I heard that there's an interesting exhibit opening at the museum downtown. My friend Greg owns Galeria Azul, and he's having an exhibition, showing twenty-five years of his artwork. I heard it's supposed to be very good."

"Thanks for the recommendation. We'll definitely plan to see the exhibition," Scooby said. "I always try to collect a little art from wherever we travel."

The mention of an art exhibition also caught Dayle's attention. She welcomed the distraction from her close call. "Really? You like to collect art, too?"

"Yeah, it dresses up my drab law office. Take a look at some of this stuff." Scooby pulled out his cell phone and let Dayle scroll through photos of the art collection in his office.

"Looks more like an art museum than a law office. What do your partners say about decorating the office like that?"

"Oh, it's just my own practice. No partners to worry about. At least not anymore."

"I see you like a mix of stuff. Some still life, action scenes, sculptures. You're a rather eclectic collector."

"I've found that the art impresses my clients. And if you know how to select the right stuff, it appreciates in value, so it's a good investment, too."

"That's certainly true. When I speak to the customers in my own gallery, I find they have various reasons for collecting. Some just want to own something unique and beautiful, some want to bring something home that reminds them of their trip, and some collect for monetary reasons, as you said." She handed Scooby his phone as the boat slowed. "Oh, we're back already."

Manuel docked the *Dorado* at the Residencias pier. Dayle gathered her dive gear, swung it up onto the dock, and climbed off the boat. She appeared slightly unsteady.

Mike seized the opportunity to remain alone with Dayle. "Terry, if you don't mind I'll blow off my second dive, too. Dayle looks like she could use a hand."

"Okay, we'll catch you next time," Terry said. As Mike climbed off the boat she exchanged suspicious glances with Joe. Neither trusted Mike's intentions.

Mike caught up with Dayle, as she and Fulvio were walking away.

"How are you feeling?" he asked.

"Surprisingly, a little shaky."

Fulvio gave Dayle a reassuring hug. "Look, Dayle, even though you're an experienced diver, an accident like that can give you the jitters."

"I suppose you're right. Perhaps a little rest and then a light dinner in town would help."

"That's a good idea. I wish I could hang around but I have to meet some clients. One of them's a real PITA."

"PITA?" Dayle asked.

"Pain in the ass," Fulvio said with a grin.

Dayle giggled. "Good one, mate. I'll have to remember that."

"Well, I have to go meet my PITA. Take care and I'll see you soon. Maybe dinner one of these nights?"

"That sounds great. Thanks."

"Mike, nice meeting you."

"Likewise, Fulvio," he replied. Walking through the sand toward their condos, Mike decided to make his move. "Listen, Dayle, that art exhibit they were talking about on the boat sounded pretty interesting. How about joining me for dinner and afterward, we'll take a look?"

Dayle thought for a moment before replying. She took a deep breath. "Sure, mate. The least I can do after you saved my life today is buy you dinner. Then we can visit the museum."

"Do you know where it is?"

"Oh yes. My last visit there almost cost me my life. It's a long story."

"Well you can tell me about it over dinner." He leaned forward and gave Dayle a short peck on her cheek before she could react. "I'll pick you up at six," he said, heading off to his condo with a wave.

Dayle stood still, watching him walk away. While she walked toward her building, she wondered why her feelings about Mike Handy were changing.

CHAPTER 18

Dayle decided to wait until Mike's car pulled up before meeting him downstairs in front of her building. Appearing too eager was not the impression she wanted to convey. "Hi," she said, closing the door and sitting just out of kissing reach. She deliberately folded her hands on her lap in the event Mike had intentions of holding her hand.

"I thought we'd go to Guido's. Nice place. It's on the main—"

"Yes, I know it well."

"Ah, yes. I forgot you've been to Cozumel before. By the way, you look beautiful tonight."

"Thanks, mate. Amazing how getting the salt water out of your hair makes a difference," she said, determined to keep the conversation light and unromantic.

Mike drove along Rafael Melgar, the main road which bordered the waterfront. Dayle looked to her left and watched the sun setting across the channel. It appeared as a blazing golden ball, turning the clouds to fire as it oozed into the sea.

Entering the town of San Miguel, Mike maneuvered around

pedestrians, mostly tourists racing to reach their cruise ships before they departed for their next port of call. He parked in front of Guido's restaurant and they went inside. They passed tables in the front part of the restaurant, which was decorated like an ordinary pizzeria. The waiter guided them through a doorway into a lush garden setting. He seated them at a quiet table for two, in a far corner of the restaurant. Dayle noticed Mike surreptitiously slip a bill into the waiter's hand and wondered if she should be annoyed or flattered that he was maneuvering for a private evening.

"How about a pitcher of sangria?" Mike asked.

"Sounds refreshing."

The waiter soon brought a large pitcher of ice cold sangria, flavored with generous portions of fresh fruit, and poured Dayle and Mike a glass.

"Cheers," she said, as she and Mike clinked glasses.

"Tell me about your last foray to the museum."

"It was several years ago. I don't really want to talk about the details, but the short summary is that I visited the museum because there was a skeleton with a decayed leather belt and gold buckle on exhibit. The buckle provided information about an investigation concerning a shipwreck that contained a shipment of gold. We put two and two together and realized the skeleton and the ship were connected. The story gets very complicated. A one-eyed dog named Pirata saved Terry, her friend Cozumel Kelly who owned the dog, and me from an assassin working for the Cuban equivalent of the CIA. The Cuban government was after the gold. I met my husband, Jeff, as a result of the incident, and we all lived happily ever after to tell about it. Okay?"

Mike sipped his wine as he listened to Dayle's summary. It was the second time Dayle had mentioned her absentee husband, so he decided to probe. "Did your husband join you on the trip?"

"No, he . . . he's away . . . on a business trip."

Mike did not believe Dayle but didn't want to challenge her explanation . . . yet. "What about your art gallery? What are you looking for?"

"I'm hoping to find some kind of signature piece that would draw publicity, besides selling for a bundle. I have some nice pieces made by several artists in Oaxaca and other parts of Mexico and Latin America. But with all the Mayan history in this part of Mexico, I thought I'd try my luck here in the eastern Yucatan. What about you?"

Before Mike could reply, the waiter came for their orders.

"I know the lasagna here is fantastic," Dayle said.

"Okay, I'm sold. Make it two."

"Let's talk about you for a change. What do you do for a real job?"

While Mike spoke about his background, Dayle thought about Joe's warning. After a quick internal debate, she decided to take a chance. "Have you ever heard the legend of the oldest known globe in the world, dating back to Columbus's time? It's the oldest known depiction of the New World, including a representation of the known Old World at that point in time."

Mike shook his head. "No, but it sounds fascinating. Tell me more."

"I've done a bit of research, beginning with some other globes housed in New York City that experts believe are based on this one. Evidently the artwork on the globe shows similarities to work by Leonardo da Vinci's students, so there might even be ties to the old master himself."

"Someone has actually seen the globe? Where is it now?"

"Yes, and I don't know, are the answers to your two questions. It was purchased by a private investor several years ago, and then accidentally destroyed in a fire. But according to legend, or whatever, the same artist had produced a second globe, which is rumored to be somewhere in the Yucatan."

"How does anyone know that?" Mike sat back, just as the waiter arrived with the main course.

"Hmm, smells great. I think you'll enjoy this."

"Looks fantastic. I'm sure I will. But please tell me. How and where did the rumor about a second globe start?"

After several bites, Dayle continued. "According to old records and ships' logs, experts have dated the globe to the late 1490s, perhaps early 1500s, when Columbus made several voyages to the New World. Letters and documents refer to some kind of navigational aid that he used. It is a known fact that he sailed to the Yucatan and had trading contact with the Mayans. It is also a known fact that one of the vessels in the fleet he sailed with on a later voyage was separated from his ship in a storm and had contact with a not-so-peaceful Mayan tribe. There was a bloody conflict that left the captain and some crew dead. The rest of the crew managed to escape with the ship but some stuff was looted, including the globe."

"And where in the Yucatan do you think this thing is? The Yucatan's a big place."

"I don't know yet. But coastal cities or towns that have strong Mayan roots seem like a logical place to start. Perhaps you'd like to join forces and help me find it for my gallery?"

"Possibly. I'm intrigued. Let me think about it and I'll let you know."

After dinner, they walked to the Museo de la Isla de Cozumel, where they noticed a crowd inside. "This must be the exhibition that Terry mentioned," Dayle said.

They saw a tall man, tanned, wearing khaki shorts, a pale-blue short-sleeve shirt, and flip-flops, speaking to several people.

"I like his smile."

They walked over and listened to Greg Dietrich explain how he made his engraved art. Dayle was fascinated and didn't object when Mike slipped away to examine some of Greg's art. He leaned over one of the displays and carefully inspected some of the smaller glass pieces featuring various sea creatures. They were illuminated as if they were swimming, trapped inside the glass.

Turtles, eagle rays, seahorses, and various other sea creatures adorned glass lamps and other large pieces. Mike had never seen such unique artwork before. Some pieces had no price tags, since they were on loan from private collections and not for sale or had recently been purchased during the exhibition. Available pieces still for sale carried price tags of several thousand dollars and higher. Mike looked around the room and made a quick mental calculation, figuring Greg's displayed art was worth over a hundred thousand dollars. He saw Dayle talking to Greg and waited for her by the exit.

"Seen enough?" Dayle asked. Before Mike answered, Dayle noticed Jamie and Scooby examining an engraved glass sea turtle lamp. "Looks like Jamie and Scooby are also interested in Greg's work. Let's say hello."

"I'd rather not if you don't mind. I'm beat and I bet you must be exhausted, too. Let's head back. Okay with you?"

"Sure. You're right. I am pretty tired." As they left, Dayle glanced over her shoulder at Scooby and Jamie, but their attention was focused on the colorful displays.

Scooby noted the price tags of Greg's art as he and Jamie walked through the exhibit. He made a quick mental calculation.

This stuff is expensive but very unique. Under the right

conditions, it might be a good investment.

Neither Dayle nor Mike talked much during the ride back to the Residencias condos, until they pulled in past the security gate. "Come up for a nightcap?" Mike asked.

"No thanks. You were correct. I'm bushed. But thanks, anyway."

Mike drove to Dayle's building. He pulled up to the entrance, jumped out, and opened Dayle's door before she could get out.

"Thanks for a nice evening, Mike," she said.

She felt his arm slither around her waist like a snake. He tried to pull her close and kiss her, but she placed her palms against his chest and pushed back, gently but firmly. "Not tonight, Mike, okay?" To her relief, the snake uncoiled.

"Sure, Dayle. I had a good time, too. I'll see you on the boat tomorrow."

She watched him drive away, confused by her feelings—flattered that Mike was attracted to her but unsettled thinking about Jeff thousands of miles away.

She wondered if her husband loved her as much as he loved going on his adventures with his SEAL team buddies.

Mike was not as confused about his intentions.

I feel the ice melting. If I play my cards right, Dayle might lead me right to that rare globe, or maybe I'll just get laid. Or if I'm real lucky, perhaps both.

He smiled.

CHAPTER 19

New York City

D r. Atcheson was reading his notes when Dr. Caruso and Chief Watkins entered the conference room. "Thanks for expediting the exhumation order on Jaslow, Chief. I really—"

Watkins cut him off. "Yeah, yeah, I accept your undying gratitude. You know my motto. When in doubt, dig 'em out." He looked around the room and shouted to his secretary outside. "I need some coffee. Anybody got some coffee? I can't think so early in the morning without caffeine! Okay, so what'd you find, Atcheson?"

"Same discolored bruise on the back of his right hand as Bavarro and a tiny puncture wound. I did a skin scraping and I'm still waiting for the test results, but since the body had been embalmed, there was no blood to test. I did open him up and found the same evidence of muscle paralysis in the diaphragm as Bavarro."

"Did the tests on Bavarro come back yet?"

"Yes. Traces of a neurotoxin. Specifically, tetrodotoxin."

"Tetrodotoxin? What the hell is that?"

Caruso opened his notepad. "It's a venom, a thousand times more toxic that cyanide. It can kill within minutes by causing respiratory arrest or heart failure."

"You said it's a venom. So that means it's not an artificially produced, chemical poison?"

"Correct, Chief."

"And what creatures produce that kind of venom? Snakes?"

"No, Chief—"

"Stop calling me Chief, dammit! You know I hate being called Chief!"

Caruso composed himself and continued. "Sorry, sir. Yes, well, certain sea creatures like pufferfish and the blue-ringed octopus produce that type of venom."

Watkins cocked his head. "What kind of octopus?"

"The blue-ringed octopus." Caruso looked down at his research notes and continued reading. "It's one of the smallest members of the octopi family. But in spite of its tiny size, one blue-ringed octopus carries enough venom to kill more than twenty adult humans within minutes. There's no antivenom, making it one of the deadliest creatures in the ocean." He looked up from his notes. Watkins stared intently but said nothing. Caruso continued. "The venom kills by paralyzing the muscles that control breathing, but victims can be saved sometimes if artificial respiration is started quickly, before cyanosis and hypotension develop. That's it."

Watkins turned back to Atcheson. "Are you on board with what Jacques Cousteau over here is telling me?"

"Yes Ch . . . sir. The venom acts by blocking the sodium channels, producing motor paralysis and respiratory arrest, just as Steve said. Most cases happen in Japan, where puffer-fish are eaten more frequently. If the flesh is not prepared properly, the victim can ingest the venom and die from food poisoning."

"And what about the goddamn octopus? Do I have to be worried every time I order fried calamari from now on?"

Before Atcheson answered, Watkins's secretary entered with his cup of coffee. "Anyone else want coffee?" she asked. They all shook their heads. After she left, Atcheson continued.

"Don't worry. Eat your fried calamari to your heart's content. The blue-ringed octopus isn't on any menus. Those deaths result when they bite. It's a shy creature, but if they're cornered, by a diver for example, they will bite. The poison is in their salivary glands."

Caruso interrupted. "Actually, Chief, calamari is squid, not octopus. However, eating too much fried calamari might result in a serious cholesterol problem, which could also prove fatal." He grinned at Atcheson.

Watkins turned toward him. "Everybody's a fuckin' comedian these days. And stop calling me Chief!"

Just then, Watkins's secretary opened the door and handed Atcheson a folder. He took it, removed a paper, and looked up. "Test results on Jaslow. Tetrodotoxin poisoning."

"Do we know what the victims ate for their last meal?"

"Jaslow hadn't eaten anything," Atcheson said. "I just found some residual alcohol in his stomach. And Bavarro had traces of wine and light food. He was at a cocktail reception, and what I found were bits of beef, chicken, and pork. No fish."

"What about your guy?" Watkins asked, turning back to Caruso.

"William Bennet was eating a salad when he died. Stomach contents were lettuce, olives, and tomatoes. But since he was cremated I couldn't test for—"

"Yeah, yeah, I know, don't remind me. But the symptoms were the same as the other two, so we can probably assume the same cause of death." Watkins pushed his chair back and got up to leave. "I meet with the commissioner in an hour. I'll give him the report and see how he wants to handle this. I'll tell him we're dealing with probable homicides, so it's his baby now."

CHAPTER 20

Cozumel

Manuel maneuvered the *Dorado* away from the pier as it pitched in the choppy surf. Mike sat next to Dayle on one side of the boat, and Scooby and Jamie sat across from them. Terry sat up front next to Manuel, who stood at the helm as he guided the boat into the channel. "Lots of waves today," he said to her.

She sat at the front of the boat and faced the group. "We have unusually strong winds from the south, gusting to almost twenty knots, so I figured we'd stay closer to home and dive Santa Rosa Wall. Everyone okay with that?"

They all nodded, so she continued the briefing. "We're almost there so you can start suiting up. We'll descend to the sandy bottom at about forty feet and then swim to the wall. The bottom is one thousand feet, but I suggest not going below eighty feet, okay?" Everyone laughed and began donning their equipment.

Dayle looked for her fins and was surprised to find them across the boat under Mike's seat, not where she had originally stowed them when she boarded. She wondered if someone had moved them. "Hey, mate, could you please pass me my fins?"

"Sure, no problem. Here you go." Mike reached under his seat and passed them across to Dayle as Terry continued her predive instructions.

"Entry technique. Mike and Dayle giant stride. Scooby and Jamie roll back." She stopped the dive briefing when Manuel cut the motors. "Okay, we're here. You can get into position, inflate your BCs, and I'll come around and give you a predive safety check."

Moments later, the divers splashed in and then popped up to the surface. "Everybody okay?" Terry asked. They all gave the OK sign and then pressed their deflator button, venting air from their BC vests, and began descending. When they reached the drop-off at the edge of the wall, Terry checked the divers again. The group had remained together during their descent, they enjoyed 100-foot visibility, and a mild current, a speed of only about one knot. She assumed this would be an uneventful dive. She remained relaxed when Dayle and Mike went a little deeper, knowing they were experienced divers.

Almost a half hour into the dive, Terry noticed the usually crystal-clear visibility was slowly diminishing, from one hundred feet, to eighty, to sixty. Grains of sand and particulates floated past them, like snow flurries. The current continued to grow stronger and whipped up the sand until it appeared as if they were engulfed in an underwater blizzard. Visibility was less than forty feet. Terry shook her metal rattle and signaled the group to keep close together and head for shallower water away from the wall's edge.

The current had changed direction, and instead of merely pushing the divers along, it was pulling them out into the deep blue channel. Terry led Scooby and Jamie away from the wall closer to the shallows and tried to find Dayle and Mike. The visibility had now dropped to twenty feet. She barely saw them in the distance, finning as hard as they could to reach the safety of the shallows.

Scooby and Jamie worked hard to make headway against the current, and Terry noticed they were tiring. She could no longer see Dayle and Mike and was concerned that the current had swept them out into the channel. She motioned Scooby and Jamie to find a rock and hold on and rest until they could catch their breath.

Dayle kicked as hard as she could, scanning the area where she had last seen Terry and the other divers. Suddenly, her right fin tore loose. She reached back to secure it, but the current swept it away. She noticed a broken fin strap flapping as it disappeared.

Crikey, I'm screwed now, she thought. *How the hell could a new fin strap just snap?*

She could not fight the current kicking with one fin, so she used a swimming motion with her hands to compensate for the lost power. But the current was too strong, and she realized she was losing the battle. The wall began to disappear from view as the current pulled her out.

Dayle looked at her depth gauge. It read 95 feet. Her experience kicked in as she assessed her options. She knew she couldn't make it back to the wall against the current, and a downwelling kept pushing her deeper. It was like fighting against an underwater waterfall.

She decided to take her chances on the surface and hoped a passing boat would pick her up if she got separated from the group. Dayle reached for her inflator button so she could transfer air from her tank to her BC vest and increase her buoyancy. If that didn't work, she knew the last step was ditching her weights. But just before she pressed the button, a hand appeared in front of her mask.

Instinctively, she grabbed the hand and kicked as hard as she could with her remaining fin. Soon the wall appeared through the sandy haze and she knew she and the other diver were making progress. She glanced at her depth gauge, 70 feet.

They passed the edge of the wall and saw another diver swimming in their direction. Dayle recognized Terry, since the diver wore a green and orange hoody and had a blue fin and a green fin. Terry extended her hand and Dayle grabbed it. She and the other diver pulled Dayle into the shallows where she saw Scooby and Jamie resting while they held onto rocks to catch their breath.

Dayle reached down and grabbed a rock, breathing hard. She wondered who had helped her get back to the wall. Mike sat next to her, grinning through his mask, giving her the diver OK sign. She returned the sign and then watched Terry inflate her yellow safety marker buoy and release it toward the surface, indicating she had decided to end the dive.

The group ascended together, surrounding Terry who held the line attached to the safety marker. They stopped fifteen feet below the surface, where Terry had tied three tiny knots on the line as a depth indicator. Their dive computers automatically went into countdown mode, so the divers would know when three minutes had elapsed. Terry held the group together until everyone gave the thumbs-up sign, indicating they were ready to surface.

Manuel was already in the area, alerted by Terry's surface marker. When he saw five heads pop up, he maneuvered the *Dorado* so that everyone was on the ladder side of the boat.

"Inflate your BCs and grab the safety line!" Terry shouted, so the divers could stay next to the boat while each one climbed the ladder.

Strong winds whipped the waves into four-to-five-foot swells, causing the boat to pitch up and down, increasing the difficulty of boarding. Dayle pulled off her remaining fin, heaved it over the side into the boat, and clambered aboard, followed by the other divers. Manuel helped each diver to the bench seats, as they staggered under the shifting weight of their forty-pound scuba tanks and weights. Terry boarded last. Standing on the ladder top, she counted heads. "One, two, three, four. Okay we're all aboard. Let's get out of here," she said to Manuel. "Great job following our bubbles under these shitty conditions. If you weren't there when we surfaced, we could have been in real trouble."

"Si. I know," he said, flashing a toothy smile.

Under power, the *Dorado* ceased pitching as Manuel guided the boat through the waves, positioning the bow to cut through the worst of the swells. Terry assessed the weather conditions and looked at her brood, all exhausted, heads down and still breathing deeply. She scanned the water, looked at the clouds, and shook her head. "Weather's getting worse. I recommend we blow off the second dive. How about it?"

"Fine by me."

"You got it."

"I'm done."

"Bloody yeah."

"Okay, I guess that makes it unanimous. Manuel, head for the Residencias pier."

Terry watched Dayle closely to make sure there were no lasting effects from her ordeal. "You okay? No aches and pains?"

"Yeah, I'm feeling all right. Just glad Mike wasn't too far away when my bloody fin tore loose. No way I could fight that current kicking with only one fin. I still don't understand how a new fin strap could just snap like that." She slipped her arms out of her BC and threw her mask into her dive bag with more than a trace of anger. She glanced at Mike, sitting next to her and elbow-jabbed him in the ribs. "Thanks, mate. Second time you saved my bacon. Looks like I owe you again."

"No problem. Just glad I could help."

Terry looked at him, puzzled. She usually trusted her instincts about people but decided she and Joe might have judged Mike too quickly. He had proven himself to be a good diver and a responsible dive buddy. After all, if not for him, Dayle might be dead.

Mike stood and patted Dayle on the shoulder as he passed by her to gather his equipment. As he stowed his dive gear, he saw her smile as she looked at him. He pretended not to notice as he knew his plan to play the hero to get close to her was working.

As that old saying goes, I'm "in like Flynn." But I bet Dayle would be totally pissed if she knew about that sliced fin strap.

CHAPTER 21

New York City

Detective Mike Monahan, known as Micko to his friends and the other detectives in his squad, finished reading the autopsy results his boss, Captain Sam Goldman, had dropped on his desk. As a scuba diver, the summary notes on the first page caught his attention.

> **Death by tetrodotoxin. Possible sources: ingestion from pufferfish or bite from blue-ringed octopus.**

He opened the file containing notes from the meeting between the examining doctors and the Chief Medical Examiner. He shook his head. "Why couldn't Sam have given me a simple, cut-and-dried shooting or stabbing?"

But Sam, walking behind him at the wrong moment, answered his question. "Because, as the senior member in my homicide division, I figure by now you have the smarts to solve the tough cases."

"Looks like the ME's boys are in hot water with their boss. They can't say for sure how the toxin got into the vics. Now I have to bail them out. This could be a tough case. Thanks a bunch, Sam. Hope I can return the favor someday."

"Sorry, Micko, I'll be retired before you have the chance." He slapped him on the back and walked back to his corner office.

"Screw you, Sam," Monahan said, smiling. "I just might put my papers in first."

"I love you, too, Micko. Might as well start interviewing. I suggest starting with whoever saw the vics last. Now hit the pavement." Sam closed the door, ending the conversation.

Monahan shook his head as he packed up his notes and headed toward the parking garage.

His first stop was the midtown office of Elaine Weatherly, Matthew Jaslow's fiancée. He called and informed her he was coming. Stepping off the elevator of the 32nd floor, he walked up to the receptionist.

"Ms. Weatherly is expecting you. Please follow me."

She led Monahan to a conference room and opened the door. Elaine Weatherly rose and shook hands.

"How do you do, Detective," she said, biting her lip, rapidly blinking her eyes. "Please have a seat."

He noticed her eyes were pale blue. Monahan assessed her body language. She seemed nervous, shifting in her chair, crossing and uncrossing her legs. He wondered if it was because she had a hand in her boyfriend's death or was just tense talking to a homicide detective. "Thanks for meeting me on short notice," he said, as he began the interview.

An hour later he sat in his car and reviewed his notes.

Vic #1 Matthew Jaslow. Weatherly & Jaslow were engaged & lived together. They attended his successful art auction at Christie's. Jaslow sold a bundle of art, mostly to one collector. On the way home, they stop to pick up some champagne to celebrate. They arrive home & the GF changes into something hot, hoping the BF will jump her bones. But GF finds BF dead on the floor. End of story. Not much to go on, but can't rule her out as a suspect. She's the last one who saw him alive.

He closed his notebook and headed for the next interview. The drive across town from Weatherly's East Side office to the restaurant where William Bennet breathed his last breath took thirty-five long minutes.

"Damn traffic and double-parked cars," Monahan fumed. "Wish I had time to give every one of these bastards a ticket."

Eventually, he arrived at the restaurant and pulled into the only open spot he could find, next to a fire hydrant. He placed his NYPD card on the dash and went inside. It was 1:00 p.m., so the place was packed with the lunch-hour crowd.

"Reservation?" asked the greeter.

Monahan just flashed his gold detective shield. "Official business. I'm here to meet one of your waiters, Juan Garcia. I called earlier so I know he's expecting me . . . Ms. Martinez," he said, reading her name tag.

"Just one moment, please."

Several minutes later Monahan saw Ms. Martinez return-ing. A young Hispanic waiter, in his early twenties, followed close behind. The waiter appeared nervous. His eyes stared straight ahead, a sheen of sweat glistened on his forehead, and his jaw muscles bulged, tightly clenched.

Poor sonofabitch probably thinks I'm from Immigration. Maybe he's got issues. I better relax him before he has a heart attack. "Hi, Juan. My name is Detective Monahan. I'm with the New York Police Department. Homicide Division. I'm conducting an investigation and was hoping you could help me. Okay?"

He offered his hand and Juan shook it weakly. His forced smile appeared more like a grimace.

"A couple of weeks ago, this man, William Bennet, had lunch here with a friend. I was told you were their waiter. Recognize him?" Monahan handed Garcia a morgue photograph of Bennet's face. He took it, studied it, and handed it back to Monahan.

"Yes, I recall that day. It was horrible."

It was a short, half-hour interview. Monahan reviewed his notes back in his unmarked police car.

> Vic #2 William Bennet. Waiter remembers him but not the friend. Never had a chance to give them the bill so no credit card statement or other info. Forgot what they ordered, except he remembers that it wasn't fish. They order a drink, start eating, and Bennet collapses. Some Good Samaritan gives Bennet CPR until EMS shows up, but he's DOA at Bellevue. Not much help.

Monahan checked his watch. *Only 1:30. Good. I can get over to Sotheby's earlier than I planned and knock off all these interviews today.* He flipped through his notebook.

> Vic #3 Arturo Bavarro.

"Okay, Artie, let's see what the good folks over at Sotheby's remember about you," he said, starting the car.

Eventually he pulled up in front of Sotheby's Auction House on the corner of 72nd and York Avenue, on the East Side. It was another aggravating ride across town, maneuvering around double-parked cars, trucks loading and unloading, and jaywalking pedestrians. He parked in a restricted area and once again placed his NYPD card in plain view. He went through the familiar routine of displaying his badge to the lobby reception-ist and asking for the person he came to interview.

Minutes later, Peter Barlow appeared, walking slowly, exud-ing an air of confidence. Monahan laughed to himself about the stark contrast to his last interviewee, Juan Garcia. Barlow was tall. Monahan estimated about six-foot-three, pale almost pink skin, with blue eyes and thin wire-rim glasses. His salt-and-pepper hair was parted in the middle and combed back. An expensive, dark-blue, pinstripe suit completed the costume.

Monahan extended his hand. Barlow hesitated, almost appearing to check if Monahan's hand was clean before shak-ing hands. Monahan caught the gesture and decided he did not like Barlow. "Hello Mister Barlow, I'm Detective Monahan. Homicide Division."

"Yes, Detective, my secretary informed me you were com-ing this afternoon. So glad you could make it on time." He smiled, revealing expensive, perfectly white, capped teeth.

"Well, we do our best not to keep the taxpayers waiting."

"Yes, of course. Let's go to my office." He led Monahan down a long hallway and invited him into a spacious office. Barlow sat behind his large mahogany desk and invited Monahan to sit across from him.

Monahan observed every detail of Barlow's office. Family photos on the credenza behind the desk featured a woman who appeared too young to be the mother of the three teenage boys in the photo.

Wonder if she's the trophy wife?

Nautical flags in glass cases lined the side wall and mod-els of racing sailboats were displayed on shelves. He noticed a fish tank in the corner. Monahan, an experienced scuba diver, recognized it was a saltwater tank, populated with expensive fish. He leaned closer to the tank, looking for a pufferfish or blue-ringed octopus, but saw none.

Too bad. I'd love to nail your cocky ass as the murderer.

"Well now, how may I be of assistance to New York's bravest?" Barlow replied with a patrician, almost condescending, accent.

"NYPD is New York's finest. The Fire Department boys and girls are New York's bravest. I'm investigating the death of Arturo Bavarro, and I would appreciate your help, sir. I was told you were one of the last people to speak with him, so I was hoping you could shed some light on his last few moments."

"Ah, yes, poor Arturo. Such a tragedy on the most successful night of his life."

"What do you mean, sir?"

"Well, he had just sold all of his artwork at extremely attractive prices. You might say the poor fellow made a killing, just before he died." Barlow laughed at his own tasteless joke.

Monahan smiled weakly. *What a dickhead.* "Can you tell me what happened the night Mister Bavarro died?"

"At a reception after the auction, I singled out the wealthy patron who had purchased most of his work. In order to acquire Arturo's work, the gentleman had forced the bidding to astronomical levels, far above what I estimated the value should be."

"What kind of food did you offer at the reception?"

"Nothing exotic. Just wine, cheese, and crackers. But very expensive wine, of course."

"Of course. No fish of any kind?"

"Just caviar. The best imported beluga caviar, of course."

"Of course. Please continue."

"After I introduced them, they engaged in a most animated discussion, enthusiastically shaking hands, smiling, laughing, that sort of behavior. Finally, they shook hands one last time and the buyer left. A little while later, after speaking with other guests, Bavarro also left. Alone. As he walked down the steps of the New York Public Library, where we held the auction, he collapsed. I'm afraid that's all I know."

"This buyer. Can you tell me his name?"

Barlow hesitated, coughed, and cleared his throat. "Detective, our select clientele expects us to maintain the utmost privacy and confidentiality regarding their identity. I'm sorry but I just can't—"

"Mister Barlow, this is a murder investigation. We can do this one of two ways. Either I obtain a search warrant and acquire your sales records, which would then become very public and embarrass your select clientele—" *probably a bunch of damn tax cheats—* "or we can do this quietly, right now. In which case, I walk out of here with a single name, without revealing you as the source of the information. Your choice." Monahan smiled, watching Barlow's Adam's apple bob up and down as he swallowed and assessed the implications.

"Well, ah, let me check my files and see what I can find, Detective."

"Thank you, sir." Monahan kept his eyes riveted on Barlow, who made a show of rifling through files in his desk drawer, until he finally pulled out a manila folder.

"Ah yes. Here are the sales records for that evening. I really just can't hand over confidential files without some kind of—"

"Just a name will suffice for now. Please make sure you don't lose that folder in case we need it."

Barlow handed Monahan the file and he copied the name in his notebook.

"I believe the gentleman mentioned that he is a lawyer. He was visiting from Fort Worth, Texas. He purchased almost all of Bavarro's art that night."

"Thank you. You've been most helpful to the investigation." Monahan got up to leave and extended his hand. Barlow stood, but his grip was wet and limp like a dead fish, much different compared to their first exchange. His eyes appeared slightly glazed. The detective was amused by the change. "Mister Barlow, looks like you've had a tough afternoon. Why don't you take a break and have some of that very expensive wine?"

Barlow managed a weak grin.

"I can show myself out. Thank you for your help."

Sitting in his car, Monahan reviewed his notes.

Need to go back and review the Jaslow case. His GF not important now. I have to visit Christie's Auction House where he sold his paintings and see if any familiar names pop up. Surprised this bozo Barlow was so helpful.

He pulled out his cell phone and dialed Christie's Auction House. After a short conversation, Monahan had charmed his way into a late afternoon impromptu meeting with the director of art auctions. He got back into his police cruiser and drove toward Rockefeller Center, back to the west side of town, feeling like a ping-pong ball.

This time Monahan found what appeared to be a legal parking spot. But after reading the parking sign indicating which days and times were legal, he wasn't sure. "Shit, ya need a PhD to figure out what these parking signs mean," he said, placing the NYPD card on the dash just to be on the safe side.

Inside, the receptionist introduced him to Heather Bancroft, pacing impatiently as she checked her watch. "How can I help you, Detective? My secretary said it was an urgent matter."

"I'm investigating the death of Matthew Jaslow and I'd like to ask you some questions about the night he died." Monahan studied Bancroft's face and body language for the signs of possible deception he was trained to look for: lack of eye contact, rapid blinking, changing breathing pattern, and blushing, among other signs.

Bancroft appeared genuinely puzzled. "Yes, Matthew's death was quite a shock. He was such a promising artist, a very nice young man, and he enjoyed a tremendously successful event. But he appeared fine when he left here. I even said good night and wished him well. I heard he died later in his apartment."

Monahan detected no signs of deception as he probed. "Was there anything out of the ordinary that night? Anything that didn't seem right to you?"

"No, not really."

Monahan remained quiet as Bancroft's expression changed, as if she struggled to recall some detail. She tapped her finger against her temple.

"But you know, I do remember one thing."

Monahan's eyes narrowed as he concentrated. He didn't want to interrupt Bancroft's chain of thought with a question.

"Matthew brought six paintings for the auction. They all sold. That's pretty unusual for a young artist exhibiting for the first time, even someone as talented as Matthew. But what really caught my attention was that they all sold for amounts significantly above our appraisal value. And our appraisers are very knowledgeable, among the top in the business."

"Any reason why they sold for so much?"

"The auction business is strictly supply and demand. One bidder kept outbidding everyone else. For some reason, he was determined to buy every piece, and he drove up the price until he was the last man standing, so to speak. Toward the end, other bidders got caught up in the action, as if they were afraid to miss out on an opportunity to buy paintings from someone whose paintings might appreciate further in value. I suppose that since there will be no more Jaslows, now they will."

"Can you tell me the name of this bidder?"

Bancroft hesitated.

"Ms. Bancroft, I know the confidential client drill. This is a murder investigation and I need to follow every potential lead. I'm not asking for details such as how much this person paid or how. I just need a name. I can return later with a search warrant."

She pulled an index card from a folder she carried in her hand. "I anticipated your question and already cleared it with my boss. Of course, if you need additional details, then we will require something official in writing." She handed him the card.

Monahan read the name. He liked Heather Bancroft. He briefly entertained the thought of asking her out to dinner but realized it would not be appropriate. "Thank you for your cooperation," he said shaking her hand.

Back in his apartment, Monahan drained a cold beer between bites of microwaved, day-old pizza while he flipped through his notebook.

Same name pops up in two of these three cases. Assume this guy was also William Bennet's mysterious lunch partner. Tomorrow's meeting with Sam and the commish should be interesting.

CHAPTER 22

Cozumel

The driver sped purposefully along Rafael Melgar toward downtown San Miguel. But he was not going all the way into town. He slowed as he neared the turn-off into the Discover Mexico Museum and pulled into the parking lot. He maneuvered his car past several tour buses that had brought customers from the cruise ships and parked in the area designated for automobiles. He strolled casually among the tourists, appearing as one of them, wearing a broad-brimmed hat and sunglasses. To complete his outfit, he wore a tropical shirt which featured a smiling parrot holding up a LandShark Lager beer and proclaiming, *Fins Up!*

He paid a fifty-dollar admission to the Alebrijes exhibit and workshop. He had done his research and knew all about Ramon Valdez and the rising value of his art. He considered the fifty dollars a good investment. He checked his dive watch. The next workshop was due to start in forty-five minutes.

He walked over to the section where various art was for sale by local Mexican artists, but he focused on the Ramon

Valdez Alebrijes collection. He admired the multicolored, phantasmagoric creatures the artist had created. They were posed in various positions: standing, sitting, or leaping. Some had horns or pronged antlers, others just had strangely shaped heads. They sported pointed tales, cloven hoofs, or clawed feet. Their wild eyes and expressions resembled the stuff of night-mares or someone's mushroom-induced dreams. He quietly purchased as much of Valdez's art as he could afford, trying not to attract attention. Twenty-three thousand dollars later, most of Valdez's art was in the trunk of his car.

He walked over to the line forming to enter the next Ale-brijes workshop. One more was scheduled afterward, but the new owner of almost the entire Valdez collection knew the last workshop of the afternoon would never be held. He had hoped that Señor Valdez would mix with the people outside the workshop, but he soon realized taking the course was the only way to get near the master.

The risk of anyone remembering him was minimal, since he blended so well with the cruise-ship crowd. The afternoon heat and humidity was intense, even in the shade. He wiped his sweaty brow with a handkerchief. As the doors opened, the crowd caught some relief as an air-conditioned breeze flowed out of the building.

He spotted Valdez standing at the door, shaking hands with the happy attendees as they filed out, each holding their own personally crafted Alebrijes treasure, worth about $2.50 in materials. He mentally calculated how much Valdez would make at the ticket price of $50 times about 50 people per work-shop, holding several workshops per day.

As soon as the hall was empty, the line moved. Once inside, the man removed his hat and sunglasses and chose a seat at a table in the rear, so he would be sitting behind most of the attendees, out of their line of sight. Once each person was seated, Valdez entered the room. He made a short presentation in English and Spanish, discussed the history of Alebrijes art, his method of construction, and ideas for how the tourists in the class could create their own art. The staff gave each person a supply of material: paper, glue, paint brushes, and paint. Valdez told them they had about a half hour to create their masterpieces since another workshop was scheduled, and everyone had to get back to their ships before they departed.

As the tourists worked, Valdez walked up and down the aisles, offering encouragement and suggestions. When he stopped at his unknown benefactor's table, he admired his creation, which looked like a psychedelic hummingbird with huge eyes and an oversized beak. The two men exchanged pleasantries, and Valdez moved on to the next person.

When Valdez announced they had several minutes to complete their artwork, the man excused himself and went to the restroom marked *Baños*, with the image of a male figure wearing a sombrero on the door. He finished his preparations, and when he came out, the exit line had already formed. Valdez thanked each person individually as they filed out. He grimaced slightly as the man near the end of the line shook his hand very enthusiastically.

The staff cleaned out the room preparing for the next group, while Valdez rubbed the back of his right hand, which began to itch. As the line for the next workshop was about to enter the room, Valdez had trouble breathing as he walked inside. A young woman was the first person to enter. When she saw Valdez's body lying face up on the floor, eyes wide open, lips blue, she screamed.

CHAPTER 23

M ike had just finished buttoning his shirt when the phone rang. "Hello?"

"Mike, it's Dayle."

"Everything okay?"

"Sure, I'm fine. No harm from today's mini-disaster. Thanks to you. I was wondering if I could treat you to another dinner. Least I could do for your heroics today. This is becoming a habit."

"Love to but I have to run some errands downtown."

"Well, perhaps I could meet you afterward? Ever been to Pancho's Backyard?"

"Yeah, Pancho's is one of my favorite haunts."

"Good. I'd like to discuss my plans for my treasure hunt if you're interested."

"Works for me. How about eight o'clock? I should be finished by then."

"Fantastic. Pancho's at eight. See you then."

He hung up the phone and assessed himself in the mirror.

"Well, here's to a successful conclusion to the evening," he said to his image.

A car pulled up to the curb on Rafael Melgar, a block north of the museum. The driver parked and strolled into the exhibition hall housing Greg Dietrich's art collection. He scanned the crowd but Dietrich was not in the room. He walked around the gallery, making notes on the pieces he wanted to purchase. He jotted down the names of the most expensive pieces, and then approached a salesperson, a young woman who had just finished speaking with another customer.

"Hola, Señor. My name is Sonya. How may I help you?"

"Follow me please, Sonya."

Together they walked around the gallery as he quietly pointed out the items he had selected. First, a pair of blue glass hanging lamps, one adorned with the etched image of an octopus, the other with a seahorse. Next, several glass vases, one engraved with a parrotfish and one showing a splendid toadfish with its frilly mouth, peering out from its protected crevice. Another vase portrayed two black-and-white drum fish with flowing fins, dancing circles around each other. A larger flat vase featured a pair of eagle rays soaring over a reef fringed with waving soft corals. The salesperson appeared breathless trying to keep up writing the orders as the customer continued, pointing out various selections. They strolled through the entire exhibit twice before he finished purchasing the pieces he wanted.

"Can we speak privately?" he asked.

"Si, Señor. Please follow me." Sonya led him out of the gallery room to a small office in the hallway. "Please have a seat." She motioned to a chair as she sat behind the desk. "You have bought a large amount of Señor Dietrich's artwork." She pulled a calculator from a desk drawer and quickly added up the buyer's purchases. "The total comes to $72,000 in US dollars. I'm sure he will be pleased."

"Yes, I'm sure he will be . . . mucho pleased."

"How do you wish to pay?"

"With my credit card," he said, pulling out his wallet and handing her his American Express card.

Sonya took her time reading the name on the card.

"I assure you it will work."

"Of course, I'm sure it will, Señor John," Sonya replied, reading the cardholder's first name. She smiled and ran the card through the machine. Sonya held her breath waiting for the card processor to respond, hoping the system would not reject the transaction, which would cost her a sizeable commission. She smiled again when the system approved the sale. "Ah, perfecto!" she exclaimed.

"When can we start putting the merchandise in my car?"

"Oh, I am so sorry. We cannot remove anything until the exhibition is over next week. Otherwise there will be nothing for the visitors to see. That has been the museum's policy from the beginning. We will, of course, mark your purchases as sold."

"Very well," he said, rising from the chair. "If you can arrange to pack everything for shipping as soon as the exhibition is over, I would greatly appreciate it."

"Of course."

"And I would like this purchase to remain confidential. I value my privacy."

"I completely understand."

He extended his hand. "Buenas noches."

"Buenas noches, Señor John."

Mike walked into Pancho's Backyard, passing a small understated sign hanging over the door. A young woman in a flowing white-lace dress greeted him.

"Dinner?" she asked.

He spotted Dayle, sitting in the back, behind decorative vegetation, sipping what appeared to be a large margarita. "I see my friend. Gracias," he said, pointing as he walked to her table.

Dayle looked up as he approached. "Hi, Mike. Finished all your errands?"

"Yes, all done. I'm famished." He motioned for a waiter who watched their table. "I'll have whatever you're drinking and let's order."

An hour later, they had finished dinner and the waiter brought coffee and dessert. "Two cappuccinos and a vanilla con amaretto."

"Perfect," Dayle said, sipping her cappuccino.

"This looks delicious." Mike took a wafer cookie and dipped it in the amaretto-soaked vanilla ice cream. "Wow, that is good!"

"So, are you going to join me on my treasure hunt?"

"Yes, I'd like to. I think we work well together. And besides helping you find your ostrich egg globe, I might find some interesting artifacts for myself."

"Good." Dayle reached into her purse, pulled out a map, and unfolded it on the table. "This is a map of the Yucatan. I've highlighted some towns along the coast close to known major Mayan cities. I figured we'd start across the channel in Playa del Carmen, and then head south to Xel-Há, Akumal, Chetumal, and so forth. According to most of the research I've

read, it seems likely that a tribe along the coast had the globe."
Dayle's brow furrowed.

"Something wrong?"

"The thought just occurred to me. If we're right and the globe is somewhere in the Yucatan, it isn't privately owned. We just can't buy it or take it. The Mexican government would likely claim it as some indigenous historical artifact. We'd never get it out of the country."

"Yeah, well, perhaps there'd be a substantial reward or something or maybe a finder's fee. Let's find it first, then we'll worry about that."

"When can you leave?"

"I figure in two or three days. I need to take care of some business and then I'm free."

"Okay, I can wait a couple of days. I just need to exchange my rental car for something more substantial, like a four-wheel drive Jeep, and get permission to take it to the mainland. Then I want to change my plane reservation to an open ticket. That's about it. Shall we go? Looks like we're the last ones in here."

"Sure. Great meal. Thanks."

"Hey, you earned it," Dayle said, as they left the table. Outside Pancho's, their cars were parked at opposite ends of the street. Before turning to walk toward her car, Dayle kissed Mike lightly on the cheek. "Thanks for the company, mate. I had fun tonight."

"It's not too late. When we get back, how about coming up to my place for a nightcap?"

Dayle hesitated, assessing the potential implications of his invitation. "I . . . I better not, Mike. But thanks. I'll call you tomorrow."

Mike's jaw clenched. "Okay, we'll talk tomorrow." He watched her walk to her car. He admired the way Dayle moved, especially because he sensed she did not realize how seductively her hips swayed as she walked.

Damn, I almost had her in the sack. Maybe next time. I wonder what the deal is with the hubby?

CHAPTER 24

New York City

Monahan slurped his coffee—black, no sugar—as he concluded his report. "So that's it in a nutshell, Captain." In the commissioner's presence, he addressed his boss in a more formal tone than usual. "This same guy is the common denominator in the first and third cases. And I bet if we had his photo, the waiter at the restaurant would ID him as William Bennet's lunch buddy."

"Where'd you say he's from?" Sam asked.

"He lives in Fort Worth, Texas. Owns a law firm, of all things. I checked him out. Made some phone calls, Googled his name, and found some interesting news stories. Seems like a sketchy character. He's respected for his legal skills, despite rumors of jury tampering. He's also made unusually large campaign contributions to judges sitting in on his biggest cases. And I guess his hobby is buying art."

"And the motive, if it is murder, Detective?" the commissioner asked, in a tone that suggested he was not accepting the coincidental deaths as murder without further evidence.

Monahan was annoyed with the commissioner's continued challenges. "I dunno, sir. According to the experts, he over-paid for the stuff he bought. Maybe he had buyer's remorse." He winced as Sam kicked his shin under the conference table.

The commissioner ignored Monahan's sarcasm and ad-dressed Sam directly. "Well, Captain, I agree you need to investigate further. Something isn't right. Be nice to know where this toxin came from and exactly how it got into the victims' systems."

"Yes, sir. Detective Monahan is booked on an American flight down to DFW later today. I'm sure he will have something to report soon." He passed a folder to Monahan, who appeared shocked, as he stared at the printout of his flight itinerary.

"Well, gentlemen, keep me posted on your investigation. Have a safe flight, Detective."

"Thank you, sir," Monahan replied glumly, as he and his boss rose to leave the commissioner's office.

"Thanks a lot, Sam," Monahan said to his boss outside the office. "I've had tickets for tonight's Yankee–Red Sox game for a month. I knew this would be an important series. I coulda left tomorrow. DFW's an American hub. They have several flights every day."

"Hey, not so loud. The walls have ears."

"I don't give a f—"

"Stop whining and start packing, Micko. Even though the commissioner didn't appear totally sold on your murder theory, he's puttin' the pressure on me to get this case resolved before the press gets wind of it. Besides, I can make sure your tickets don't go to waste."

Sam held out his hand and grinned. Monahan pulled two tickets from the inside pocket of his jacket and shoved them into Sam's front breast pocket and walked away. Sam tried not to laugh out loud listening to Monahan grumble his way toward the elevators. He smiled, wondering how Monahan would eventually extract his revenge.

Three hours later, Monahan watched Jamaica Bay recede as his Boeing 737 climbed out of JFK airport, banked, and headed southwest toward Texas. He opened his file on the respected attorney and read about his background. After he finished, he looked at his watch and realized the baseball game he had to miss was probably in the second or third inning. He shook his head and pushed the attendant call button. At least he could make the department pay for a Scotch on the rocks. After he finished his Dewar's White Label, not his brand of choice but at least free, he pulled the shade down to keep the setting sun out of his eyes. He slept for the remainder of the flight.

A detective met him at DFW airport.

"Detective Monahan? I'm Sergeant Tom Brennan, Fort Worth PD. Good to meet you."

"Likewise, Sergeant. It's been a long day. Can we grab a bite to eat? The peanuts sucked. And you can call me Micko."

Brennan laughed. "Okay, Micko. I know a nice little place on the way. You can fill me in on the details."

After enjoying juicy, medium-rare steak sandwiches, the two men drove together to the suspect's residence. "Sure is an interesting case you have there. Never heard anything quite like it before."

"Yeah, I could do with less interesting. Give me a run-of-the-mill shooting any day."

"I hear ya, buddy. Here we are," Brennan said, pulling into a long, circular driveway. By the time they arrived, the sun had set and the white stone building took on a golden hue in the twilight. The two officers walked to the front door and tapped, using the brass knocker on the nine-foot tall, dark wood door. After three attempts, they circled the property looking through windows for signs of life or other entrances. "Looks like no one's home. But we did obtain a search warrant, since you came such a long way to see your person of interest."

"Your Texas hospitality is much appreciated."

They circled back to the front door and Brennan produced a set of lock picks. "I'd hate to break down such a beautiful, expensive door," he said inserting the first pick into the lock. After using three different picks, the lock clicked and the officers entered the premises. "Fort Worth Police Department. Anyone home?" Brennan's words echoed in the cavernous entrance hall. A chandelier hung fifteen feet above their heads, framed by skylights from a cupola thirty feet above them.

Monahan whistled. "What a shack!" They drew their guns and began a methodical, room by room search of the first floor. They were satisfied no one was downstairs.

"Okay, let's go upstairs." Monahan followed Brennan up a circular stairway, featuring marble steps with an oak and wrought iron bannister. At the top of the stairs, the landing flared out. Bedrooms with open doors were at opposite ends of a long hallway. In the middle of the hallway were several other rooms with closed doors. "Might be more bedrooms, an office, or maybe the proverbial bonus room."

"You mean his man cave?" Monahan asked.

"Yeah, let's take 'em one at a time." Brennan opened the nearest door and stepped into a large master bedroom.

Monahan stepped over to the dresser and picked up a framed photo of a couple wearing wetsuits. "Looks like they were on a dive vacation. I wonder if she's the wife or a girlfriend?"

All the other rooms were empty as they came to the last closed door. "You hear something?"

Monahan concentrated. "You mean like a whirring noise?" He pointed down to the crack at the door sill. In the darkened hallway, they noticed a light from inside the room shining through the bottom of the door. Monahan flipped a small button on his weapon. "Safety off."

"Safety off," Brennan acknowledged.

Monahan gripped the door knob and twisted. It turned. He whispered to Brennan. "Unlocked. Okay, it's show time." He burst through the door and dropped to one knee. His gun swept the room in an arc. He looked toward the light source. He blinked as two, large, blue eyes stared back at him.

"Holy shit!"

CHAPTER 25

"Look at this setup," Monahan said, looking at the fish tanks lining the wall. He turned his attention back to the pufferfish still staring at him. "Hey, buddy, you're cute."

"Yeah, he is a cute little feller," Brennan said. "Biggest blue eyes I ever did see. I had tropical fish when I was a kid but not like these."

"Me, too, but I just had freshwater tropicals. These are saltwater fish. Pretty expensive hobby. Those large tanks with a variety of fish are community tanks. Nice collection. They look like they're at least fifty gallons each. But these four smaller tanks are probably twenty- or thirty-gallon affairs." He stepped closer. "Well, well, what do we have here? Only pufferfish in these two tanks. And these other two tanks have partitions. I wonder . . ."

"What the hell is that little thing?" asked Brennan, looking at a creature that could fit in the palm of his hand.

"That, my friend, is the deadly blue-ringed octopus. I recognize them from when I was scuba diving in the Pacific.

They aren't native to here. He must have bought them from some aquarium store that sells exotic stuff. He's got them partitioned off from each other." Monahan stepped to the other side of the room, next to a long table and overhead lamp. He flipped on the lamp, illuminating the work area. He picked up a small glass beaker, about four inches tall and two inches wide at the top. A thin membrane was stretched tightly over the open top. "What's this thing?"

Brennan walked away from the tanks and Monahan handed him the tiny glass jar. "That looks like a smaller version of what we use when we milk venom from rattlers."

"You do what with who?" asked Monahan.

Brennan laughed. "Ain't you never milked a rattler, boy?" he said with an accentuated Texas drawl.

"Hey, I'm from the Bronx. We know about rats, not rattlers."

"Well, when we need to collect snake venom to make antivenom, we take a rattler and hold it just behind the head, so it can't turn and bite you. Then we put its mouth over a glass jar covered with a thin membrane like you see there. We let the snake sink its fangs through the membrane and presto. The snake's venom drips into the jar. Then the medical boys take the stuff and do their magic and make an antivenom."

Monahan noticed a pair of rubber-tipped, long forceps on the table, lying next to another miniature beaker. Then he watched a blue-ringed octopus climbing along the side of the glass tank, using the suckers along its tiny eight arms for traction. He walked over to the tank and looked closely at the sharp beak on the underside of the creature, pressed against the glass. "Son of a bitch," he said, looking at Brennan.

Before Brennan replied, they heard the front door open. Both detectives froze, making no noise. They heard footsteps coming up the stairs. "He's home," Brennan whispered. They drew their guns and silently positioned themselves on either side of the door. A man holding a bag entered the room and stepped toward the fish tanks.

"Hands up! Turn around slowly!"

In one motion, the man dropped the bag and raised his hands. He turned around as slowly as he could. When he saw two guns aimed at his chest, he stammered. "I . . . I don't have any money. Ta. . .take what you want." His eyes flicked back and forth to each gun.

"Fort Worth Police. Who are you?" Brennan asked, still in a shooter's stance.

"My name's Ernie Jackson. I'm a neighbor. I live down the road. I feed the fish when the owner's out of town. He travels a lot."

Micko smiled as he holstered his gun. "Yeah? I wanna see how ya feed 'em, Ernie."

"Huh?" Ernie said, hearing a Bronx accent in person for the first time.

The cell phone on Sam's night table rang and rang until he woke up and answered it. "H'lo," he said, groggily, trying to focus on the digital clock next to the phone.

"Who won the Yankee game?" a vaguely familiar voice asked.

He rubbed his eyes and concentrated, trying to place the voice. "Micko? Is that you? What the hell are you calling me for now? It's two a.m. here."

"I wanna know who won the game."

"The Yanks, six to three. Okay? Can I go back to sleep now?"

"Don't you wanna know how he did it?"

"How who did what? I got no time for riddles, Micko. I'm

tired and I got an early morning meeting with the commissioner tomorrow."

"Good. I just thought you might want to tell him how our suspect poisoned his victims. But if you'd rather go back to sleep, okay. Good night, Sam."

"No! Wait! Don't hang up!" Sam bolted out of bed. "Whad-ja find out?"

"Besides collecting art, our boy has another hobby. Saltwater tropical fish. He's got a few pufferfish and several blue-ringed . . . octopi, as we say in the octopus business. And he even knows how to milk the damn things."

"He milks them?"

"You know, like how scientists milk poisonous snakes to extract their venom. Evidently, he collects the venom when he needs it. I don't know how long the shelf life of this stuff is, but he collects it and he must have figured out a way to inject it. Maybe he uses a special ring with a tiny needle or something. Wouldn't be too tough to shake someone's hand and then use your other hand to scratch the back of your vic's hand. Wanna try it sometime?"

"Very funny. Did you arrest him?"

"He wasn't home. Place looked deserted, like maybe he's away. But we're gonna visit him at his office tomorrow. In the meantime, we emailed his photo to you. See if the waiter at the restaurant can ID him as William Bennet's lunch date. That should clinch it for the commish."

"Okay. Good work. Sometimes you even amaze me."

"Thanks, Sam. That's very touching."

"Oh, and Micko?"

"Yeah?"

"The game was great. Too bad you missed it."

"Screw you, Sam!"

The next morning Brennan found Monahan waiting outside his hotel. "Hope you weren't waiting too long."

"No. I just got down here. How far to the law firm?"

"Pretty close, only about a thirty-minute drive."

When they arrived at a modern looking, eight-story white building in downtown Fort Worth, they walked into the lobby and stared at the building directory.

"This place is crazy with law firms. There it is. Fifth floor," Monahan said. "Looks like the only one with no partners or associates."

They took the elevator to the fifth floor and walked through a pair of glass doors. "You do the talking, Tom. No one understands my accent down here. I don't get it."

Brennan laughed. "Yeah, we Texans never know what the hell you New Yawkers are talking about."

"May I help you?" a college-age receptionist asked. Both officers flashed badges, and Brennan took the lead.

"Official police business, ma'am," he began in polite Southern fashion, explaining he and his partner needed to speak with the owner of the law firm on a confidential matter.

"Oh, I'm sorry, gentlemen. My boss is out of the office."

"Do you know where he went and when he'll be back, Ms. . . . ?"

"Ms. Johnson. I'm sorry, I don't have that information. I wish I could help you." She turned to answer another call and her body language indicated she thought the conversation was over. Monahan decided to change her opinion.

"I assume he has a secretary. We'll speak with her. Now, we'd appreciate it if you would please call her . . . Ms. Johnson."

Ms. Johnson appeared flustered by Monahan's brusque, New York manner.

"Yes . . . yes, he does. I'll see if she's available."

"Thanks," Monahan said, flashing an insincere smile. A minute later, a tall woman opened a thick wooden door.

"Hello, gentlemen, I'm Jenna Wallace. I understand you asked for me. Please follow me." She brought the two men into a conference room, where they all sat down. "Is there anything I can do for you?"

"No, ma'am," Brennan said in a relaxed, unassuming manner. "I'm afraid we have to speak with your boss confidentially. When will he return?"

"I really don't know. He's out of town for an undisclosed period of time."

"Do you know where he is?"

"No, I'm afraid he's out of the country."

Monahan lost patience with the slow, polite pace of the conversation and jumped in. "Ms. Wallace, this is a very important matter. Instead of playing twenty questions, can you please tell us exactly where out of the country he is now?"

She looked at Brennan for friendly, hometown help, but he avoided eye contact, pretending to check his watch. "He went to Mexico for a vacation." Before Monahan could ask the next obvious question, she blurted out, "I'm not sure exactly where in Mexico. He mentioned something about exploring the land of the Mayans or something like that."

"Can you contact him or his wife?"

"I'm sorry, he did not give me any contact information. He had no pending business and said he needed a vacation and wanted to remain unavailable for a while. He will likely return next month."

"Thank you," Monahan said. "If you hear from him or his wife, please have him call either of us." He handed her his card, as did Brennan.

Brennan drove Monahan back to the airport. "Good working

with you, Micko. We'll lock the house down. Lots of evidence in there."

"Great, Tom. Good working with you, too." He got out of the car, started walking, but suddenly stopped. He waved as Brennan pulled away. "Hey! Make sure that guy Ernie doesn't forget to feed the fish."

Brennan waved back. "Will do," he said, laughing.

After passing through security, Monahan checked his watch. His flight didn't board for an hour, so he decided to update Sam. He dialed his boss's number.

"Micko, how's it goin'? Did you make the collar?"

"No. Our boy was conveniently out of the office. Actually, out of the country. He took a trip to Mexico. They don't expect him back for a month."

"Too bad. Hey, I have some interesting info for you. We showed your suspect's photo to that waiter you interviewed. He ID'd him as William Bennet's lunch buddy at his last meal."

"Bingo!"

CHAPTER 26

Cozumel

The doorbell rang as Terry and Joe relaxed after another day of diving.

"I'll get it, hon," Joe said, as he sprang up to answer the door. "Dayle, what a surprise!"

"Hi guys, I just stopped by to say hello. The day off from diving really helped. Between the actual diving and my mishaps, I was really bushed. I needed a break."

"Are you diving with us tomorrow?" Terry asked.

"No. I'm taking some time off to hit the mainland, pick up some local art, and see if I can find out anything about that mysterious globe."

"Going alone?" Joe asked.

"No, I asked Mike to join me."

Joe's eyebrows arched.

"Now before you say anything, let me explain. I really would like some company, and I feel comfortable with him. He strikes me as a pretty responsible bloke, and he's reliable in a pinch. Damn, he did save my life twice, you know."

"She does have a point," said Terry. "And we really don't have anything concrete to base our suspicions on, other than your old NYPD gut instinct."

Joe held up his hands, palms out. "Okay, I can see I'm outnumbered. I know I'm just relying on my usually reliable gut, but the guy just strikes me as off. I can't help it. Just be careful, Dayle, okay?"

"Sure. I understand. Initially he really turned me off, but I've gotten to . . . like him, I guess."

"Well it's easy to see he likes you, for various reasons," said Terry.

"I've handled tougher cases," Dayle replied with a raised eyebrow. "In fact—"

The door burst open and Jackie and Peter ran in. "Hi, Mom, hi, Dad. Hey Dayle, what are you doing here?"

"That's quite a greeting, sport," Joe said, tousling Peter's unruly brown hair. "Forget your manners?"

"Sorry, Dayle. Good to see you."

"Good to see you too, Peter."

"So how was school today?"

"Really cool, Dad. We had a field trip today."

"Where'd you go?"

"Chankanaab Park," Jackie replied, before Peter could answer. "We heard the ghost. It was so cool."

"What ghost?" asked Dayle.

"Tepeu," said Jackie.

Peter jumped in. "According to local legend, he was some Mayan dude, just a lower-class commoner, who made it with the chief's daughter, Akna, back in the day."

"The chief, Coyopa, found out that Tepeu had defiled his virgin daughter, so he arranged to sacrifice him to the goddess because a lot of bad luck had befallen the tribe," added Jackie.

"He blamed all the bad luck on Tepeu leading his daughter astray."

Peter continued. "But the goddess, Ixchel, I think that was her name, was so pissed about the whole thing that she demanded the chief also give her his most valuable possession, whatever that was, in addition to sacrificing Tepeu's life. The object was supposed to have some kind of magical powers, and Coyopa believed it gave him greater knowledge about the earth and universe than anyone else knew at the time."

"And this all happened in Chankanaab?" Dayle asked.

"Well, the tribe lived on the mainland, but all the sacrifices were always done every year at Chankanaab in a lagoon where Ixchel hung out," explained Peter. "The lagoon was a sacred place."

"So, what's all the ghost stuff about?"

"Well, after the chief had Tepeu killed, all the people still hung out on the beach. They were saying final prayers, or whatever, getting ready to row back across the channel. All of a sudden, they heard his spirit moaning really loudly. Like, the sound was just coming from everywhere. The people were scared out of their minds. And now even today they still hear him every so often."

"When did this happen?"

"Sometime in the 1500s," Jackie said. "So anyway, the natives have been hearing Tepeu moaning for revenge for hundreds of years. They would even scare their misbehaving kids, telling them Tepeu would come and take them away if they were bad."

"And you heard Tepeu's ghost today?"

"Yes, it was really loud. But now, scientists have explained the noise. Everyone knows the ground here is very porous because the island is made of limestone. The island contains cave-like formations, especially around Chankanaab. Most can be accessed from inland, where the cave ceiling has collapsed, like a natural sinkhole."

"They're called cenotes," Peter pointed out. "Pronounced like, say-NO-tays. The best cenotes to explore are on the mainland. They were the main source of fresh water for the ancient Mayans. They considered them sacred."

Jackie threw her brother a dismissive look with her piercing green eyes, just like her mother's. "They eventually empty out into the sea, so in some cases you can enter the cave system from underwater if you can find the opening. As far as the weird noises are concerned, a bunch of conditions have to be just right for Tepeu to do his thing. The tide has to be really low, and the currents have to flow at just the right direction to expose the tops of some of these caves, which in some cases are totally underwater. Then the wind has to blow in the right direction, and really strong, like when we have a storm. When the wind blows through the exposed cave openings, it travels underground and then comes out through all these openings, like blowholes, near the lagoon, where Ixchel lives. It makes this whooshing, moaning sound. Really eerie."

"And that's the legend of the ghost?" Dayle asked.

"Yep. It doesn't happen very often. And because so many factors have to coincide at just the right time, no one ever figured it out for many years. That's why we went today. They projected the tides, wind, and currents would be perfect today, and they were right."

"That's a fascinating story. So, the island acts like a giant woodwind musical instrument?"

"Yeah, I guess you could say that."

"Hey guys, I love the fact that you're now experts on Mayan history and folklore, but don't forget we're eating early tonight. Dayle, you're welcome to stay for dinner."

"Thanks, Terry, I'd love to!"

"I'm taking some of our divers . . . I think just Scooby and Jamie . . . down to Galeria Azul—Greg's art gallery—tonight. They're leaving soon and wanted to buy some nice gifts for friends back home. I heard Scooby was very interested when he saw what kind of art Greg makes when they visited his exhibition at the museum. I promised to pick them up around seven o'clock and drive them to the gallery. Dayle, you can join us if you like."

"Sounds like fun. After seeing Greg's exhibition at the museum, I'd love to see his gallery. Mike said he's busy taking care of some business in town, so I have no plans."

After dinner, Terry and Dayle drove to the Hotel Cozumel resort where Scooby and Jamie were staying. Jamie met them outside. "Sorry for the delay. I needed to take a long shower. Scooby will meet us downtown. He wanted to get his regulator checked out at a scuba repair place near the art gallery, so he took the rental car. He said he'll meet us at the gallery."

"No problem, Jamie. We'll just hang out there if he's late," Terry said.

CHAPTER 27

G reg was etching a hawksbill sea turtle on a glass vase when he heard the doorbell. He opened the door to a pleasant-looking tourist.

"Hi, you're Greg, right?"

"Yes, how can I help you?"

"My name's John. Sorry to interrupt you, but I'd like to look through your gallery and possibly purchase some items, if you have time."

"I can always make time for a sale," the affable artist said, with a smile. "Have you visited my exhibition at the museum?"

"As a matter of fact, I did. I was hoping to purchase some of your work there but it was sold out. I mean, I saw your work but everything had a 'sold' sign on it."

"Yes, I heard that someone bought out the place. I'm thrilled."

"Well, you should be. I really like your work. It's beautiful and very unique."

"Yes, it is unique. Thank you. I don't think anyone else works in this glass medium like I do. One thing I have to explain, though, is that while the museum takes credit cards, I don't. Here, it's strictly pesos or dollars."

"No problem, I came well prepared with cash."

"Most of my work is in this room," Greg said, leading his new customer into a back room, housing much of his art.

Many thousands of dollars later, the gallery walls were bare, and ceiling hooks, where colorful, expensive lamps had hung, were empty.

"Do you want me to wrap everything for you? I can pack it so it won't break in transit. Is it all going or staying on the island?"

"If you can help me load everything into my car, that'll be fine."

They loaded the artwork mostly in the backseat, with the less fragile items in the trunk.

"John, thank you very much. You've got my head spinning with this purchase. I'll have to work plenty of overtime to refill the gallery." They shook hands briefly and Greg walked back inside the gallery. He was surprised to see John had followed him back inside.

"I think I left my glasses somewhere. Ah, here they are," he said, finding them on the counter where he had purposely left them. "Greg, I just can't thank you enough," John said again, grasping Greg's hand with both of his.

Greg winced as John pumped his hand enthusiastically.

"Goodbye, Greg. And good luck."

Greg's customer left but decided to remain in the area for a little while in case someone else wandered into the gallery.

When Terry pulled up in front of the Azul sign hanging over the entrance to the gallery, she spotted someone standing in front, leaning against a parked car. "Looks like your husband beat us here," she said to Jamie. "Hi, Scooby, been here long?"

"No, I just got here a couple of minutes ago. Looks like the gallery is closed. I guess we should leave." He opened the car door and got in. "Jamie, are you coming?"

Terry said, "Wait a minute, Scooby. Don't be in such a rush. Let's check before we leave."

Terry, Dayle, and Jamie piled out of her car and Terry rang the bell, but no one answered the door. She checked her watch. "That's strange. It's only eight o'clock. Greg never closes the gallery this early." She tried the door and it swung open. "That's weird. Greg always locks the door." They went inside. The gallery and display cases, normally decorated with Greg's colorful art, were empty.

"Wow! Someone cleaned out the place." She called out, "Greg? It's Terry. I brought some friends. Are you—"

"Oh my God! Terry!"

Terry whirled around. She saw a pair of legs protruding from behind the counter. She ran behind the counter past Jamie and saw Greg, lying face up. His eyes were open but focused as if he was trying to communicate. His color was ashen, lips blue. "Cyanosis! He needs oxygen," Terry correctly determined. "Help me move him!" she shouted to Jamie, who grabbed Greg's hands while Terry took his feet.

They dragged him to the center of the room where Terry had room to work on him. She immediately began CPR, compressing his chest repeatedly. "Dayle, I have oxygen in a DAN emergency pack in the trunk." She flipped the keys to Dayle and continued CPR. "Jamie, we passed a police car a block back. See if you can find him!"

Scooby heard the commotion and came inside the gallery just as Jamie ran out. Dayle ran back inside with the suitcase-size

Divers Alert Network medical emergency equipment pack, but Terry did not want to stop administering CPR. "Open it and get me the oxygen, fast! Can you set up the mask?"

"Sure." She took out the small, pure-oxygen tank and hooked up the hose and face mask. Then she clamped the mask over Greg's face while Terry continued chest compressions. A couple of minutes later, Greg's color had improved and his lips turned from blue to pink. Just then, two policemen walked in.

"Ambulancia rápido!" Terry shouted to them.

One of the cops pulled out his radio and made the call.

An hour later, a doctor approached Terry, Dayle, Scooby, and Jamie in the hospital waiting room. "It's still touch and go, but we've managed to stabilize him. I think he might make it. Do you know what happened?"

"No. We found him unconscious on the floor. I assumed heart attack. But it was weird. His eyes were open and it looked like he was trying to focus, as though he wasn't unconscious."

"Check his right hand," Jamie said. Everyone turned toward her.

"Excuse me?" said the doctor.

"Terry, remember on the boat when I told you sometimes I notice small details that many cops, and even doctors, miss on a body?"

"Yes, I recalled you mentioned that."

"Well, when I took his hands and helped you drag him to the middle of the floor, I felt a slight bump on the back of his right hand. I looked closer while you were doing CPR, and it seemed like a welt but with a scrape of some kind. It appeared irritated, like when you brush your hand against a jellyfish or a hydroid."

"Let me examine him again. I'll be right back," the doctor said. When he returned, he said, "We found a small puncture wound. Very strange. We scraped some skin cells and we'll run some tests. In the meantime, there is nothing more you can do right now. You've already saved his life. He's lucky you had that oxygen bottle in your car."

"Thank goodness I had just bought a new DAN emergency pack for the boat. The one I have is getting old. I planned to replace it and use the old one as a spare."

"Well good thing you had it tonight. I'll call you as soon as we know something."

"Okay, thanks. I'm so relieved that he'll recover."

"Well, as I said, he's not out of the woods yet but he is improving."

"Quite a night," Terry said, shaking her head as they left the hospital. Jamie and Scooby got into their rental car. "I'll call you in the morning. Nice job, Jamie," Terry said. Then she dropped Dayle off at her condo at the Residencias. "I'll let you know as soon as I hear something."

"Thanks. Good night." Dayle walked toward her building and recognized Mike's car parked in front of his building, about fifty yards away.

Back at the condo, she turned on her computer and checked email. "Maybe I'll hear something from Jeff," she said hopefully. The only messages were junk mail advertisements and several updates from Felix back at her LaLa gallery. The screen blinked and a new message popped up. Her heart leapt but then plummeted when she saw the message was from Mike.

Ready for Adventure?

She clicked on the message.

Hi Dayle! Looking forward to our treasure hunt. Talk to you tomorrow.

She smiled for a brief moment, thinking about the prospect of her search for the globe with Mike. But then she shook her head and took a deep breath. "Jeff, where are you? What the hell's going on?"

CHAPTER 28

Fallujah, Iraq

"Incoming! Incoming!" one of the SEALS shouted.

Jeff Becker jumped behind a stone wall just before the RPG round exploded, lighting up the night for a brief moment.

"Shit, that was close. I don't think our top-secret mission is top secret anymore."

"Roger that!" his team member shouted back. "Hey, boss, you got a plan B?"

Jeff had been recruited to lead a small, elite team in a series of classified missions in Iraq because of his background as a former CIA officer and ex-Navy SEAL. The goal of the missions was to blunt the resurgence of ISIS forces and assist people who had been helpful to the United States and Western allies. Their lives were now in danger because of their efforts. Jeff's SEAL team had been involved in a series of missions to "neutralize high-value targets" (kill important enemies) and to "extract high-value assets" (rescue important friendlies). Tonight, a CIA stealth helicopter had inserted them into a fortified compound to hold off an ISIS force until Iraqi army reinforcements could arrive tomorrow, and then evacuate a family deemed critical to the war effort. But, as had happened all too often in a conflict where today's friends turned into tomorrow's enemies, someone had tipped off the ISIS fighters.

"Yeah! Plan B is to get that copter back here ASAP and get us and our Iraqi friends out now instead of tomorrow. We can't wait for the Iraqi army to get here in time. Billy! Call in that copter now. Rocky! Go inside and assemble that family and tell them to get ready for immediate extraction. Gary! Help me return as much fire as we can and hold these guys off!"

Plan B was working, and the helicopter crew informed Jeff they were only ten minutes away. But then trouble. Three vehicles were driving at high speed toward their barrier.

"Suicides coming!'" Jeff shouted to his men. "Knock 'em out!" They poured as much fire as they could at the three targets. One car exploded, then another. But the third crashed through the barrier and drove into the building where the family waited for rescue. The building exploded into a cloud of thunder and flame.

"Shit!" Jeff exclaimed, feeling the shockwave through his chest. They ran into the rubble and searched for survivors until the helicopter arrived. They only found mangled bodies.

"Can't wait, sir! We're taking enemy fire!" the pilot shouted.

"Okay, we're out of here."

Just then, Jeff heard a cry, more like a whimper. He moved several large rocks and saw a hand. The hand moved. He moved more rubble and uncovered a woman's face. She attempted to speak despite the crushing weight of the building on top of her. Her eyes kept darting to the left, and her fingers pointed weakly. Jeff leaned forward, trying to understand her words.

"Sharif . . . Sharif," was all the woman could say before the life left her eyes.

He looked to where she had pointed and lifted several large pieces of masonry. He saw two large, brown, terrified eyes looking at him. He moved another slab and pulled a small, bloodied boy from the rocks. He was still alive. Jeff guessed the boy was about three or four years old. During his time in hell, Jeff had seen more than enough children maimed and killed before they'd had a chance to start living. At least he could save this child. He gathered the boy in his arms and ran to the copter. He threw him into the hands of another SEAL already aboard, and then jumped in. "We got four?" he asked.

"Affirmative!" one SEAL shouted back.

"Go! Go! Go!" Jeff screamed to the pilot, who lifted off as a hail of small-arms fire pinged off the helicopter.

He looked at his team, sprawled out, breathless in the belly of the helicopter. Sharif trembled in the arms of one of the SEALS. Jeff looked over at the boy.

"Sharif!" he shouted, trying to get the boy's attention. "You okay, buddy?" Jeff had no idea if the boy understood, but he hoped some form of communication might calm him.

Sharif looked at Jeff, then squeezed his eyes shut. A tear slipped down his cheek and his lips quivered. "Mama," was the only sound he made.

"A real bad day at the office, boys," Jeff said to his team.

CHAPTER 29

Cozumel

The next morning, Terry and Joe drove to the hospital to check on Greg's progress. The receptionist ushered them into a small waiting room. "Doctor Gomez will see you in a moment."

Terry and Joe exchanged glances, wondering if they would soon receive good or bad news. A young man, Terry guessed about thirty-five years old, opened the door and greeted them.

"Hola, Señora and Señor Manetta. I am Doctor Gomez." Sensing their anxiety, he bypassed further social graces and immediately provided details about Greg's condition. "Señor Dietrich is resting comfortably."

Terry exhaled, relieved to learn Greg was alive.

"He is very lucky that you were there, and extremely lucky that you happened to have 100% pure oxygen available."

"What happened? Was it a heart attack?" Joe asked.

"No. As far as we can determine, he ingested, or was somehow given, a dose of a neurotoxin which causes muscle paralysis." He looked at Terry. "When he was brought in, you mentioned his eyes were open as if he was awake."

Terry nodded, trying to assimilate and process the information.

"You were correct. Señor Dietrich was conscious. We ran tests on the skin cells from the wound on his hand that your friend noticed and found traces of tetrodotoxin. It can cause a state of paralysis similar to curare, where the victim is awake and aware of his surroundings but cannot speak or communicate. Death is caused by suffocation because the primary muscles that control breathing—the diaphragm—are paralyzed. Most victims usually die within minutes. But you arrived shortly after the poison affected him, and the only treatment is aggressive CPR with oxygen, which you provided."

"Will he live?" Terry asked.

"Yes, I believe so. By continually forcing oxygen into the victim's system until the poison is metabolized and excreted by the body, the patient will survive. That is what we are doing with your friend."

"Is Greg conscious yet? Can we see him?"

"No. Señor Dietrich has not regained consciousness yet, but you can visit him. Come with me."

Terry and Joe held hands as they followed Dr. Gomez into an elevator.

"I've heard of tetrodotoxin," Terry said. "I believe it's found in pufferfish, which we have in Cozumel, and also in the blue-ringed octopus, which is native to the Pacific and not found here."

"Yes, that is true. If the flesh of the pufferfish is not properly prepared for cooking, the poison can be ingested by eating it."

Joe interjected. "Well, as far as we know, Greg did not eat pufferfish that night. And no one eats the blue-ringed octopus. Victims get the poison only if the octopus bites them. So how did it get into his system?"

The elevator door opened and the doctor talked as they walked through a hallway.

"Thanks to your friend Jamie's suggestion, when we examined Señor Dietrich's hand, we found a puncture wound on the back of his right hand that contained traces of tetrodotoxin."

"Are you telling me this was attempted murder?"

"I'm not qualified to make such a pronouncement. That is for the police to decide. All I can say is what caused his condition and how the tetrodotoxin likely entered his system."

They stepped into a private room and Terry gasped when she saw Greg. He was unconscious and hooked up to a ventilator. The only noise was the rhythmic pumping and hissing of the machine, breathing for him.

"We are forcing high-oxygen content air into his lungs as the tetrodotoxin works its way out of his system. Once we are sure that he can breath on his own, we will disconnect the ventilator. We expect him to make a full recovery."

Joe stepped closer to the bed and attempted to examine Greg's right hand, but it was bandaged. Suddenly, Greg stirred and moved his head from side to side, as if trying to throw off the mask covering his mouth and nose.

"Doctor?" Terry said, startled.

"He is okay. That is a normal reflex as his breathing muscles recover, trying to breathe on their own. It is actually a good sign. We may be able to disconnect the ventilator by tonight or tomorrow. There is nothing more we can do here now."

"Thank you for everything, doctor. We'll check back tomorrow."

"My pleasure. We will notify you if there is any change in his condition."

Outside the hospital, Terry turned on her cell phone, which she had switched off because of hospital regulations.

She started to dial Dayle's number to give her an update on Greg's condition when a message popped up. "Hey, I got a message from Dayle."

Hi Terry. Tried calling you but phone was off. Hope all is OK. Left Cozumel on the car ferry with Mike about twenty minutes ago. Will head south and then return in a few days. Hope we can connect.

"Damn!"

"What's up?" Joe asked.

"Dayle tried calling me while my phone was off in the hospital. She took off with Mike on the car ferry."

Joe pursed his lips.

"What's wrong? You don't look happy."

"I still don't trust the guy. Now she's alone with him, and we don't know exactly where they are. And with cell phone coverage so spotty, it'll be almost impossible to contact her."

"I think you're overreacting to your old NYPD instincts, dear. You still don't have any real proof that he—"

"My NYPD instincts never let me down in over twenty years on the job or here. One thing I learned is that people show their true colors when there's a lot of money at stake. And if that globe is the real deal, there's a lot of money at stake."

"Let me at least call her or message back about Greg's condition and that we got her message."

After a few minutes of failed connections, Terry gave up. "Can't reach her. Maybe they're on the ferry or someplace where there's no signal."

Dayle and Mike sat in her Jeep as the ferry pitched through wind-generated swells. She glanced at Mike, who kept swallowing as he focused on the horizon. "Looks like we're about halfway across the channel. You okay?"

"Yeah. Just a little queasy with all this rolling. Wish those swells would calm down."

"As we get closer to the mainland, they should. Let's take our mind off that and plan our route." She pulled out a map of the Yucatan coastline and unfolded it. "We land here at Calica, about five miles south of Playa del Carmen. Then we can take this highway, Carretera 307. The only towns where I think we'll find out anything about Mayan history connected to the globe would be along the coast. The legend says a coastal tribe stole it from a ship in Columbus's fleet on one of his later voyages. What do you think?"

"Makes sense to me. How many towns are there along the route?"

"Let's see. I'm more familiar with the inland and western part of the country, but based on our situation, I think we should go south and hit Xcaret, Akumal, Xel-Há, and finally Tulum. I think it'd be a waste of time to go farther south."

"What about that major Mayan city where they held a lot of ceremonies and sacrifices? I think it was called Chichen Itza?"

"That's a biggie, all right. But it's pretty far inland. I think focusing on Mayan tribes that lived closer to the sea would be more productive."

"I think the water's getting calmer. There's the dock up ahead. We should be off this boat soon."

A half hour later, they rolled off the ferry and headed south, toward Xcaret. "Glad that's over," Dayle said. "I'm getting pumped about our little expedition. I really feel lucky. How about you?"

"Me, too," Mike said, grinning at her. "I think we really will find that damn globe."

CHAPTER 30

New York City

It was seven o'clock in the evening when Monahan walked into his boss's office. "I came as soon as I got your call. Surprised you're still here. Thought it was past your bedtime."

"Funny, Micko. Now that we're getting closer to solving this case, the commissioner is busting my balls. How was your flight?"

"Thanks for asking. Bumpy, but otherwise noneventful. And the Scotch was good. Did you notify the Mexican officials that we'd like them to find our suspect?"

Before his boss answered, the door opened. Monahan glanced over his shoulder and beamed when he recognized the detective who walked in. "Bill Ryan! What the hell are you doing here? Thought you put in your papers last year."

They shook hands. "Good to see you, Micko. I did. But I missed the action, so I got a gig in the DA's office as an investigator. A little extra dough doesn't hurt and it keeps me from getting bored."

Monahan glanced from Bill to Sam. His boss thought he looked confused.

"I asked Bill to give us a hand. Our friends south of the border asked for some assistance on this one. And Bill knows the lay of the land in the area of Mexico where you're headed."

"Yeah, I remember hearing about some of your capers down there. You have friends in Cozumel, right?"

"Yes, one of our retired NYPD brothers named Joe Manetta and his wife, Terry, live there. We've been involved in a couple of interesting cases together over the years. Even though it sounds like your guy is headed to the Yucatan mainland, based on that offhand remark from his secretary about him exploring the land of the Mayans, Cozumel is pretty close. It's just across the channel, only about ten miles away."

"So, I figured if you needed a little help, Bill was the man to ask," Sam said.

"Me? You're sending me to Mexico?"

"I know how you get when you're closing in, like a bird dog on the hunt. But if you want me to send someone else, I can."

"No! I'm goin'. Just surprised that you're sending me."

"Like I said, they asked for a little help tracking this guy down. And we'd have to send someone to bring him back anyway. So, I thought since you gave me the Yankee tickets . . ."

"Hey, that's great. Maybe I'll get in some diving while I'm there."

"Since we're meeting with the commissioner tomorrow morning, I'd like to bring Bill up to speed on where we are now with the case."

Sam passed folders out to both detectives. "Have a seat and let's get started."

Cozumel

Terry and Joe had just finished a late dinner after two day-time dives, followed by a night dive. Jackie and Peter were still on the east side of the island, helping the conservation society supervise another turtle nesting session. When the phone next to Joe rang, Terry looked over and saw his chin resting on his chest. Joe had nodded out.

"Next time no tequila after dinner for my hero," she said loudly, hoping to wake him.

But when Joe began to snore, she jumped up and answered the phone. "Hello? . . . Yes, Doctor Gomez! Is everything all— I'm so glad . . . Greg said what? . . . I'm sorry, could you please repeat that?" She kicked Joe's foot and put the phone on speaker.

Joe flinched, startled from his deep sleep. "Huh?"

"Greg kept repeating the name John, John, over and over again. He was quite delirious, tossing his head from side to side as he tried to speak. But that is a good sign, indicating that he is coming out of his coma. Do you know who he could be talking about?"

"No, I don't know anyone named John." She glanced at Joe, but he just shook his head again.

"I think there is a good possibility you can speak with Greg by tomorrow if you would like to come to the hospital," Dr. Gomez said.

"Joe and I have a small group for tomorrow morning's dive, but we could stop by in the afternoon."

"That would be fine. In fact, the timing is even better since that will give him a few more hours to recover. How about three o'clock?"

"Better make it closer to four if you don't mind. By the time we clean and store all the dive equipment, I think we'll need more time."

"Fine. I'll be expecting you around four o'clock. Good night."

"Good night, doctor."

Terry hung up and looked at Joe, who was now fully awake. "You know anyone named John?"

"Yeah, Ter, lots. But not in Cozumel. Here I know a few guys named José," he said, smiling.

"You know what I mean. Get serious!"

"No. Can't think of anyone offhand."

"I wonder if this John is the last person Greg met before his encounter with tetrodotoxin. And the fact that his gallery was just about empty when we arrived has me puzzled."

"You think it was a robbery-murder scenario?"

"You're the ex-cop. What do you think?"

"I've seen people killed for much less. I guess we'll have to wait and see what Greg can tell us. Who's diving tomorrow? You said it was a small group."

"Just Fulvio, Jamie, and Scooby. Fulvio heard about another cave full of glassy sweepers somewhere near Chanka-naab and he's been bugging me to take him to find it. Scooby likes to stick to the no flying until twenty-four hours after diving rule."

"Okay. Well I'm bushed. If we're diving early tomorrow, how about turning in?"

Terry smiled and put her arm around Joe and pulled him close. "Sure, but we don't have to go to sleep right away, do we?"

Joe grinned, kissed her on the lips, and then kissed her neck. Terry shivered. "Oh, I think we can stay up awhile," he whispered in her ear. She took his hand and led him up the stairs. He followed, watching Terry's long auburn hair sway with each step. He caught up at the top step and nuzzled the back of her neck, enjoying the softness and smell of her hair.

"Damn, your hair is like the ocean. Soft and calm one day, wavy and wild another."

Terry sighed and took a deep breath. At the foot of the bed she turned and pulled Joe down on top of her. Their eyes locked, lips brushing, barely touching. "Amazing how it doesn't get old, does it?"

"No, it doesn't," he said, as he reached under her blouse and unhooked her bra.

CHAPTER 31

The next morning, they met Jamie and Scooby at the marina. As soon as they boarded the *Dorado*, Fulvio's car pulled up.

"Thanks for driving down here, Fulvio. Since we're diving north of the Residencias Pier today, this makes things easier," said Terry.

"No problem," Fulvio said, climbing aboard with his equipment bag slung over his shoulder. "As long as I find my glassy sweepers." He dropped his dive equipment on the deck and greeted Jamie and Scooby as the boat pulled out of the marina.

"So, I guess we're on glassy sweeper patrol today?" Scooby asked.

"Yep. And if we find them, you'll be very impressed. You'll see."

Fifteen minutes out, Manuel knew they had reached the dive site and cut the twin outboards. "We're here," he said to Terry.

"Thanks. Okay, we're just off Chankanaab, about where the cave should be," Terry said. "We'll drop in here, descend to the bottom. It's about sixty feet deep here, but it gets more shallow closer to shore. Swim toward the shoreline. It's a rocky wall, not a sandy beach, so look for an opening. Some of the openings lead into the lagoon, but others might just be a dead-end cave. Keep together and don't go exploring alone. Swim-throughs you can handle, but you guys aren't cave certified. Cave diving is where accidents happen."

The divers splashed in. Fulvio used a giant-stride entry, while Terry, Joe, Jamie and Scooby back-rolled in. Everyone bobbed to the surface and acknowledged they were okay, so they descended and met on the bottom. Terry started swimming toward the shore and they followed. Several minutes into the dive, Terry still could not see the rocky wall, despite 100-foot visibility. As she led the group along the bottom, she noticed her depth gauge register fifty-five feet and then fifty feet, so she knew they were headed in the right direction, not out into deeper water. Finally, the wall appeared, fuzzy like a mirage, and then more defined as they swam closer.

Swimming along the wall, the divers noticed the visibility change as the water took on a shimmery, wavy appearance, like the air over a hot desert highway. She realized it was a halocline, caused when fresh water mixes with salt water. They shivered as a burst of cold water enveloped them, intensifying the visual distortion. She recognized the effect was due to a thermocline, where cold fresh water from under the island poured into the sea.

Terry turned to the group when she decided they were close to a cave opening. She gave the OK sign to each diver, making sure no one was panicking due to the disorienting change in visibility and temperature. Everyone acknowledged with the correct OK sign, so she continued swimming closer to the wall.

At a depth of about twenty feet, Terry found what she was looking for. She pointed to an opening in the wall and swam inside. The cave was dark and visibility reduced to less than twenty feet. Then she saw light because the cave was more like a swim-through than a true cave formation. The group followed and the light enveloped them as they entered the lagoon. Visibility returned to 100 feet again, and they watched brightly colored parrotfish and angelfish dart around the lagoon. Terry checked her depth gauge, which indicated they were still only twenty feet deep. Diving so shallow was like a long safety stop, so she knew she could extend the dive and not worry about decompression time. Farther along, she pointed toward the cave opening where they had entered, indicating it was time to leave the lagoon and continue their search for the glassy sweeper cave.

Jamie had entered last, so she led the group on the way out. Swimming faster, she exited the cave first and turned left at the opening in the direction they had been going. By the time Terry and the other divers exited the cave, they could not see Jamie. At first concerned, Terry suddenly saw Scooby about sixty feet ahead of them, waving wildly toward the wall. Due to the gradation of salinity and temperature, Jamie looked like a fuzzy doll in the shimmery visibility.

Fulvio reached Jamie first and realized she had found another cave, much smaller than the first. It was barely large enough for two people. Once again, it appeared to be little more than an indentation in the wall rather than a true cave or swim-through. He cautiously swam inside and proceeded into the darkness.

Soon he felt feathery movement around his head and face. He turned on his dive light and saw that a living, pulsing mass of coppery, pinkish-colored fish had enveloped him. He swam a few feet farther through the metallic mass, which parted like a screen, to reveal two large green moray eels intertwined at the back of the cave. They turned toward him, mouths open, revealing needle-sharp teeth, as they breathed. Their eyes reflected dark blue in his dive light. He stopped and finned backward to avoid startling the eels. Then he relaxed and rested on the cave bottom, as though in a trance, enjoying the company of his glassy sweepers. Thousands of the tiny fish, each barely two inches long, swam around, over, and under this large bubble-blowing creature from another world.

Jamie looked back at Fulvio, who appeared in a Zen-like state, as if the tiny fish had mesmerized him. She snapped some still photos and took several seconds of video. Then she backed out, letting Scooby and the other divers have a turn observing the mass of fish, with Fulvio in the middle.

Terry entered the cave last. She smiled watching Fulvio floating among his fishy friends. She checked her dive computer. They had been down for over an hour. She decided they should head back to the boat, so she shook her metallic rattle to get Fulvio's attention and motioned for him to follow her.

The noise snapped him out of his trance. He acknowledged with a hand signal and swam out behind her. Terry led the group several hundred yards away from shore into deeper water, inflated her yellow marker tube, and sent it up to the surface. Manuel saw it and aimed the *Dorado* toward the buoy. He waited near the buoy until the divers popped to the surface following their three-minute safety stop. Then he positioned the boat to retrieve his passengers.

"Hey, that was pretty cool, Fulvio," Scooby said. "I'm glad you convinced Terry to make this dive."

"Yes, that was even better than my glassy sweeper dive on Punta Tunich. A lot more fish. Did you see the two morays in the back of the cave?"

"Yep. Very cool. Did you see 'em, too, Jamie?"

"Yeah, that was a great dive! I got some good photos of Fulvio and his little fish friends, too."

"And you also spotted the cave first," said Terry. "We should call it Jamie's Glassy Sweeper Cave."

"Okay, that's how we'll write it in the logbook, even though it wasn't a true cave," Scooby said, laughing.

Terry agreed. "Yes, these formations aren't caves in the strict sense of the term. I wouldn't take you into a real cave unless you were cave certified." She turned toward Manuel. "Let's head for the closest pier and hang out for an hour while we decide where to go for our second dive. Jamie, can I see your camera a minute? I want to see the photos you took of Fulvio and his glassy sweepers."

"Sure thing. Take a look." Jamie handed the camera to Terry.

She put the camera into review mode and scrolled through the pictures. She laughed at one shot. "That's a great picture of Fulvio and his thousands of little shiny buddies." Then something caught her eye. "Would you mind emailing these photos to me when you get a chance? I'd like to check out something."

For the group's second dive, Terry selected a shallow reef near the marina called Paradise. She assumed Jamie and Scooby wanted to finish diving early so they would have twenty-four elapsed hours before their flight to ensure they would not encounter any decompression issues. The dive proved uneventful but still enjoyable. There were plenty of small critters to see, so Jamie practiced her macro photography. After the dive, the group split up at the marina. Fulvio drove home, while Jamie and Scooby said goodbye to Terry and Joe.

"Thanks for some great diving, Terry," Jamie said. "Scooby and I really loved the experience. And he even bought some nice art from your friend, Greg, at the museum exhibition. That was an unexpected bonus. I hope he'll be all right."

"Thanks to you, I think he'll make it. You really saved his life." She hugged Jamie and then Scooby. "Glad you enjoyed yourselves. Next time bring the rest of your gang."

"Okay, that's a plan," Scooby said. "In fact, we decided to stay a bit longer so we can check out some hotels where we can all stay next time."

Terry and Joe wanted to see Greg as soon as possible, so they brought their dive gear home and left it soaking while they went to the hospital. At the hospital, Dr. Gomez met them with some bad news.

"I'm sorry but Señor Dietrich has had a relapse. He slipped into a coma again this afternoon." He saw the expression on Terry's face and tried to reassure her. "But your friend is stable and breathing on his own, so we believe this is just a temporary setback. I will call you when there is a change in his condition."

"Thank you," Joe said, holding Terry's arm. "Please keep us advised."

"I will, and thank you for coming down anyway. Adios."

Later that night, Terry downloaded the photos Jamie had emailed to her, more to keep her mind occupied from thinking about Greg than anything else. She started to examine them when the phone rang. "Joe, would you get that please? I'm busy here."

"Sure, I have it. Hello? Bill, is that really you? Damn, how ya doing? . . . It's been ages since we've seen you. . . . You wouldn't believe how big the kids are now. What are you up to? . . . A case down here? . . . Oh, on the mainland. Well that's not too far away. . . . Sure, if you have any questions, just call us. . . . Yeah, be great to see you when you're finished. . . . Okay, I'll tell Terry. Hopefully we'll see you soon."

Terry looked up from her computer. "I thought Bill retired."

"Well, he did. From the NYPD, that is. But you know Bill. Can't sit still. He's coming down on business."

"Did you invite him to stay with us?"

"He's consulting on a case with another detective over on the Mayan Riviera. They're tracking down a person of interest. He'll let us know when he's done and if he can, he'll hop over for a visit."

"That's great. I can't wait to see him." She looked back at her computer with a puzzled expression. "Would you come here and take a look at this photo Jamie took of Fulvio in the cave at Chankanaab today?"

Joe leaned over Terry's shoulder as she showed him the photo. "Here's Fulvio, surrounded by thousands of little fish. But look up here in the corner. What's that?"

"Looks like . . . is that light? But where could it be coming from?"

"Good question. I think maybe we should go back to that cave formation and take another look. It might be nothing more than a blemish on the lens or perhaps just another swim-through into the lagoon. But if it is, I'm curious to see where it leads."

CHAPTER 32

Akumal, the Yucatan Mainland

Mike sipped his coffee and checked his watch, waiting for Dayle in the hotel lobby. He waved when he saw her enter near the front desk.

She waved back and walked over to where he was sitting. "Good morning, mate. How'd you sleep?"

"Pretty good. The mattress was a bit lumpy but we're not here for the creature comforts. I wish we had just driven through straight to Tulum instead of wasting time in Xel-Há and here."

"Well, I thought it would be helpful starting in some of the touristy places on our way, just to speak with the locals about any traditions they might have heard concerning the globe. Sorry we came up dry on that strategy. Let's head out for Tulum right after breakfast."

"Fine by me. I'm hungry. Let's eat and run."

After breakfast, they drove south toward Tulum, the ancient Mayan walled city overlooking the Caribbean, famous for religious rituals. Arriving at the site, Dayle pulled into a large parking lot filled with tourist buses, vans, and taxi cabs. "Okay, mate. We're here. Let's hook up with a tour. Looks like the next one starts in half an hour."

"A tour? You want to waste time on a tour?"

"You can't just start digging for the globe. We have no idea where it might be or even if we're on the right track. These tour guides are pretty informative and well trained. You never know what we'll learn."

Mike raised his eyebrows. "Okay, let's give it a shot."

They bought tickets and waited with a group of twenty tourists. Soon, a young man approached.

"Hola and welcome to Tulum. I am your tour guide. Please follow me." The guide stopped in front of a stone building and began his introduction. "Tulum was a seaside port, maintaining trading routes all the way down to Belize. Spanish explorers discovered the city in 1518 and . . ."

Dayle poked Mike in the ribs. "Hear that? The timing is right."

". . . the city survived until the end of the sixteenth century. But soon after, diseases from the Old World killed many inhabitants and the city was eventually abandoned. Please follow me."

The tour proceeded from building to building. Dayle sensed Mike was losing patience but kept him moving along. Finally, they stopped at a temple. As the guide explained the significance of the building, Dayle noticed an upright stone slab near the entrance to the temple. It was shaped similar to the dimensions of a gravestone but taller. She waited until the guide had finished talking about the temple. "Excuse me, but what is that?" she asked the guide, pointing to the object.

"That is called a stele, pronounced just like steel, the metal. They had many purposes." He stepped closer to the stone slab, almost as tall as he. "The Mayans used them to mark important commemorative events as territorial boundaries, to post government proclamations, and to indicate land ownership, among other things. Most are decorated with carvings, paintings or writing. This particular stele was damaged when it was recovered, and much of the text is worn away so we do not know its original purpose. But the text indicates a Mayan date that corresponds to a Western date sometime around the 1500s."

Dayle tried to jab Mike's ribs again when she heard the date, but he blocked her elbow with his arm.

The tour guide pointed to an engraving in the stone. "This stele shows a Mayan king or noble person, dressed in full ceremonial clothing. His image is framed with a long Mayan inscription, but we cannot determine what it says because of the extensive erosion caused by wind and water. He appears to be holding some important object up, either to venerate it as holy or to show it to the populace, who would have been gathered for some major event." The guide waited for several minutes to let the group inspect the stone slab and take photos.

"Please follow me to the next building, dedicated to an important Mayan goddess."

As the group followed their guide, Dayle and Mike stayed back to examine the monolith more carefully. Dayle focused on the object the Mayan king held in his hand. "Blimey, look at this! If that isn't a globe, you can feed me to the salties."

Mike leaned forward and looked around to make sure no one was watching. Then he pulled out a magnifying glass and examined the globe. "Looks like I won't be feeding you to those Aussie saltwater crocs. There's a very faint outline, but you can make out patterns, like land masses and oceans. I'll take a photo." Mike leaned closer to the stele and held the phone as close to the image of a globe as focusing would permit. "Got it. Let's go somewhere and talk. We don't need any more tours. This proves the damn globe was here around the same period as the Spanish conquistadors in the late fifteenth or early sixteenth centuries."

They walked to a shady spot near a moss-covered building. "What do we do now?" asked Mike.

"I suggest we stroll around on our own and look for any more of these steles. If we can find one with more detail, perhaps a better inscription, we can ask one of these tour blokes what is means."

"Sounds like a plan. We might as well kill the rest of the day here and see if we learn anything else." They walked around the ancient ruins and stopped at the edge of the cliffs overlooking the multihued, blue Caribbean Sea.

Dayle looked down the steep rocky bluff and watched the foamy surf crash against the base of the cliffs. "Whoa, that's a long way down. Makes me a bit dizzy."

Mike stepped closer and put his hand on her shoulder. "Be careful, Dayle. I don't think the locals would like it if a tourist got a little too close to the edge and lost her balance. Might be bad for business. Besides, I still need you. Proving the globe exists and was in this vicinity is one thing. Finding the damn thing is another matter."

"I appreciate your heartfelt concern, Mike," she said, laughing, just as her foot dislodged a large piece of rock. He grabbed Dayle's arm and pulled her back from the edge.

"Oh!" she exclaimed, as she watched the rock tumble down and disappear into the sea. "Thanks, mate. Perhaps they *should* warn the tourists not to get too close to the edge."

"Yeah. Let's get back to the hotel. Then we can decide our next steps."

Mike dropped Dayle off at the hotel entrance. "Thanks, mate. I'll see you later." She began walking inside when he called out.

"Hey, I'll just be a minute parking the car. How 'bout coming to my room for a drink?"

Dayle looked back over her shoulder. She was tempted and lonely, and she knew Mike wanted more than just a drink. But she hoped she would find an email from Jeff.

"Nah. Thanks, anyway. I'll see you later." Back in her room she closed the door and leaned against it with a sigh. "Jeff, I feel disconnected. I need you. I need us." She turned on her laptop and went right to email, but there was still no message from Jeff. She shook her head and bit her lip. Dayle was about to sign off when a new email popped up, which caught her attention. The from-address line read: Cozumel 4 You. Dayle clicked on the email with anticipation. She knew Laura Wilkinson's *Cozumel 4 You* newsletter always contained interesting Cozumel tidbits, local happenings, events, and occasionally some local gossip.

If you wanted to know what was happening on the island, Laura Wilkinson was one of the main go-to people. One story headline immediately caught her eye.

CHAPTER 33

Akumal

Dayle was about to click on the story in *Cozumel 4 You* when she heard someone knock on the door. "Who is it?"

"It's me. Mike."

She opened the door and returned to her computer. Then she clicked on the link.

Sacred Mayan Crossing Will Be Re-enacted This Weekend

Mike came into her room and stood behind Dayle. Then he leaned over her shoulder and watched the screen as she scrolled down.

Several hundred participants will join the annual Sacred Mayan Crossing, which will be re-enacted this weekend. The three-day event recreates ancient ritual pilgrimages by the Yucatan peninsula's original inhabitants from Xcaret to Cozumel. The celebration will start at Xcaret, where participants re-enact rituals to the goddess Ixchel. They will wait for the first rays of dawn, when they launch their wooden canoes toward Cozumel. After paddling the twelve-nautical-mile crossing, they will make offerings to the goddess. She sends a message back with the natives when they return to Playa del Carmen on the mainland.

Here in Cozumel, the celebrations will take place at Chankanaab National Park and be overseen by the Fundacion de Parques y Museos Cozumel (FPMC). For more information . . .

Her curiosity piqued, she Googled "Cozumel Crossing" and was astounded by what she saw. More than ten stories with variations of "Cozumel Crossing" popped up on her screen, some featuring pictures of the annual re-enactment of the crossing, while others displayed actual Mayan drawings of the event. In one of the older Mayan representations, a man sitting in a canoe dressed in ceremonial garb held a golden urn and was surrounded by young men paddling. The caption read:

The Mayans brought valuable items from the mainland to Cozumel. They presented them as offerings to the goddess Ixchel, who they believed resided at a sacred place called Chankanaab.

Dayle's mind raced as fast as her fingers could type. First, she copied and saved several of the Mayan drawings. Then, she fired off an email to Terry. She looked over her shoulder at Mike. "What do you say tomorrow we stop at Xcaret again before heading back to Cozumel?"

"I'd say that's a good idea, especially if it could help us figure out what that guy in the canoe is holding inside that urn." He leaned closer and placed a hand on her shoulder. Their lips were inches apart. Dayle tried to stand but before she could, Mike kissed her firmly on her lips. She fell back in the chair.

"Mike, I . . ."

"Don't say anything. Just stay with me tonight. Your room, my room, I don't care where."

Dayle's mind raced, as her conflicted thoughts spun out of control. She was attracted to Mike. He had saved her life twice. But she and Jeff were still married. She loved her husband, but she wondered if he really loved her. She worried if Jeff's life was in danger. Someone could be shooting at him at this very moment. But she felt angry that he had left her to pursue his adventure.

Dayle was still trying to make sense of her feelings when Mike kissed her again.

Cozumel

Terry arrived back at her house with a truckload of gear to wash and prepare for tomorrow. Contented, she thought of how well the dives had gone today.

"Hi, hon. How was the diving?" Joe asked as he entered the house.

"Fine. I had all experienced divers, so there was no drama. Just easy dives and lots of interesting critters to see. I wish every day was like that. No, on second thought that would probably get boring. Did you see Greg today?"

"Yep. I stopped at the hospital and Doctor Gomez told me he was out of the coma and could talk. I went to his room and he was awake but still a little groggy. He recognized me, though. He kept mumbling about this 'John' character that he met just before he collapsed at the gallery. I think finding him will answer a lot of questions."

"By the way, Bill's coming to the island."

"Oh? Is he finished with his case?"

"No. Bill and his partner are kind of stuck. They started off in Cancun and have been working their way south trying to find their guy. They're over in Playa del Carmen for a couple of days so he called and asked if we were free for dinner. I told him we were. I'm just waiting to hear back from him. Maybe we can have dinner downtown tonight?"

"Sounds good. Where?"

"How about La Cocay? We haven't been there or seen Kathy in a long time."

"Okay, when Bill calls, see if he's in the mood for great food and atmosphere."

Later when the phone rang, Terry answered the call expectantly. "Bill! Great to hear from you. What ferry are you taking? . . . Okay, great. Listen, I know how much you enjoy Joe's cooking, but since you'll be downtown, Joe and I would like to treat you to dinner. How about La Cocay? . . . Great. . . . Yes, you can bring your friend. We'll pick you up at the ferry pier at seven. Look forward to seeing you."

"Are we all set, Ter?" Joe shouted from the upstairs bedroom.

"Yes. I'll call La Cocay and make reservations for seven-thirty."

"Can't wait to hear about his case. I guess we'll learn the details tonight."

CHAPTER 34

Terry and Joe arrived at the ferry pier and saw Bill waving. "Hey, wonderful to see you!" he exclaimed as he hugged Terry and then Joe. He turned and introduced a younger man standing behind him. "This is Detective Michael Monahan, NYPD. I'm working for him. By the way, we call him Micko. Anything more formal makes him nervous."

Joe shook his hand. "All right then, good to meet you, Micko."

"Thanks. Good to meet you, too. Bill's been filling me in about your joint exploits. Sounds like you've had some amazing adventures together." He nodded, extending his hand toward Terry. "Mrs. Manetta."

"Please, just Terry. I don't like formalities either."

They piled into Joe's truck and drove to La Cocay, one of their favorite restaurants on the island. Kathy, the owner, greeted them at the door. "Welcome, friends. Wonderful to see you again."

"Good to see you too, Kathy," Terry said.

"Outside?" she asked.

"Definitely," Joe said.

She escorted them past the interior seating area to a table located in the outside garden area.

"Is this okay?"

"Perfect."

"Can I get you something to drink? As I recall you like red wine. Merlot, cabernet, or Chianti?"

"Merlot for me," Terry said.

Kathy turned to Joe.

"I'll have a cab."

"Margaritas, for us. Rocks and salt," said Bill.

"Perfect. By the way, do I detect a New York accent?"

"You sure do. Brooklyn for me."

"I'm from the Bronx," Micko said.

Kathy laughed. "Well, this is old home week. I hail from Queens."

A waiter soon brought their drinks, balanced on a large tray. "Are you ready to order?" he asked.

"Is the filet mignon still outstanding?" Bill asked.

"Good memory," Joe said. "Make it two, please. Medium rare, right?"

"Good memory," Bill replied. "Thanks."

"Grouper for me," Terry said. "With the salad."

The waiter looked at Micko. "I'll try the scallops, and a salad for me, too."

"Might as well make it four salads," Joe said to the waiter, as they handed their menus back.

After the waiter left, Bill raised his glass. "Here's to friendship."

"Same here, Bill," Terry said, clinking glasses with Bill, then draining her glass and ordering a refill.

"I bet you guys must have some stories to tell," Monahan said, grinning.

"Oh yeah," Terry said, already feeling the effects of a second glass of wine on an empty stomach. "In fact . . ."

Joe rolled his eyes, sat back, and let Terry regale Monahan with stories about the adventures the three had shared.

"Micko, over the years we've battled Mexican drug lords, pirate whalers from Iceland, Islamic terrorists, and assassins from the Cuban secret service. And those are the dull parts!"

Monahan's eyes widened. "I had heard a little about your exploits, but I never dreamed you three would have—"

The waiter interrupted him. "Excuse me, here are your salads."

Everyone leaned back as the waiter served their salads. "So, ex-partner, how's retired life been treating you?" Joe asked, as he attacked his salad.

"Never been busier. Been doing well, even though I never found a mermaid like you did."

"So, what brings you two gents to Cozumel?" Terry asked.

"Well," Bill said, "as you know, I'm retired and doing some overpaid consulting work for my former employers. Micko's been working a tough murder case, actually a multiple murder case."

Monahan continued. "We have reason to believe our suspect left the U.S. and is traveling somewhere in this area. We subpoenaed his credit card records and the merchant category codes on his MasterCard indicated he took an American Airlines flight to Cancun. The Yucatan's a big place, but based on interviews with some of his staff, we think he's staying somewhere on the mainland, probably along the coast. We requested help from the local authorities to find him and they invited us down. My boss, Sam Goldman—"

"Sam's your boss? How the hell is he? I remember Sam when he was just coming up the ranks. I left the department around that time," Joe said.

"Good guy to work for. Sam recalled Bill had some experience down here and worked on some cases with you a while back. So, he suggested that Bill accompany me."

"Yeah, he wanted me to teach Micko how to make a good margarita."

Joe laughed. "So, what's your case about?"

Bill nodded to Monahan. "I told you Joe always cuts to the chase fast."

"We're pretty sure we're dealing with a very clever serial killer, who—"

Two waiters arrived with four steaming entrees.

"This food smells awfully good," Joe said.

"Spoken like a true Italian," said Micko, lifting his fork as they all started to eat. "Several months ago, we had several deaths that were puzzling but didn't seem all that suspicious at first."

"Puzzling?" asked Terry.

"Sudden deaths that seemed like heart attacks. Routine stuff. They ended up being classified as unexplained by natural causes. But then, a sharp-eyed ME . . ."

Terry tilted her head, inquiring.

"Medical examiner. He spotted a strange coincidence. He noticed a link between the victims. They were all young, too young to suffer those kinds of deaths. And most importantly, they were all artists. And, they all had recently held very successful expositions of their works, which sold for unusually high prices at the events. So, the ME went back and redid the autopsies. He determined their deaths, the heart failures, were likely caused by respiratory arrest." Monahan looked at Joe, who was leaning forward, eyes narrowed, concentrating on every word.

"Did he determine what caused the respiratory arrest?" Joe asked.

Bill smiled, thinking about how his former partner still retained his investigative instincts.

Monahan nodded. "Yes. He found a small puncture wound on one of the victims. He retested the tissue samples, looking for something specific. And he found it. He tested another vic. Same result. A third vic had already been cremated, but from reading the autopsy notes, he figured that if they had tested him, they probably would have found the same result. They both . . ." He stopped eating. No one touched their food as he continued. "They both had been injected with a neurotoxin."

Joe shot a glance at Terry, who looked back at Joe.

Micko and Bill both caught *"the tell"*— a slight shift in body language or eye glance that detectives are trained to spot, indicating a suspect or witness knows something, is hiding something, or holding back some piece of vital information. Monahan was puzzled by their reaction.

Bill watched the exchange as Monahan used Joe's favorite investigative technique against him. He stopped talking and recalled early in his career that Joe had taught him when you hit a nerve, keep your mouth shut until the suspect or witness confesses or blurts out a key piece of information.

But what the hell could Terry and Joe know about this? Bill wondered.

After a silent moment, Joe spoke. "So, your medical examiner concluded that the neurotoxin caused the respiratory arrest, which caused the heart failure, which at first glance just appeared to be a run-of-the-mill heart attack."

"Correct."

"There are a lot of neurotoxins out there. Did they determine which one?" Joe suspected the answer before Monahan confirmed it.

"Tetrodotoxin. Which is found in—"

"Pufferfish and the blue-ringed octopus," Terry said, finishing Micko's sentence.

This time Micko and Bill exchanged glances. "You two seem pretty knowledgeable about the subject. I know you're both experts in undersea life but—"

"A good friend of ours, an artist on Cozumel, suffered respiratory arrest from tetrodotoxin recently after holding a very successful art exhibition," Terry said.

"Did your friend die?"

"No, thank God. He was in pretty bad shape, near death, but we found him soon after he ingested, or was injected with, the poison. Luckily, I had a DAN Emergency Pack in the car, so I was able to administer pure oxygen. Then, we brought him to a hospital just in time. They knew how to treat him, so he's alive. It was touch and go for a while, but they think he'll make a complete recovery."

"Lucky for him they knew how to treat it. This toxin works real fast."

"Actually, there was a lot of luck involved. Jamie, one of the divers who was with us when we found Greg, that's our friend's name, is a mortician. She's seen a lot of deaths, suspicious and otherwise. She noticed the wound and alerted the doctors." Terry picked up her glass and sipped her merlot, as Bill and Micko looked at each other.

Bill nodded and Micko took a photo out of his pocket. He handed it to Joe.

"Son of a bitch!" Joe handed the photo to Terry. Micko and Bill saw her eyes go wide. She dropped her glass, spilling the wine all over the table.

"Mike Handy!" she said, staring at the photo.

"You two know this guy?" Micko asked Joe.

"Yeah. He's been diving with our group. I had my suspicions

about him from the start. Something about him just didn't feel right."

Micko took the photo from Terry before she dropped it onto the wine-stained tablecloth. "Do you think we can show this photo to your artist friend? If he can ID Handy as the person who slipped him the neurotoxin, it's a slam dunk."

"We're planning to see Greg tomorrow morning," she said. "Why don't you meet us at the hospital then?"

"Okay, that's a—"

"Do you know where Handy is now?" Bill asked, interrupting his partner.

"Oh my God! Joe, he and Dayle are on the mainland. We need to warn her!"

"Who's Dayle?" Micko asked.

"She's a good friend of ours. Originally from Australia but now she lives in Roatan, Honduras with her husband. Besides running a dive operation there, she also opened an art gallery called Latin American Lifestyle and Art."

Bill asked, "Dayle? Is she the same woman that Cuban assassin targeted a few years back, who married that CIA guy, Jeff, who was assigned to protect her?"

"One and the same," said Joe.

"That was quite an adventure. I remember it well."

"Another one of your joint capers?" Micko asked.

Bill nodded. "Why are they traveling together on the mainland now?"

Joe answered while Terry used a napkin to blot her spilled wine. "Dayle wants to purchase some art for her gallery. She likes to buy original, indigenous pieces from local artists. Right now, she's also looking for a unique object, some kind of ancient Mayan representation of the New World as it was known around Columbus's time. It's supposedly been painted or inscribed on an ostrich egg, of all things. Actually, it might have been produced in Europe. There's even been some mention of a link to the master himself, Leonardo da Vinci, as the creator of the globe. How the Mayans got their hands on it and where it is now is part of the mystery."

"I can see how something like that would pique our guy's interest," Micko said. "If they do manage to find this object, I think your friend is in a lot of danger. Handy's already killed several people for artwork with no historical importance, worth a lot less than the value of what you're describing. This globe, or egg or whatever it is, could be priceless. In fact, I would be surprised if she made it back to Cozumel alive."

Joe saw Terry pull out her cell phone. "Who are you calling?"

"Dayle! I need to tell her she's in danger and she should just get the hell away from Mike. Damn, it's going right to voice mail. She must have the phone off."

"Hang up and don't leave a message!"

Terry pressed the disconnect icon on the screen. "Why not?"

"You don't know if Handy might hear your message. Let's figure out how to safely contact her. I doubt she's in immediate danger tonight, especially if they haven't found the globe yet. I think we should check on Greg first thing tomorrow morning and see if he ID's Handy as the guy who poisoned him. Then we can come up with a game plan and contact Dayle," said Joe.

CHAPTER 35

Akumal

A ray of sunlight pierced the space between the curtains, shining on Mike's face. He blinked and rolled over.

Shit, what a lousy night. Me with a hard-on and this bitch gets a sudden conscience attack 'cause she's worried someone might be spraying her hubby with an AK47.

He looked at the time. 9:00.

I need some coffee.

He dressed and went downstairs to the lounge. He saw Dayle already sitting at a table, staring into a steaming cup of coffee. A map was spread out on the table in front of her. He walked over and pulled out a chair. "Good morning. Mind if I join you?"

"Hi, Mike. No, of course not. About last night, I—"

"Forget it. No need to explain. I get it. You're not over your husband yet, even though he left you to go on some adventure jaunt with his buddies." He saw Dayle's eyes flash.

"That's not fair. Jeff didn't leave me to go on some joyride for kicks. He's on a dangerous mission fighting for a cause he believes strongly in. If I thought for a minute that—"

"All right, Dayle, no need to debate the point. But it just seems to me that he believes his mission is more important than you, and . . ."

Dayle's eyes narrowed as if she was about to explode, and Mike realized he was treading on dangerous ground.

"Let's forget about it and just focus on *our* mission, okay?"

Her eyes softened and the tension lines around her lips relaxed. "That makes sense to me, too. Thanks for understanding."

Good thing I changed the subject, he thought. "I see you have a map. What are you planning?"

"Just figuring out the best route to Xcaret. That should be our last stop before heading back to Cozumel."

He leaned over her shoulder to look at the map and inhaled her perfume. *Damn, she turns me on.*

"Makes sense. It's lucky you saw that story in the *Cozumel 4 You* newsletter. We'll be there in time for the ceremonial crossing. Seems like a good opportunity to learn more about the ceremony, and maybe even what they were carrying in that urn pictured in the sculpture we saw in Tulum." He checked his watch. "Almost nine o'clock. How about grabbing a quick breakfast, packing up, and then getting on the road?"

"Sounds like a plan." She smelled the aroma of eggs, pork, and potatoes and glanced over her shoulder. "Looks like the breakfast buffet is open. Let's eat, I'm starved."

Cozumel

Terry and Joe met Bill and Micko in the lobby of the Flamingo Hotel, where the two detectives stayed overnight.

"Good morning guys. Ready to head over to the hospital?" Joe asked. "I'd really like to settle this issue so we can focus on helping Dayle."

"Yep." Bill turned to his partner. "You have Handy's photo?"

"Got my rogue's gallery right here," he replied, patting the breast pocket on his tropical shirt, decorated with palm trees and lyrics from Jimmy Buffett songs.

"Don't tell me you're a parrothead?" Terry asked.

"Fins up!" Micko said, with a broad grin. "After all, aren't we in Margaritaville?"

"That we are," Terry said, forcing a smile. She was worried about Dayle but grateful that Micko's sense of humor eased the tension temporarily.

They piled into Terry's Jeep for the short trip through town to the hospital and arrived in fifteen minutes. Dr. Gomez met them in the reception area. "Greetings my friends. You are a little early for visiting hours but not a problem." He glanced at the two strangers and then at Joe.

"These men are police detectives from New York City," Joe explained. "They may have information about the man who attempted to kill Señor Dietrich."

"Ah, that would be wonderful. Señor Dietrich is doing much better this morning. I was told he just finished breakfast. Let me call the nurse and see if he can have visitors now."

The four exchanged hopeful glances while Dr. Gomez spoke to the floor nurse. "You may see him now. Please follow me."

Terry and Joe entered the room first, with the two detectives behind them. Greg was sitting up, watching television.

"Hey, good to see you guys!"

Terry leaned over the bed and kissed his cheek. "So glad to see you getting better."

"I'm feeling stronger every day. The doctors expect a full recovery, and I should be out of here in a few more days."

"That's fantastic," Terry said.

Joe introduced Bill and Micko. "They're working a case that had some similarities to your experience and they just want to ask you some questions."

Greg's eyes widened. "Really? Something like this happened in New York, too?"

Micko took the lead and stepped forward. "Yes, sir. The big difference is that the victims in New York aren't alive to help identify their assailant, but you are. You were very lucky."

Greg stared at Micko. "What's the connection to my case?"

"It seems the assailant used the neurotoxin tetrodotoxin to kill his victims, just like he tried to do to you. That's a pretty unusual poison to use. Tough to obtain and difficult to administer. The other victims had a scratch on their hands, just like I'm told you did. That was a lucky find, and the fact that Terry's dive customer Jamie spotted it probably saved your life. Finally, they were also artists, just like you. Different from the art you create, but artists, nevertheless. It seems the assailant purchased a large supply of their work just before they died."

"Well, someone did recently purchase a large amount of my work that was on display at a local museum. And shortly after that, someone came to my gallery, the night I got sick, and just about cleaned me out. I never sold so many pieces at one time. I was ecstatic."

"Do you know the identity of the buyer?"

"Well, no. I never met him before. But he said his name was John."

"I see. Do you think you would recognize John if you ever saw him again?"

"I think so. I got a good look at him and he was in the gallery for a long time."

Micko reached into his pocket and withdrew three wallet-sized photographs of similar-looking men. He handed them to Greg. "Do you recognize anyone in these photos?"

Greg looked at the photos and immediately showed one to Micko. "This is John. No doubt about it. I never saw the other two before. He's the guy who bought all my artwork."

Micko took the photo and handed it to Joe.

Joe's eyes went dark. He gave it to Terry.

"Mike Handy!" she exclaimed. "That settles it. I'm calling Dayle now!" She pulled her cell phone from her purse but Joe grabbed her arm.

"Just wait a minute. Let's discuss next steps downstairs. We can—"

"You know this guy?" Greg asked, interrupting Joe.

Micko spoke next. "To answer your question, yes. We've ID'd Mike Handy as the suspect who killed our three victims in New York. We tracked him to Fort Worth, Texas, where he lives, and now down to this area. We're pretty sure he's on the mainland now with a friend of Terry and Joe, Dayle Standish, looking for a very rare and valuable piece of art. My next step is to meet with the local authorities. Thanks to your help we should have no problem getting their cooperation to help us arrest this guy. But we want to move fast before Dayle becomes victim number five, at least that we know of. We have no idea how many people he might have already killed. I think the only thing keeping her alive is that he needs her help to find what they're looking for."

"I can't believe it," said Greg, shaking his head.

"Believe it! Thanks for your help. And the best of luck with your recovery. That neurotoxin is nasty stuff." Micko turned to Joe, Terry, and Bill. "Let's get moving. We have some planning to do."

The group left Greg and Dr. Gomez and met outside next to Terry's Jeep.

Micko said to Terry, "We need to find out where they are. Why don't you ask Dayle how their search is going, where they are, and when they might be returning? Just small talk. But tell her you need to discuss something privately, and ask her to call you back when she's alone. But act real casual about it, so even if Handy overhears the conversation, it won't set off any alarms."

"Okay, I can make some girl talk."

"Good. I don't want to chase this weasel all over the mainland and take a chance on losing him. I'm thinking that when we know they're returning, we meet them coming off the ferry. Bill and I can make the arrest. He has no clue who we are and won't be suspicious."

"Yeah, especially if you're wearing your Jimmy Buffett shirt," said Bill, smiling.

Micko continued. "The Mexican police can back us up. As long as they remain out of sight until we make the collar, Handy won't try to run. Then we can take our bad boy back home. Everybody on board with the plan?"

Everyone nodded their assent. "Okay, Terry. Make the call."

Terry stepped back inside the hospital lobby away from the street noise and called Dayle's cell phone. It rang several times and then went to voice mail.

Damn, where the hell are you, Dayle? Why aren't you answering your phone?

She decided to leave a message and hoped Dayle would return her call. "Hi Dayle. It's Terry. Just wondering . . ."

Terry left a message and went back to the Jeep, where Joe, Micko, and Bill waited. "Dayle didn't answer so I left a voice mail. Joe, it's almost 11:00. I have an afternoon dive group. Bill, can we drop you guys off at your hotel? I'll call you as soon as I hear anything."

"Sure. We have to send our report in anyway. Not much we can do until we know where they are or when they're coming back."

They drove back to the Flamingo Hotel and dropped off the two detectives.

"Say Terry, can I ask a favor?" Micko asked, as he got out.

"Sure."

"I haven't been diving for a while and never in Cozumel. Mind if I join your afternoon group today?"

"You're a certified diver?"

"Yep, for many years. In addition to diving in New York waters, I've been to Truk Lagoon several times, too. I dived most of the deep wrecks there." He flashed his PADI certification card. "But I didn't bring any equipment with me."

"If you can handle Truk in addition to the currents, cold water, and low visibility of diving in New York, I'm sure you can handle Cozumel. I can give you rental gear. Meet us at the marina at 1:00. It's a quick cab ride from your hotel. See you later!" Terry waved, pulling away from the curb.

CHAPTER 36

Xcaret

Dayle and Mike had been driving north on the highway to Xcaret when her cell phone rang. She glanced at the caller ID. "Oh, it's Terry. Wonder what she wants?" She put the phone down on the console. "I don't like chitchatting and driving. Especially in a foreign country. The last thing I need is an accident."

"Want me to answer it?" Mike asked.

"No, let it go to voice mail, then play it." After the phone pinged that a voice mail message was received, Mike hit *Speaker* and *Play*.

When Terry's voice came from the speaker, Mike's heart skipped a beat.

"Hi Dayle. It's Terry. Just wondering how you guys are making out on the mainland, and where you are now. Any hot leads? Also, do you know when you're returning to Cozumel? If we can meet you at the ferry, we can all go to Guido's for lunch or dinner, and you can fill us in on your adventure. Oh, before I forget, can you call me when you're alone? I want to discuss something privately with you, girl to girl. Okay? Bye."

"Wonder what Terry wants to chat about?" Dayle said.

Mike sensed trouble. *I need to disable that damn phone somehow.* "Oh, she probably wants to tell you about something interesting that she saw diving today."

"Yeah, you're probably right."

Mike pulled out his cell phone and pretended to call someone. "For some reason, my phone's not connecting. Can I try yours?"

"Sure. Here."

"Thanks." He checked the power level. The screen indicated 28%. *If I can kill the battery, that'll buy me some time.*

While he pretended to have a problem dialing, he opened every app that would drain the battery quickly. "Nope, can't reach my office. Oh, well. Guess I'll try again later."

An hour later, they pulled up to the Occidental Grand hotel in Xcaret.

"Hope they have rooms available. Looks pretty crowded," Dayle said.

"I'm sure they will. Does look crowded, but the place is huge. Let's check in and get down to the waterfront. I don't want to miss anything."

They checked in early, at noon. The only room available was a two-bedroom suite. They took it, then walked down to the beach, where hundreds of people surrounded local residents adorned in Mayan costumes. The natives stood next to several large wooden canoes, accompanied by the sound of conch shells, drums, and the chants of Mayan priests. The scent of incense wafted through the air. A master of ceremonies narrated the scene in both English and Spanish to the assembled tourists using a loudspeaker, breaking the magical, ceremonial mood.

"Ladies and gentlemen, this concludes the first day of our festivities. Tomorrow, as the first rays of dawn appear, a couple of hundred oarsmen will recreate the ancient ritual pilgrimage of the Yucatan's original Mayan inhabitants, as they rowed across from Xcaret to Cozumel. Or, as the Mayans called it, either Cuzamil or Kùutsmil. Both pronunciations translate into Land of the Swallows. The celebration will start here early in the morning.

"First, the participants will re-enact ancient rituals devoted to Ixchel, the goddess of the moon, fertility, and childbirth. Then they will launch their canoes for the twelve-mile crossing over to Cozumel. There, they will make offerings to Ixchel at the sacred lagoon of Chankanaab. The goddess will then send a message, which the canoeists will bring back to the people on the mainland. We will see you all tomorrow at dawn."

As the crowd dispersed, Dayle decided to call Terry back. "Oh damn! The bloody phone's dead. I'll have to charge it up and call Terry later."

"Too bad. Do you know where your charger is?"

"In my backpack. I think I left it on the sofa in the room."

"I have to go up to the room, anyway. Give me your phone and I'll charge it up for you."

"Okay, thanks. Here. I'm going to take a stroll along the beach. See you later."

Mike took the phone and went up to their suite. He rummaged through Dayle's backpack until he found the charger and plugged in the phone. He waited until the Apple logo appeared. He started to compose a text message to Terry, asking her not to contact Dayle until Dayle contacted her first.

Cozumel

Terry was about to give a dive briefing to Micko and the afternoon dive group as Manuel increased power to the *Dorado's* twin motors. She checked her phone, worried that she still had not heard back from Dayle. She called again but got a message that Dayle's phone was not available. Terry felt desperate. "Micko, I don't know what to do. We have to warn Dayle."

"Okay, send her a text. There's less chance of Handy seeing a text message than hearing a voice mail. Either way it's risky, but I don't see any alternative."

Xcaret

Mike was about to send his message to Terry, supposedly from Dayle, but Terry's text beeped in first.

> Dayle, we found out Mike Handy poisoned Greg. He'll kill you if you find the globe. Get away from him ASAP!

"Shit!" he exclaimed, staring at the message. Mike's mind raced, figuring out a way to buy time. He erased his original message and replied back to Terry the way he imagined Dayle might compose a message, with her Aussie pluck.

> Crikey! Thx mate! Don't text or call back. The bloody bastard might see or hear the message before I can get away. I'll contact you first.

He decided to act natural while he figured out a plan. He left the phone on the desk in the living room area of their suite and went to join Dayle on the beach.

CHAPTER 37

Dayle and Mike arrived at the beach just before dawn. The only other people on the beach were the oarsmen, tending to their canoes. Soon other tourists filtered down from their rooms.

"Welcome to the re-enactment of the ceremonial crossing. This morning . . ." came the narrator's voice.

In the waning darkness, they heard the Mayans chant to the beat of ceremonial drums. Rows of marchers appeared, all dressed in colorful native costumes. Many wore headdresses adorned with feathers tipped with gold. The rising sun's piercing rays broke the horizon, bathing the east-facing beach in a golden hue. The gold-tinged headdresses appeared to explode with light.

The assembled crowd remained totally silent, watching the natives re-enact the centuries-old ceremonies. Incense drifted through cool morning air, prompting some tourists to sneeze as the sharp scents wafted across the beach. The narration, though helpful to the uninitiated, seemed intrusive.

"Amazing," Dayle whispered in Mike's ear, as he nodded.

After almost an hour of chanting and dancing, one of the participants, who appeared to play the role of a chief or high priest, suddenly let out a loud cry as he looked up, arms outstretched, palms facing the brightening sky, now a pale blue. Silence descended over the dramatic scene. Without further commands, the natives moved to their canoes.

"Please direct your attention to the center of the formation," said the narrator. "You will notice . . ."

Dayle ignored him as her eyes fell on the largest craft in the middle of the fleet. Several of the more ornately dressed natives assembled next to it. One tall native, wearing the largest headdress, held an urn. Four oarsmen stepped into the front of the canoe and four in the rear. A young girl, Dayle estimated in her late teens, sat in the middle, followed by a young man about the same age, and behind them, a middle-aged woman and the tall native. From his regal bearing and costume, Dayle assumed he was the king. Behind the king sat another man, dressed as a servant.

"Looks like the royal family," Mike said quietly. He heard Dayle gasp.

"Oh!"

He turned toward her. "What's wrong?"

"Blimey, it's the stele!"

"The what?"

"The stele! The stone monolith at Akumal. Remember? They're re-enacting the same scene that we saw carved in the stone!"

By this time, all the canoes had pushed off from the beach, except the large canoe carrying the royal family. As it slid off the sand a moment later, they watched the chief raise the urn toward the heavens.

"This year's ceremony depicts the sacred sacrifice the Mayan chief Coyopa was forced to make when an indiscretion by his virgin daughter Akna required him to . . ."

Dayle tuned out the narrator as he droned on. Her body went rigid as the story Jackie and Peter told her about the Ghost of Chankanaab slammed into her brain.

"Mike! I know where the globe is. It's somewhere in Chankanaab!"

"Please join us tomorrow afternoon as we welcome the natives home and hear the message that they will bring back from the goddess . . ."

"Let's get out of here and get back to Cozumel." She took Mike's hand and pulled him through the crowd.

"Are you sure?"

"Let's check out and get rolling. I'll explain while we pack."

Back in their suite, Dayle explained the story Jackie and Peter had told her about the legend of the Ghost of Chankanaab.

"I admit it's an interesting theory, Dayle, but—"

"No 'buts' about it, mate. It's the only logical theory that fits. First, the timing is right. The legend dates back to Columbus's time as well as the estimates of the globe's age. Next, the sacred object supposedly gave Coyopa greater knowledge about the earth and universe than anyone else in this part of the world knew. What else could do that except some kind of representation of the earth that was far ahead of the Mayan beliefs at the time? They still believed the earth was carried on the back of a giant turtle or some similar myth."

Mike's raised eyebrows indicated he still had doubts, so Dayle pressed on.

"We know the goddess Ixchel demanded his most treasured object if he would not sacrifice his daughter. What else could have been more valuable and unique to him? Third, historians know that during Columbus's fourth voyage to the New World in 1502, one of his ships encountered Mayan trading canoes. Who knows what might have transpired when the European explorers and Mayans met each other back then? The globe must have been the object inside the urn that Coyopa carried to Chankanaab. That lagoon is riddled with underwater caverns, some of which might have sunk and been forgotten over time. We have some diving to do!"

"Okay, okay, Dayle. You convinced me. We'll go to Chankanaab and find that globe." *At least I will. Since I know where the globe is, I don't need you any longer.*

Then, Mike's thoughts turned to his bigger problem. He knew it was not safe for him to return to Cozumel now that the authorities had identified him as Greg's attacker. He decided to handle the immediate issue and figure out a plan later.

First thing's first. Time to get rid of Dayle.

Mike heard Dayle packing in her room. He went into the bathroom and opened a special zippered pouch in his toiletry kit. First, he took out a thin, flesh-colored latex glove and slipped it on his left hand. Next, he found his specially equipped ring and slipped it on. Then he carefully adjusted the ring so the barb was on the underside, where it would contact Dayle's skin.

He removed a small metal capsule and slowly unscrewed the tip, attached to a tiny sponge applicator, concentrating as he coated the almost-microscopic barb on the ring with blue-ringed octopus venom. He smiled.

"Hey, Dayle, I have a question," he said as he walked out of the bathroom.

CHAPTER 38

Dayle didn't reply, so he walked into her bedroom. *This is too easy. I can make it look like she had a heart attack sleeping in her bed. No muss, no fuss.*

But the room was empty. Mike spun around and ran back to the living room. Empty chair, empty sofa. No Dayle. Then his eyes fell on the desk where he had left her phone. The charger wire was still attached to the wall plug, but the phone was gone. He stared at the empty space on the desk, as if willing the phone to reappear. Then, he realized that he never deleted Terry's message.

He heard the elevator bell ring and ran to the elevator just as the doors closed. He pounded the button with his fist and watched the floor indicator blink 3, 2, 1. He bolted to the stairs and ran down the three flights as fast as he could. But when he reached the parking lot, he saw Dayle running toward her Jeep.

Just as he caught up, she jumped inside, locked the door, and turned the ignition key. Mike grabbed the door handle just as she hit the accelerator and peeled out, leaving him on the ground, enveloped in a hazy cloud of blue smoke and gravel dust. He stood and almost pounded his fist against his leg, until he remembered that he was still wearing his poison ring.

"Wouldn't that just make my fucking day complete!" he muttered under his breath.

He ran back to the front desk and asked to rent a car, hoping he might catch up to Dayle, but none were available. Instead he requested a taxi and went back to his room to finish packing. He knew that the car ferry from Calica ran less frequently than the people ferry from Playa del Carmen, so even though Dayle had a head start, he could beat her back to Cozumel and make plans.

Driving as fast as she could, Dayle looked back in her rearview mirror, afraid Mike might be pursuing her. Relieved, she saw only an empty road behind her. She blinked and sighed deeply. She remembered the deadly fury in his eyes back in the parking lot.

"Yeah, now I can see that bloody bastard as a killer," she said aloud to herself. She glanced down at her phone on the console and dialed Terry.

"Dayle!" Terry exclaimed, seeing the caller ID. "Are you okay?"

"Just a little shaken up and out of breath. I just had a bloody close call. Your text message saved my life."

"I know you said not to call or text you until you returned from—"

"What? I never sent you that message!"

"You di—Wait. Did Mike ever have your phone?"

"Yeah. The battery died and he offered to bring it up to my

room and charge it. So . . ."

"So, he must have seen my earlier text to you, and he knew the game was up. He was waiting until he knew where the globe was before he killed you."

"And we had just figured it out only about an hour ago."

"What? Where?"

"It's somewhere in the Chankanaab lagoon."

"How did you . . . oh never mind. You can tell me later. Where are you now?"

"Heading for the car ferry at Calica. I'll be there soon but I think I'll have about a three-hour wait for the ferry."

"Okay. Joe and I'll meet you at the pier when you arrive. Drive safely."

"Will do, mate. I'll be looking out for Mike, too."

"I doubt you'll run into him. He'll probably head for the ferry out of Playa because they run more frequently. I'll notify the police to keep an eye out for him there and at the ferry pier in San Miguel. See you later. Stay safe."

"Okay, thanks. See you later."

An hour later, Mexican police stationed at the ferry pier in downtown San Miguel took up surveillance positions as the high-speed boat from Playa del Carmen, ten miles across the channel from Cozumel, pulled up to the pier. As soon as the crew maneuvered the heavy metal gangplank into position, passengers streamed off, pulling, carrying, or dragging their luggage toward a line of waiting taxis, as the drivers hawked business. Many travelers had made the hour-long trek from Cancun by van, bus, or cab to the Playa ferry terminal instead of flying directly into Cozumel Airport. In the chaos, no one paid any attention to the tired-looking gentleman, walking with a limp and a cane, slowly dragging his rollaboard. Head lowered, his face shielded by a wide-brimmed hat, the man crossed Avenida Rafael Melgar and made his way up one of the narrow side streets toward an old hotel. He knew they would be grateful for any business and would ask no questions as long as he paid the bill.

Almost three hours later, Terry waved when she spotted Dayle's rental Jeep driving off the large car and truck ferry, several miles south of downtown San Miguel. Dayle tooted the horn, turned onto the local street, and pulled over as Terry and Joe ran up to her Jeep. She jumped into Terry's waiting arms, finally breaking down.

"I'm so relieved," Terry said, holding Dayle's heaving shoulders. She raised a tear-stained face.

"Blimey, mate! You have no idea how relieved *I* am," she sniffled.

"You're staying with us tonight. No arguments," Terry said. "We don't want you staying alone."

"No problems on that. I don't want to be alone tonight. Not with a killer in paradise on the loose." Dayle shifted her embrace to Joe.

"Welcome home," he said, as her shoulders heaved again. Terry sat in the back with Dayle as Joe drove. Finally, on the way south toward Joe and Terry's house, Dayle had finally cried her eyes dry. She took a deep breath.

"Good timing. I'm all out of tissues," she laughed. "So, what the bloody hell happened? How did you find out Mike was really the bloke who tried to kill Greg?"

Hearing Dayle's spicy language return reassured Terry that her friend was regaining her plucky spirit. "We had a surprise visit from a couple of New York City detectives. You remember Bill Ryan from a couple of years ago?"

"Of course I remember Bill. He's one of the Yanks who whisked me out of New York when that Cuban assassin tried to kill me there. What's he doing here?"

"Bill is assisting another detective on this case. They've tracked Mike from New York, down to Texas, and into this part of Mexico."

"All the way from New York?"

"Yes. It seems he has a bad habit of killing artists there after purchasing a large quantity of their work."

"Crikey! You're shittin' me!"

"Three other artists to be exact," Joe said from the front seat. "I guess Mike figured out a new investment strategy. Buy up their work and then kill them, creating a foolproof supply-demand situation. When he saw Greg's unique artwork, he decided to give it another go."

"I guess I was next on the hit parade, pardon the pun."

"Yep. Once you figured out where the globe was, you were expendable."

"How did you two figure out that part of the mystery?" Terry asked.

"Well, it was a combination of research, instinct, and luck. We . . ."

By the time Dayle had explained how she and Mike had determined the probable location of the globe, Joe was turning off the main road and slowly threading his way past the dirt potholes created by recent heavy rains. After bouncing along for several minutes, their house appeared in a clearing near the beach.

"Good to be home," Dayle said, smiling.

"I can't wait to show you something interesting," Terry said.

As soon as they entered the door, Jackie and Peter rushed over to hug Dayle.

"Oh, I can't tell you two how good it is to see you again," she said squeezing both children in one embrace. "In fact, you two actually helped me figure out the probable location of this mysterious globe that we've been searching for."

"Cool. Can't wait to hear what a genius I am," Peter said, wincing as Jackie threw a sharp elbow into his ribs.

Terry brought a small pouch from her bedroom and pulled out a photo. "Take a look at this." She handed Dayle the photo Jamie had taken of Fulvio gazing at his beloved glassy sweepers inside a small cave. "See anything unusual?"

Dayle stared at the photo for several seconds. "No, just Fulvio having an orgasm enjoying the company of his favorite fish. Oops, sorry!" she said, with a sheepish grin, hearing Jackie and Peter giggle.

Terry laughed. "I think they've heard the word before. Look here." She pointed toward the corner of the frame. "See that? At first, I thought it was just some kind of imperfection in the shot, like a reflection from the strobe. But if you look closely, it looks like . . ."

"Like a light from some source," Dayle said, finishing Terry's thought. "That means sunlight must be filtering through the ground into a cave, like a cenote."

"Yeah. There are some cenotes in the area. You can enter many of them directly from the surface, penetrate them, and then work your way back out. But here the surface is not open. It might have been open and accessible 500 or 600 years ago. However, with earthquakes, land shifting due to rains, floods, and hurricanes, who knows? Obviously, it must have been more easily reachable at some point, since the natives could only freedive. They didn't have masks or any equipment."

"Well, mate, let's go diving!"

"My thoughts exactly," Terry said. "It was Jamie who took the shot. But I'm sure I can count on Fulvio to help us. He'd rather go diving than work any day."

"Joe's famous paella will be ready in about thirty minutes. Let's have drinks and discuss a dive plan for tomorrow," Joe called out from the kitchen.

"Oh, he's the perfect man," Dayle quipped.

"Shhh," Terry said, with a conspiratorial smile. "You'll spoil him."

CHAPTER 39

The next morning Dayle, Terry, and Joe made a quick stop at the Residencias Reef condo so Dayle could pick up some of her dive equipment before heading to the marina where the *Dorado* was moored. Joe and Terry walked her to the condo she was renting.

"Looks like it's in good shape," Terry commented. "I recommend the place to people asking for a nice, clean, beachfront condo. They all seem to like it."

"Yes, I've been happy staying here. Saluting the sunset with a glass of wine works for me."

"No sign of Mike Handy," said Joe, scanning the beach from the second-floor balcony.

"I think you have my reg and BC, right Terry?"

"Yep. All washed, dried, and ready for diving."

"Good, so let me see if I have everything." Dayle checked the contents of her dive bag. "Wetsuit, mask, fins, snorkel, dive computer, drybag. And my waterproof and crushproof Pelican camera case for my new SeaLife camera. Okay, I'm good to go."

On the way out, they walked past one of the two heated pools on the property and glanced over at Mike Handy's condo in an adjacent building. They noticed a policeman standing on the balcony. When they reached the parking lot, they saw two more policemen sitting in a patrol car.

"I don't think Mike's gonna be enjoying his beachfront condo for a while," Joe said, getting into his truck. "They found a roomful of Greg Dietrich's art ready to be shipped back to the States, along with several pieces of Alebrijes art from that artist, Ramon Valdez, who suddenly died at the Discover Mexico exhibit. I heard they re-examined his remains and found tetrodotoxin in his system, too. We can add another victim to Handy's list." They drove to the new marina and lugged their equipment to the boat, a long walk from the parking lot.

"I sure miss the old Caleta Marina," Dayle said, carrying her dive equipment.

Terry nodded. "Me too. This place was not designed by anyone with any sense about boats and diving, but don't get me started on that rant." She saw a familiar, white BMW parked nearby and smiled. As they walked toward the boat, a taxi pulled up and two men got out. One was dressed for diving in a wetsuit pulled down to his waist to keep cool.

"Hi, guys," Terry said, waving. She glanced toward Dayle. "Looks like you'll get to meet some New York dicks."

"Who?" asked Dayle, with a wide-eyed expression.

"Dicks. That's American slang for detectives," Joe explained, laughing. "You hear it a lot in old movies."

"I'll keep that one in mind," said Dayle, flashing a mischievous grin.

Joe introduced her. "Dayle, this is Detective Monahan, and I think you already know Bill Ryan from your past adventure here."

She hugged Bill. "Hello Bill. It's so good to see you again, even if not under the best circumstances."

"Likewise, Dayle. You look great. But we have to stop meeting like this," he said.

"Seriously!"

She turned toward Micko. He extended his hand. "My friends call me Micko."

"Okay, mate. Then consider us friends. Nice to meet you, Micko."

"I have to get back to town," Bill said. "I'm scheduled to meet the Federales in about an hour and see if we can figure out where Handy might be hiding. No one saw him return from the mainland. For all we know, he could still be over there, perhaps making his way back to the States. He can't fly home. We've got that exit all covered. Happy diving, Micko."

"Thanks, partner. I'll let you know if we find anything."

Bill got into the waiting cab and headed back to San Miguel to meet with the police, while everyone else walked to the boat. When they arrived, they saw Manuel loading the last of the scuba tanks. Most were scratched and dented.

"It's amazing these things don't explode the way they're thrown around and banged up down here," remarked Micko. "We're so careful in the States to handle them with care. Sometimes we even put tank boots to protect the bottom of the tanks."

"Sometimes accidents do happen. Ask Dale. She had a close call recently."

Terry saw Fulvio sleeping on the bow, arms and legs spread out. "When I saw the BMW in the parking lot, I knew my bow ornament would be around here somewhere."

Fulvio opened his eyes and stood up. "Glad you all finally made it. I was just getting some sun waiting for you."

"Friend of yours?" asked Micko.

"You could say that. Meet Fulvio."

"Eh, how ya doin', Fulvio." They shook hands.

"Good to meet you. Sounds like you're not from anywhere near here."

"You've got a good ear for accents," Micko replied with a grin. "From the Bronx, New York."

"Oh, I thought perhaps New Joisey," Fulvio replied with an exaggerated accent, as they laughed.

Manuel guided the *Dorado* out of the marina uneventfully and into the channel. He swung the boat south toward Chankanaab, a short distance away. Since it would be a short ride, he proceeded slowly, allowing Terry and Joe time to give their dive briefing.

They passed a panga, a Mexican fishing boat used by local fishermen. It was just a twenty-foot long, leaky, wooden rowboat powered by a single outboard motor. The bow rose higher than a conventional rowboat to carry the weight of fishing nets and fend off waves. Even going slowly, the *Dorado* created a wake that upset the panga, causing it to pitch. The two fishermen shook their fists at Manuel, but he waved back with a smile. He glanced at Terry standing next to him at the front of the boat. "I wonder why they're out here now. They usually go out fishing later in the day or at night if they're poaching in protected waters."

"Who knows?" She shrugged.

Dayle, Fulvio, and Micko sat on padded bench seats along the gunwale as Terry began the briefing. "Okay, we'll stop in front of Chankanaab Park and get as close as we can to the area where the caves are to minimize our swim. Manuel will have to keep hovering offshore because we can't anchor out here. He also can't follow us for the entire dive like he normally would, so we'll have to swim to the cave and then back out to the boat. Last time we were here, we explored two caves."

Micko interrupted Terry's briefing. "Excuse me, but I'm not cave certified. Are all of you?"

"Don't worry about that. These aren't really caves. They're more like long swim-throughs that lead into open lagoons. Or, in this case, I suspect we might surface inside a cenote."

"Very cool. I've heard a lot about diving in cenotes, and I've always wanted to try it."

"I think the Mayan gods might grant your wish. One of these swim-throughs led us directly to the lagoon on the interior of the island. That's the one most tourists who come to Chankanaab explore when they dive with the house dive operation here. I don't want to waste our time exploring that one, but we'll use it as a marker to find the cave we're looking for."

"Yes, I want to find my glassy sweeper cave as soon as possible," Fulvio said.

"The cave where Fulvio had his love affair with the glassy sweepers is close, only about seventy feet south of the main cave. But it's almost impossible to find by itself because of the halocline, which causes the water to look so shimmery you can't see details right in front of you. The bottom out here is about sixty feet deep, but no need to go down that far. If we descend to about thirty feet, approach the wall, and follow it south, we should find the opening we're looking for. Check your depth gauges or computers. The bottom will get shallower as we approach the caves. Any questions?" asked Terry.

She looked at each diver. No one raised a hand.

"You'll need these dive lights," Joe said, handing each diver a main light, about the size of a flashlight or a lantern light, and then a smaller back-up light, about the size of a mini flashlight. "Okay, everyone test your lights." He waited until each diver turned on both lights several times. "All okay?"

Each diver nodded, and Terry continued.

"Okay. The cave is small. Only big enough for two people at a time. Fulvio went in the farthest. Tell us what you saw."

"When I went in to play with my little coppery-pink friends, maybe about twenty feet or so, I kept going, shining my light on them until they parted like a screen. Suddenly, I saw four blue eyes staring at me. Two large, green moray eels were hiding in the back of the cave. At least I thought it was the back, but I'm not sure. It was dark and it looked like there was a solid wall behind them. I didn't try to go past the eels to see if the cave continued."

"Good move," said Micko, smiling at him.

"I think the cave kept going a little farther," Terry said. "Jamie took these photos of Fulvio communing with nature inside the cave. See that grayish light just past his head?" She handed the photos to the divers and waited until they returned the photos. "I think that's a natural light source, indicating the cave opens up above the surface, like a cavern. I think it's worth exploring. Fulvio, since you've been inside the farthest, you'll lead the group once we reach the cave."

"Me?"

"Yes. Now's your chance to prove to the world that you're really the world famous Fulvio of the Deep, not Chicken of the Seven Seas! If you can get past the moray eels, just keep going and see if the cave opens up inside a cavern. If the cave ends there, it won't be difficult to turn around and back out."

Dayle patted Fulvio on the back. "Don't worry, Fulvio, we'll protect you. Then she asked Terry, "Since Chankanaab is such a popular place, why wouldn't anyone have found a cave or cenote in the park area in recent times?"

"Don't forget, 500 years of hurricanes, earthquakes, and floods have covered the opening. If the Mayans stopped using the cave, the memory might have been lost to history. The formation of the cave is tricky. It even fooled Fulvio into thinking it just stopped. Without Jamie's lucky photo, we wouldn't have kept searching any farther."

The group exchanged excited glances, anticipating their entrance into a magical realm, unseen by human eyes for hundreds of years, which possibly held a historic relic worth millions. The mood was broken when Manuel cut the motors and said, "Okay, we're here. Everyone suit up!"

Joe positioned everyone for diving. "Dayle and Micko, you'll giant stride off the stern. Fulvio and I will roll off the side. When we're all in position, Terry'll jump in first to check our location and the current."

Everyone took the spots Joe assigned, and Terry and Manuel brought each diver his or her tank with attached BC and regulator. Terry walked around to each diver for a predive safety check. "Air on, BC inflated, tank full, weights attached, all buckles secure?" When she checked Dayle's equipment, Dayle felt her adjusting the trim-weight pouch in the back of her BC.

"Anything wrong?" Dayle asked.

"No, I just thought you might need an extra pound or two."

"Oh. Why?"

"I noticed you're carrying your camera case instead of just the camera. How come?"

"I usually carry the camera without the case. But also lugging the dive lights is more than I want to handle, so I'm leaving the camera in the case to protect it. Is that why you gave me some extra weight?"

"Yeah. Since those Pelican cases are watertight, I figured it would make you a little too buoyant."

"Thanks, mate, I should have thought of that. I'm sure the extra lead will help."

When Terry was satisfied that each diver was ready, she prepared to jumped in to check that Manuel had positioned the boat in the correct location. She spotted the panga following slowly in the distance. As she hit the water, she wondered why the boat was in the area, since fishing was not permitted in the immediate vicinity.

CHAPTER 40

Terry looked down at the bottom and saw the current was mild. "We're good," she said.

Manuel shouted, "Okay everyone, get ready!"

They all knew the drill. That was the signal for the giant-stride divers at the back of the boat, Dayle and Micko, to stand, and for Joe and Fulvio to sit on the sides of the boat. After securing their masks and regulators with their hands, they would splash in on the count of three. "One, two, three, go!" said Manuel.

The four divers hit the water simultaneously.

They all surfaced together and Terry asked, "Everyone ready?" She waited until all the divers acknowledged with the appropriate hand signal. "Okay, see you on the bottom."

The divers pressed the deflator button on their BCs and slowly descended, clearing their ears every few feet as they descended to prevent ear squeeze and possible eardrum and inner ear damage. When they had reached sixty feet, Terry motioned the direction to proceed and they followed her.

When Terry saw their depth reducing from sixty feet to fifty and then forty, she knew they were going in the right direction. She also confirmed her visual cues with a compass reading, which indicated they were heading east. Joe followed up at the rear of the formation, ensuring that no one accidentally drifted off in the wrong direction.

Soon, the water took on a shimmery quality and cool fingers of brackish water stroked their bodies.

Must be the haloclines and thermoclines, Dayle figured. *I guess we're getting close to the caves.*

Her depth gauge indicated they were now at a depth of thirty feet.

Terry continued until she saw a wall pierced by a gaping black maw, the entrance to the lagoon they had visited on their last dive. She motioned for everyone to stop and made sure everyone saw the cave opening. When she faced the cave, she pointed to her right, south on her compass.

Everyone followed her, trying to read their gauges and stay close to the wall so they wouldn't miss the opening to their target cave, only about seventy feet away. Terry continued until she estimated they had traveled at least seventy feet, but there was no opening in the wall. She looked ahead but could only see about fifteen feet due to the shimmery, cloudy water.

She wondered if she had miscalculated the distance when she heard a metallic rapping sound. Someone was signaling by banging on their tank with a metal object. She looked back over her shoulder and saw Micko, rapping a brass hook against his tank and pointing up at the wall. They saw the cave opening, just above them. They had been too deep and didn't see the opening in the poor visibility. She smiled, gave him the OK sign, and pointed upward to make sure everyone saw the cave.

She motioned to Fulvio to enter first. He moved toward the opening and then halted. Six large, silvery barracuda, none less than four feet long, stood guard at the entrance. They eyeballed the divers and didn't seem predisposed to move anytime soon. They hovered, as they opened and closed their jaws, revealing needle-sharp teeth.

Terry checked the time, twenty minutes underwater, and her air supply—2,200 pounds of pressure, still plenty of air. She knew the other divers were experienced and should also have sufficient air remaining. But she jiggled her metal rattle to get their attention and held out her air gauge toward each diver, the signal to report your air supply. None had less than 2,000 pounds, about two-thirds remaining, so she was satisfied.

A shadow passed over her head. She looked up and saw Micko, heading straight for the barracuda school, waving his arms. They seemed startled that a strange-looking, bubble-blowing fish swam toward them, waving its fins. The largest barracuda, at least five feet long, sped away, followed by the other five. Micko motioned for Fulvio to proceed.

Fulvio gave him the OK sign and entered the cave. Ten feet inside, he turned on his dive light and was rewarded with an explosion of silvery-pink and copper color. His glassy sweepers were still here.

Dayle flipped on her light and followed next. Fulvio had stopped to enjoy watching his little fish and get his bearings, so Dayle's legs remained halfway outside the small cave, surrounded by the remaining three divers. Fulvio proceeded a little farther and pushed past the school but remained off the bottom in the event the moray eels waited at the back of the cave. The fish curtain parted, revealing that the eels were not at home.

He pressed on, allowing Dayle to fully enter the cave. His light reflected off the back wall and he started to back out, thinking he had reached a dead end. He saw Dayle behind him, motioning for him to go farther inside. Swimming along a slight curve in the cave wall, he moved ahead another several feet. That's when he saw what looked like a sliver of daylight.

Dayle bumped into his fins just as he turned off his dive light, making the dim daylight appear more prominent. He moved toward the light and let himself drift upward. He froze momentarily when his tank scraped the ceiling. Then he relaxed and exhaled a little extra air from his lungs to reduce his buoyancy to descend a few inches.

Clear of the ceiling, Fulvio continued ahead for several more feet. He realized why no one had ever found the cave. Unless someone pushed you from behind, the normal instinct was to turn around at what appeared to be a dead end.

Back at the cave opening, the other divers saw Dayle's fins disappear into the blackness. Micko followed her, and Joe motioned to Terry to enter next. She acknowledged, thinking Fulvio must be making forward progress since three people were now inside the cave.

The light was getting brighter and Fulvio let himself drift up a few more inches.

No ceiling! he thought, excitedly, as his scuba tank did not scrape against anything above him.

He played his light around and saw the narrow tunnel open wide into a strangely beautiful world of stalactites piercing the water from above and stalagmites rising from the bottom. He moved ahead several more feet and then let himself rise several inches. Suddenly he felt cool air around his head and when he looked up, his mask was above water.

He swam forward several more feet to give Dayle more room and then heard her bubbles breaking the surface. He advanced a few more feet and inflated his BC, letting himself float vertically in the water. He pulled off his mask just as Dayle surfaced next to him.

"Oh my God!" she exclaimed.

CHAPTER 41

Dayle looked above her. She saw they were inside a cavernous space, perhaps a hundred feet across. The rocky ceiling was shaped like a dome but not smooth. Hundreds of stalactites, many over several feet long, hung from the ceiling wherever they looked. Some pierced the surface of the water, descending to the floor of the cavern. She estimated the height of the dome was at least twenty feet over their heads. Several thin streams of daylight filtered through the porous limestone, providing a mystical ambiance. She was startled as several bats flitted above her head. A stream of bubbles erupted through the still water, and Micko surfaced next to her. He pulled off his mask.

"Wow!" It took several seconds for his eyes to adjust to the dim light. "This is amazing. Like another world."

"A world five hundred years ago," Dayle said. "Are Terry and Joe coming?"

"Right behind me."

Terry announced her arrival with an explosion of bubbles,

and Joe surfaced a few seconds later.

"Great navigation job, Fulvio," he said.

"Gracias, amigo," he replied. "This exceeded my expectations. Look!" He pointed to a horizontal stone slab. "What's on that table-shaped rock?"

"That's not a table, Fulvio. It looks more like an altar," Dayle said. The filtered sunlight reflected off a gold object in the middle of the altar. It was about one-foot high, including a tapered top, half as much in width, and had flat sides sculpted almost in a circle. The group finned closer to the slab.

Joe, taller than the rest, found solid ground first. "I can stand."

As everyone moved closer, they all found themselves able to walk. When they finally reached the stone slab, the water was only waist-deep.

He continued. "I bet this was dry ground 500 years ago. The top of the cave where we entered might have even been exposed when the water level dropped with storms and tides. And the wind streaming through the porous limestone ceiling must have created quite an eerie sound. This was definitely some kind of ceremonial altar. Look." He pointed to several bones scattered on top of the altar. "I can't tell if those are animal or human." As he reached to pick up one of the bones, Dayle grabbed his arm. "Wait! Let me take some photos first. This is an archeological site. Everything should be photographed in situ before we move anything." She opened her Pelican camera case and removed her camera.

She snapped some photos of the bones on the altar, several wider interior shots of the cavern, and then she photographed the golden urn. "And now let's examine that urn and see what's inside."

They stared at each other expectantly. Joe stepped forward but as he reached for the urn, his foot slipped.

"What the . . . something shifted under my feet." He put his mask back on and stared into the black water. "I can't see anything." He stood and unsnapped his dive light from a metal D-ring on his BC. He flipped the light on and ducked his head beneath the surface again. Then he knelt down and reached for the object he had disturbed, resting on the bottom. He stood and pulled off his mask, his eyes wide as if he had seen a ghost. "This wasn't just a ceremonial altar. This was also a sacrificial altar," he said, lifting up a human skull.

Everyone remained silent until Dayle spoke. "The altar of the Goddess Ixchel."

They all turned on their dive lights, put on their masks, dipped their heads below the surface, and played their lights along the submerged floor. Everywhere they looked, they saw human skulls and various bones from numerous individuals. A moment later they stood erect.

"Joe, can you put that skull down exactly where you found it so I can take photos of the area? This place is an under-water graveyard." After Dayle was finished photographing the bones, she surfaced and took a photo of the urn. "Now let's see what's inside."

Joe stepped forward gingerly, shuffling through the bones. He reached for the urn. "Uh . . . this thing is damn heavy. It must be solid gold." He braced himself and lifted the urn several inches, placing it near the edge of the altar. They all leaned closer to examine it.

"It almost looks like one of those incense holders we used for church services when I was a kid," Micko said.

Dayle looked at him with an inquisitive expression. He grinned. "Former altar boy. Irish Catholic."

Dayle took more photos and then Joe rotated the urn, looking for a latch or someplace where it would open. Finally, he found two interlocking pieces opposite a crude hinge. He forced the pieces gently, until they slid apart.

"Ready?" he asked the group, as they craned their necks.

He grasped the bottom of the urn with one hand and the tapered top with the other. At first nothing moved. Joe took a deep breath, applied more pressure, then a little more, and slowly the hinge, unmoved in over 500 years, yielded with a creak. He stopped and looked at the group. It seemed that they all had stopped breathing. He pulled the top back, revealing the contents of the urn.

CHAPTER 42

Dayle broke the silence first. "Blimey, it really is a globe!"
"It's beautiful," Terry said.
"Look at all the detail!" Fulvio remarked. "The oceans and the known continents of Columbus's time. You can see most of Europe, Africa, Asia, and part of South America. But where is North America? All I see are two small islands."

The globe sat in the urn so that the top two-thirds was exposed and the bottom third sat in the base, resting on the remains of some kind of cushioning material.

"Is that a seam where the equator would be?" Micko asked.

"Yes," Dayle said. "During my research, I read that in order to make the globe round and not egg-shaped, the artist took two similar sized eggs and cut them in half. Then, he only used the round halves, gluing them together to make a round globe, and discarded the rest. Let me take some photos." She took several shots as Joe rotated the urn. "Joe, if the globe is loose, can you lift it out carefully so I can photograph the rest?"

"I'll try." He touched the top and gently rocked the egg.

"It moves. I thought it might be stuck with all the moisture. I guess the urn protected it pretty well. I'm surprised that it survived all these years without decay." Using two hands, he held the sides and carefully lifted the globe as Dayle photographed the southern hemisphere and polar region. "It actually feels pretty sturdy."

"Well, the shell is much thicker than a chicken eggshell," Terry said. "Don't forget, it had to withstand the weight of an ostrich sitting on it. I've read that those birds can weigh over two hundred pounds."

They examined the egg, the gold urn, and the cavern for a few more minutes. "How about we take the globe and the urn and get out of here? I should notify the proper authorities so they can protect the cave and study it in more detail. This find will really put Cozumel on the map."

"I guess once the government knows about the globe, it will have to stay in Mexico," Dayle said, with a wistful air of resignation.

"I don't know, Dayle. That's not my call. But you'll get credit for the discovery. Think of the value of the publicity."

"Terry, before we leave I have a small favor to ask," said Fulvio. "Would you mind if I went first and took Dayle's camera? I'd like to snap a few photos of my glassy sweeper friends before we disturb them again. I just need about two or three minutes."

Terry laughed. "Okay, Fulvio, I think you've earned the right after navigating us into the cave. Okay with you if he borrows your camera, Dayle?"

"Sure mate," she said. "But before you leave, how about taking a group photo, and then a group selfie?"

"Glad to oblige," Fulvio replied. After he took several shots, he put on his dive mask, checked his regulator and dive light, and prepared to submerge.

Before he left, Terry asked everyone to check their air supply. "We have a good half-hour swim back to the boat. Do you all have at least half a tank of air left?"

Everyone checked their gauges and computers and nodded.

"Okay, if we're all good, then Fulvio, you go ahead. We'll give you a three-minute head start so you can play with your little fish friends."

"Gracias," he said as he sank back underwater.

Terry checked her dive watch and started timing him after the last of his bubbles disappeared. "Okay, let's make sure we have everything. Take a good look around. After this story breaks, we won't be getting back in here so easily."

"I'll carry the urn," Joe said. "This thing must weigh at least ten pounds. The globe must be worth millions, but this urn will bring a pretty penny, too."

"Wanna take off ten pounds of lead to compensate?" Terry asked him.

"Nah. I'll just add extra air to my BC."

She checked her watch. "Okay, Fulvio's had enough time. We're out of here. Let's go. Dayle first, then Micko, Joe, and me. Lights on."

They submerged and finned out of the cave, kicking slowly in order to avoid disturbing the bones that covered the underwater cave floor. Dayle noticed a flash up ahead, which meant Fulvio was still taking pictures, but by the time they reached the school of glassy sweepers, he was out of the cave. They swam single file through the thousands of tiny fish and soon found themselves outside the cave, where Fulvio waited for them.

Terry moved to the lead and they followed her back through the haloclines, thermoclines, and finally into clearer water. The current had picked up during their time inside the cave, and everyone had to work harder as they swam along the wall. Terry found the large cave, which had served as their landmark on the way in. Now it served as their reference point back to the boat. Terry stopped to make sure the group was still together. She inquired if everyone was in good shape, pointing to each diver and making the diver OK sign, and they all replied using the same sign. Then she checked her compass and headed out toward deeper water.

When she reached the area where she assumed the *Dorado* should be waiting, she sent up her yellow marker buoy. Then, she signaled the group to ascend to fifteen feet for their three-minute safety stop. After everyone indicated three minutes had elapsed on their dive computers, Terry gave the thumbs-up ascend sign and they surfaced together next to her marker buoy. They saw the *Dorado* drifting about a quarter mile away. Terry grabbed the marker buoy and waved it.

"What's Manuel doing? Sleeping?" she said. Finally, she saw the boat moving in a wide circle until the bow pointed in their direction. When the *Dorado* turned, she saw the fishing panga next to it, where it had been hidden on the far side so she didn't see it at first. As the *Dorado* made its way slowly toward them, the panga followed, keeping pace. The two boats were moored together.

Terry wondered why.

CHAPTER 43

When the boat reached the divers, they assembled on the side where the ascent ladder hung in the water. They hung onto a safety line that ran the length of the boat, waiting their turn to board. Dayle went up the ladder first and clambered aboard. She stumbled, trying to balance the weight of the tank on her back as the boat pitched. She wondered why Manuel wasn't helping, as he usually did.

"Hey mate, how about lending us a hand?" she said, reaching over the side as Joe, hanging on the safety line, handed her the urn.

Fulvio climbed the ladder next, and he heard Dayle exclaim, "Oh my God!"

He turned and saw where she was looking. Manuel was shackled to the helm, with just enough slack in the chain so he could both steer and reach the throttle.

"What the . . ." Fulvio said, just as Micko reached the top of the ladder. One of the floppy-hat Mexican fishermen emerged from the front cabin pointing a gun at Manuel. He pulled off his hat.

"Mike Handy!" Dayle screamed.

"Everybody up the ladder now! No games or the captain here gets a bullet in the brain." Fulvio helped Micko aboard, then Terry, and finally Joe.

"Everyone take a seat and don't move." Dayle sat, holding the urn in her lap. Handy smiled. "I think I know what's in the urn. I recognize it from the drawings we saw. Thanks, Dayle. Good job."

"How did you find us, you bloody bastard?" she spat.

"Don't be so harsh. After all, I did save your life a couple of times. I found a local fisherman down on his luck, so I retained his services. I've been keeping tabs on the *Dorado*. Didn't take a genius to figure out who you'd use to help search for the globe. When I saw Terry's boat stop in front of Chankanaab, I figured today was the big day." Then he saw Micko and aimed the gun at him. "I recognize everybody except you. Who the hell are you?"

"Detective Monahan, NYPD. You're under arrest for the murders of Matthew Jaslow, William Bennet, and Arturo Bavarro."

Handy staggered momentarily. "How the hell did you . . .? You're here to arrest *me*? In case you haven't noticed, *I've* got the gun, asshole."

"And the Mexican cops are looking to arrest you for the attempted murder of Greg Dietrich," Terry said.

"*Attempted* murder?" he asked.

"Yep. We got to him just in time. Greg's alive, and he identified you."

"I guess that investment won't pan out. Oh well. Win four, lose one."

"You can't wisecrack your way out of this one," Terry said. "Your options are running out. You'll never leave Cozumel, and you're the bad-news poster boy at all the airports."

"Who said I'm going back to Cozumel?"

"You'll never make it across the channel in that," Terry said, pointing to the panga.

"Then I guess I'll need a bigger boat." Handy chuckled. "Sometimes I crack myself up." Everyone just stared at him, and his mood turned dark. "Manuel, head across the channel toward the mainland but take a heading a little south of Playa del Carmen. About there." He indicated a southwest direction.

"What happens to us now?" Terry asked, trying to keep Handy talking and perhaps distract him so someone could jump him. She glanced at Joe, who knew what she was thinking.

"All kinds of accidents can happen to those flimsy pangas way out here in deep water, especially if they're overloaded with too many people."

"Are you counting on an accident to cover this up?" Joe replied, inching to the side so Handy would have trouble keeping everyone in sight simultaneously.

"No, I guess not. How many are you? Seven? I've got enough bullets."

"Seven? I count six," Terry said.

Handy nodded toward the fisherman steering the panga.

"Him too? You're gonna kill a poor fisherman who doesn't even know what he's mixed up in?"

"One Mexican more or less won't make much difference." He shrugged. "Maybe I can use him for chum."

Micko looked confused. He looked at Terry. "Chum? I've only seen nurse sharks around Cozumel. You don't chum for nurse sharks."

"Bull sharks hang out near Playa," she said.

Dayle leapt to her feet. "You cold hearted bast—"

Handy smacked her hard across her face. She fell to the pitching deck, stunned. Dayle staggered to her feet, and Micko helped her back to her seat. She pressed her hand against a bleeding lip. "So that's your big plan? Feed us to the bloody—"

"I've really had enough of your sharp Aussie tongue, Dayle. Now please shut up!"

It was the distraction Joe hoped for. He lunged for the gun, but Handy quickly sidestepped and clubbed him with the gun as he fell past. He aimed the gun at Terry, who had stepped forward, then back at Joe, sprawled on the deck holding his head. He looked around. "Let's have no more antics from anyone. The next hero is a dead hero."

Dayle glared at him. "You're lower than a piece of chewing gum on the bottom of my shoe."

Handy rolled his eyes. "Oh, Dayle, sometimes you're so dramatic." He scanned the water, noting they were halfway across the channel, where he knew the water went to more than 1,000 feet deep. "Well my friends, in a few more minutes I'm afraid we must part company."

Everyone remained silent, wondering how he planned to orchestrate a feeding frenzy once he sunk the panga and left them in the water. He estimated they were still in deep water, but not far from where dive operators conducted bull shark encounters for customers crazy enough to swim with an aggressive shark species that scientists discovered have more testosterone than great whites.

"Slow the boat, Manuel." Handy motioned to the panga driver to pull up alongside the *Dorado*. "Okay, one at a time, everyone into the panga."

They filed into the smaller boat. The panga driver appeared confused, not understanding why he had just taken on so many new passengers. Dayle was last in line. She rose, still holding the urn. Mike stopped her.

"Oh, I'll take that before you go. I've been shopping for buyers, anticipating you'd eventually find the globe. I have two private collectors who've already offered me five million dollars. Who knows how high they'll eventually bid? Maybe ten million?" Handy noticed a strange glimmer in her eyes.

"Sure, mate. Catch." Just as she wound up, Fulvio realized what she planned to do.

"No, Dayle!" he shouted.

Handy glanced from Dayle to Fulvio and back to Dayle. Before he could react, she tossed the heavy urn as hard as she could over his left shoulder, just out of his reach. He lunged, but holding the gun with his right hand, all he could do was tip it with his other hand. The urn splashed into the water and began sinking.

In that brief second, Handy's avarice took over. The only thought in his mind was saving more than five million dollars. He dived in after the urn, swam down fast, and grabbed it at about fifteen feet. Joe had resealed it as best he could in the cave, so it was slightly airtight and sank slowly despite its ten-pound weight. But it began to fill with water, sinking faster by the time he reached it.

Handy desperately clutched the urn in one arm, as he frantically tried to swim back to the surface with the other. He let the gun go but not the urn, now totally filled with water and more negatively buoyant. Its weight pulled him deeper, even as he kicked and clawed for the surface. By now his lungs burned for air, and as he looked up at the sun glowing through the water, he knew that's where he would find air. But he still refused to let the urn go.

Finally, he realized he had to release it and swim with both hands if he ever hoped to reach the surface. He dropped the urn and watched it plummet into the depths. Then he looked up and kicked as hard as he could, but his Mexican fisherman's clothes were now waterlogged and heavy. His efforts grew weaker. He was less than ten feet from the surface, but the reflex to breathe eventually overpowered the logic to keep his mouth closed, and he breathed in a mouthful of water. As his lungs filled with water, he began to sink again. The sunlight above dimmed, replaced by the bright light induced by an oxygen-starved brain.

Shit, I really fucked up, Handy thought, before he blacked out.

Terry saw he was drowning and dived in. She swam down and reached him at fifteen feet. She grabbed his outstretched arm and kicked for the surface. Her strong legs, conditioned by years of rescuing divers caught in Cozumel's strong currents, began to win the battle against Handy's negative buoyancy.

They broke the surface together. She gasped for air, then flipped his body over to keep his face out of the water and started rescue breathing. A few seconds later, Handy vomited seawater. Coughing and breathing hard, Terry grabbed the side of the panga, grateful for a short reprieve. She never noticed Handy, barely conscious, drifting toward the *Dorado's* stern, until she heard Joe shout.

"Mike, watch out! You're—" Joe jumped overboard and swam toward Handy, but before he could reach him, the current carried him into the *Dorado's* twin spinning propellers. The props fouled briefly as they cut through clothing, then sliced through flesh and bone.

Terry averted her eyes and clamped her hands over her ears as Handy's blood-curdling screams cut through the air.

"Oh, shit!" Joe shouted, shielding his eyes from a spray of blood. Then he heard Terry shout.

"Joe! Get back in the boat! Hurry!"

He turned toward the panga and saw three triangular dorsal fins approaching. Joe wrapped his arms across his chest, expecting razor-sharp teeth to tear into his body, but the fins passed by. They all watched the sharks converge on Handy and engage in a gruesome tug of war, turning the water from aquamarine to a bloody froth. The three bull sharks pulled the dismembered body farther out into the channel. Seconds later, snapping jaws pulled it under, and Mike Handy disappeared forever.

Everyone made their way back aboard the *Dorado*. Terry took a bolt cutter from her tool kit and cut the shackles holding Manuel to the helm. "Are you okay, Manuel?"

"Si, Terry. Gracias," he said, rubbing his bruised wrists.

"Good. Let's head for the marina, muy pronto! Joe, would you please cut the panga loose and let that poor fisherman go on his way? He doesn't know how lucky he is."

As the *Dorado*'s engines accelerated, Fulvio asked, "Terry, do you have GPS on board?"

"Yes, of course. Why?"

"So you can write down our coordinates, and perhaps we can come back later and try to locate the globe."

She suppressed a smile. "Well, I don't know, Fulvio. We're still pretty far out. The channel here is almost three thousand feet deep. That's way below recreational and even technical diver limits. It would probably take a deep-sea submersible craft to reach the bottom. Besides, the globe could never survive those crushing depths."

"Then that beautiful, priceless globe is really lost forever. Oh my God! At least five million dollars lost, not to mention the value of that solid gold urn." Fulvio held his head in his hands.

He heard Terry chuckle and looked up just as Micko suppressed a laugh. He saw Joe grinning, and then Dayle smiled, even with the pain of her swollen lip.

"What's so funny?"

Dayle reached beneath the seat and retrieved her Pelican case from her dive gear. She opened it, facing Fulvio. There sat the ostrich egg globe, intact.

He gasped. "How? Why? Who?"

Joe put his arm around Fulvio's shoulder. "After you left us in the cave and took Dayle's camera to shoot your finny buddies, Dayle suggested transferring the egg to her Pelican case assuming the urn wasn't pressure resistant or waterproof, which Mike found out the hard way it wasn't. Her idea made sense to us, so I took the empty urn and she carried the globe inside her Pelican case.

"The Mayans were able to bring the globe into the cave intact without protection five hundred years ago because the water in the cave wasn't as deep as it is now. Taking it out of the cave now required some kind of protection or the water pressure would have crushed it. We didn't deliberately plan on not telling you, we just didn't have the chance. But I'm sure glad we didn't. Your genuine reaction really sold it to Handy that the globe was still inside the urn."

Fulvio rolled his eyes, smiled, and shook his head.

CHAPTER 44

Dayle stayed in Cozumel with Terry and Joe for another two weeks, until the media craze died down. There were interviews, radio and television specials, and a special photo story in *The Portolan* magazine, which had started Dayle's quest for the globe in the first place. "Where are we going tonight?" she asked Terry.

"Since you're heading home to Roatan tomorrow, we thought everyone should get together for a post-treasure hunt dinner at Pancho's Backyard tonight. Micko and Bill are still in town. With their number one suspect dead, there's no need for them to rush back to New York, so they won't be leaving for a few more days. Fulvio is free, and Greg is feeling much better so he'll join us, too. We made the reservation for nine o'clock so no one needs to rush."

"I'm glad Greg's recovered enough to join us. It'll be good to see him again." She looked off and sighed. "As I expected, the Mexican government claimed the globe as a national treasure, especially since we found it on government property.

They were nice enough to grant me a modest stipend for my trouble. I did get some nice publicity for my art gallery on Roatan. And we did have one hell of an adventure, didn't we?"

"I'll drink to that," said Terry. "By the way, any word from Jeff?"

"No, not recently. He did email me that he was on his way home, but he'd be delayed. He didn't say why. That was a week ago. I really don't know what's ahead in our future."

"I hope you know that Joe and I are rooting for you two. I hate clichés, but as they say, love will always find a way. We sure hope you guys find your way together." She looked at Joe. He nodded his assent.

"Thanks, mates. Your support means a lot," Dayle said, her eyes tearing up. They all stood and hugged.

Terry pulled an envelope from her pocket and handed it to Dayle. "Oh. Before I forget, Jackie and Peter wanted to give this to you, but they had to leave early."

"For me? How sweet." She opened the flap and pulled out the card. "It's an invitation." She flipped the card open. "To a birthday party?"

"Remember you mentioned that you wanted to attend a sea turtle nest release? If we hurry, we can watch about one hundred baby sea turtles emerge from their nest. The kids arranged it with the Ecology Department of Cozumel."

"Oh, how wonderful. Let's go!"

They piled into Terry's Jeep and headed south, past Punta Sur and then north up the east side of the island. They pulled off the road at the turtle camp sign at San Martin, where Peter and Jackie waited with other volunteers.

"Hey, what kept you?" Peter asked.

"We were getting worried you might be late," said Jackie.

"Not a chance, Jackie. I wouldn't miss this for the world.

Thank you both so much for this wonderful surprise," Dayle said, hugging them.

"Follow us!" Peter said as he and Jackie got into the conservation society truck. "The release is at Chen Rio."

After a short ride along the coast, they pulled over to the roadside and walked across a bicycle path to the beach, where ten other turtle enthusiasts had gathered. Peter and Jackie staked out a path with ropes to prevent the spectators from interfering with the turtles' march to the sea. Turtle volunteer Patrick Crane, a transplant from London, greeted them and explained what was about to happen.

"Welcome to our sea turtle nest release. You're about to witness one of the most wonderful events of nature, as baby green sea turtles race from their nest into the sea. Beneath that stake in the ground, baby turtles are ready to leave their nest. Pantera, the volunteer over to my right, has devoted twenty-five years of his life to the turtles. We call him the boss of the turtles. He has the honor of uncovering the nest. Take as many photos as you want, but please no flash. The brightness might confuse the turtles, since their instinct is to move toward light."

Pantera scooped out the sand covering the nest. Soon he uncovered over a hundred turtle hatchlings, already squirming under the soft sand. Now freed, the baby turtles scrambled out of their buried nest and clambered over the sand, sea grass, and other obstacles, racing across the beach toward the bright foamy surf.

Dayle was amazed, watching the tiny turtles, each smaller than the palm of her hand, scamper toward the water. She remained transfixed as one last baby turtle finally made its way into the ocean, propelling itself with tiny flippers. She turned to Terry, tears in her eyes.

Terry hugged her. "You okay?"

She sighed. "I was just thinking about a baby."

Dayle watched the turtles disappear into the ocean. "I hope they all survive."

Patrick heard Dayle. "With so many predators out there, the odds are stacked against them, but some will." He smiled to reassure her.

Joe and Terry held hands, watching the turtles. He kissed her, then looked at his watch. "Let's head for Pancho's. My stomach's calling me."

Terry rolled her eyes and punched Joe's shoulder. "That's my man! Some things never change."

CHAPTER 45

Atlanta, Georgia
THE WINE BAR, HARTSFIELD INTERNATIONAL AIRPORT

Jeff Becker and his team were traveling in camo fatigues since the airline had misrouted their luggage on a previous connection. After clearing Immigration and Customs, they still had several hours to catch connecting flights on their way home from deployment. They wandered into the International Terminal Food Court and glanced at the choices. Instead of eating at the usual fast-food locations, they walked over to the circular wine bar, which looked more appealing, especially with pleasant piano music playing in the background.

The bar was crowded, but they found four empty stools together. The server, a pretty young woman with long dark hair, greeted them and handed out menus. Jeff saw that she wore two name tags, *Natasha Bailey* on one and *Tasha* on the other. They ordered drinks while they decided on food.

After looking through the menu several times, Jeff looked up and called Natasha over. "Tasha, I'll have the antipasto platter, please. And also another cabernet. That wine is really good."

g right up," Natasha replied with a smile. She saw
mpanions were still mulling over their choices and
e Jeff's order.

Donna Woods, the manager, watched the four men carefully. She noted the look in their eyes. These men weren't on
their way to hell; she knew they had just returned. She whispered something in Natasha's ear, and she nodded.

Donna walked over to the servicemen. "Good evening, gentlemen. Whatever you order, your money's no good here. It's all
on the house. Welcome home, and thank you for your service."

The men smiled and nodded. One soldier said, "Thank
you, ma'am, we really appreciate that." He glanced around
the food court and watched some people gulping down meals
at the fast-food outlets, while others rushed through the airport, clutching boarding passes, trying to find their departure
gates. "Your place here really is like an oasis in the desert."

"Thanks," Donna replied with a friendly smile.

A couple sitting across the bar from Jeff caught his eye.
Between sips of wine they talked, their lips almost touching,
and kept their eyes locked onto each other. He recognized
the look in the woman's eyes, and he knew she loved the man
intensely. It was the same look he saw in Dayle's eyes whenever
they were about to make love. He thought about how much he
missed her.

The couple kissed briefly and the man got up and walked
over to the piano player, Michael Boggioni. He leaned over
the piano and said something. Michael nodded and smiled.
The man placed a bill into the tip jar and returned to the
stool. Michael began to play a romantic Frank Sinatra ballad,
Strangers in the Night. As the notes drifted across the bar,
the couple clinked glasses and leaned into each other. The
woman whispered something and smiled, but Jeff noticed

tears glistening as they trickled down her cheeks. The man also tried to smile, but his eyes betrayed his sadness. Jeff realized they were two lovers departing to separate destinations. He felt their pain.

Boggioni's set was finished after the song. When Kathy Beers, the other regular pianist, arrived to relieve him, he decided to relax at the bar with a frothy cappuccino before going home for the evening.

Donna stepped over to the piano. "Kathy," Donna winked, "play something nice for us."

Kathy had observed the four men and assumed they were military but didn't know which branch of the service, so she began playing a medley of military anthems. When Kathy played *Anchors Aweigh,* the four Navy SEALS slipped off their stools and stood at attention, facing the piano. The hundred or so patrons in the adjoining food court outlets realized something special was happening and observed the four military men standing next to the piano. They stopped eating, stood, and applauded.

After Jeff and his team finished eating, they shook hands and hugged. They thanked Donna, Natasha, Kathy, and Michael, said their goodbyes, and wondered if they would ever see each other again. Then they stuffed several bills into the tip jar resting on the piano and headed off to find their separate flights home.

CHAPTER 46

Roatan, Honduras

*I*t sure feels good to get back home and underwater again, Dayle thought, leading the day's dive.

The dive group was composed of five divers, all with an advanced rating, so Dayle kept her supervision to the minimum, making sure no one wandered too far away or ran out of air. Other than that, she gave them their lead. They were diving the wreck of the *Anguila,* which she hadn't dived on since she was forced to stab the poor green moray eel that had mistaken a stupid diver's finger for a piece of food many months ago.

The dive was almost over, and Dayle had signaled the divers to assemble at the ascent line for their three-minute safety stop. Something beneath the wreck moved, and she decided to investigate. She peered under a slab of metal and saw the green moray. A scar at the corner of its mouth extended for several inches. Other than the healed wound, the eel appeared completely healthy. Dayle smiled so broadly that her mask leaked a few drops of water.

Oh, I'm so glad you survived!

She wanted to hug the eel but knew that would be pushing the limits of good judgement. She blew it a kiss and returned to the dive group. As they hung on to the ascent line during their safety stop, Dayle hoped seeing the eel again was a good omen.

When Dayle returned home, she began preparing lunch when the doorbell rang. She looked out the window and saw a DHL delivery truck parked in the driveway. She gave the driver a tip and examined the package. It was postmarked from Cozumel, and it weighed several pounds.

Intrigued, she took it into the kitchen and immediately opened it. The sturdy package resisted her attempts until she found an opening in the tape and cut it. White foam "popcorn-packing" material spilled all over the floor. She gasped when she finally opened the package. It was an engraved glass egg, a replica of the ostrich egg globe, perfect in every detail. She was stunned.

"Blimey, this must be worth thousands of dollars."

It was an exact replica, except for one detail. The initials GD and the date were etched on the bottom, in the empty south polar sea area of the globe. The sender had also enclosed a note:

Hello Dayle,

Hope this little surprise gift finds you doing well. I know how much you wanted a signature piece for your LaLa gallery. I hope my replica of the ostrich egg globe fills the bill. Thanks to you, the original now sits in the Museo de la Isla de Cozumel in downtown San Miguel.

The museum authorities granted me private access to the globe so I could copy it accurately. Of course, my engraved initials and the date will prevent anyone from trying to claim this egg is another old original. This was the least I could do after all you went through. I hope you enjoy it and it brings you much good luck.

Best wishes,
Greg

"What a wonderful, generous gesture," Dayle said, wiping a tear from her eye. "That Greg sure is a nice bloke." She brought the glass globe inside and carefully placed it back in the protective package.

She fixed herself a Scotch on the rocks and was answering emails when the doorbell rang again.

"Twice in one day? I must be getting popular."

A dark-blue, official-looking car was parked outside in the driveway. Apprehensive dread enveloped her as she opened the door. A tall man stood outside, wearing a U.S. Navy uniform.

"Jeff . . ." she heard herself say, hopefully. But it wasn't Jeff. *My mind is playing tricks on me.*

"Excuse me, ma'am? My name isn't Jeff."

"No, of course not. I'm sorry. I'm just . . ." her voice trailed off, afraid of what a stranger in uniform coming to the door might mean.

"Are you Mrs. Jeff Becker?"

"Yes, I am. But if you're looking for Jeff, he isn't home now."

He held what appeared to be a telegram in his hands. Dayle blinked, as her eyes teared. Her knees weakened, and she grasped the doorframe for support. She anticipated hearing the words, *The Navy regrets to inform you that . . .*

"I was hoping to catch Jeff at home, ma'am, but I guess he's been delayed en route. I wanted to leave this letter for him. I just need you to sign for it. Can you please see that he gets it?"

She exhaled. "Yes, yes, I will. Thank you."

He handed her a clipboard and pen. Dayle signed on the "received" line, but her hand trembled so much she didn't recognize her own signature. Like a robot, she handed the clipboard back to the tall, uniformed officer.

The officer handed her the envelope. "Thank you, ma'am. Good day."

Dayle was still too dazed to ask questions before the uniform left. She glanced at the letter, tempted to open it. It was not a Western Union telegram but sent from an official U.S. government agency. She slid a fingernail under the unsealed end flap, but then had second thoughts.

Since it was marked confidential, she decided to let Jeff open the letter. Still shaken, Dayle went back to her drink, drained the glass, and sat down at her desk. She placed the letter next to the computer and finished replying to personal emails and taking dive reservations. Then she went into the bedroom and tried to relax.

She picked up a novel she had recently started, a dive thriller titled *Dangerous Waters*. Dayle didn't recall drifting off to sleep until she heard the doorbell again. She shook her head thinking she was still dreaming, but then realized someone really did ring the doorbell.

She walked unsteadily to the door and opened it. A tall man dressed in camo fatigues stood in front of her. She blinked and his familiar face came into focus. "J . . . Jeff?" Instinctively, she reached out and gently touched the familiar scar on the side of his head. "Jeff!" Strong arms enfolded her and pulled her into a tight embrace. He kissed her fiercely on the lips. Dayle's intensity matched his and she kissed him back. Her fingers grasped his hair and she pulled him toward her.

"Oh, Jeff. I've missed you so much! I was afraid I'd never see you again."

"My only fear was the thought of living the rest of my life without you. I'll never leave you again. I promise."

Dayle drew back and looked at him again. She smiled, wiped a tear from his cheek, and then her own.

"Mind if I come in?" Jeff asked with a grin. "The neighbors might be watching."

Dayle laughed. "Come on in, stranger." She took his hand and led him inside. They hugged, and she was about to kiss him again when she saw the envelope on the desk. "Oh, this came for you just before you arrived." She handed Jeff the letter.

When he saw the return address, his body tensed: U.S. Department of State. He opened the envelope and read the contents silently.

"What is it?"

"Looks like I'm going back to Baghdad."

Dayle's eyes lost focus and she trembled. Her lips tried to formulate a question, but the words wouldn't come out. A photo and some forms were enclosed with the letter. He handed the photo to Dayle.

She looked at a young boy, she estimated about four years old, with curly brown hair and large brown eyes. The intense longing in his expression unsettled her. The boy's eyes, staring into the camera, were locked onto her eyes. "Who is he?"

"His name is Sharif. He's a war orphan. He's the reason I was delayed so long in getting home. I had to pull a lot of strings, file a ton of paperwork, and call in some overdue favors. But this letter says we finally got clearance to adopt him."

He stopped talking and waited for Dayle's reaction. There was none. "But only if you agree." Dayle still said nothing. Her expression remained noncommittal. Jeff continued with a stammer. "I . . . I thought this was a great chance for us to start living as a family. You know, like a real family. They sent some adoption papers here that we both need to sign." He fumbled with the envelope. "Then I can fly over to the U.S. Embassy in Baghdad and bring him home." Jeff didn't breathe during the silence that followed. "What do you think?"

Dayle shook her head. "No."

Jeff tried to speak. "But . . . I thought . . . I don't . . ."

Dayle stepped forward, put her arms around Jeff's neck, and pulled him close. Her lips brushed his ear. She whispered, "Mister, if you think I'm letting you go back over there by yourself, you're crazy. Let's go and bring Sharif home. Together. Like a real family."

ABOUT THE AUTHOR

Author Paul Mila explores a cenote near Tulum in the Mexican Yucatan.

Paul Mila has expanded his horizons from Brooklyn to Baja and beyond. In 2002, he traded in his corporate suit for a wetsuit and now devotes his time to writing, scuba diving, underwater photography, and speaking to groups about ocean conservation.

He has enjoyed photographing and diving with Caribbean reef sharks in the Bahamas, humpback whales in the Dominican Republic and Tonga, and a wide variety of sea life around the world, including his home waters of Long Island, New York, and his favorite dive location: Cozumel, Mexico. Diving in the same waters as the characters in his books enables Paul to write exciting, realistic dive adventures, and to accurately describe the beauty and wonder of our undersea world for nondiving readers.

Killer in Paradise is the fifth novel in his dive/adventure/thriller series. Paul has also co-authored *Bubbles Up*, a nonfiction collection of ocean adventures and sea creature encounters, with Judith Hemenway, and published the entertaining and informative children's book, *Harry Hawksbill Helps His Friends* through Best Publishing Company, www.bestpub.com.

Paul and his family reside in Carle Place, New York. When not diving, Paul writes thriller/adventure novels, teaches underwater photography at a local dive shop (Scuba Network), and coaches tennis. You can contact Paul via email at paul@paulmila.com, visit his website at www.milabooks.com, and check out his newsletter, *The Sea-gram*, at http://www.sea-gram.com.

AFTERWORD: Facts and Fiction

Most novels contain a degree of factual events. Here are the "Facts and Fiction" for *Killer in Paradise*.

Facts

The **ostrich egg globe** really does exist. It resides in the private collection of a Belgian map collector.

The Portolan is an actual magazine, published every quarter by the Washington Map Society. The magazine featured a story about the ostrich egg globe, Issue Number 87, Fall 2013. The photo from the magazine prominently shows South America on the globe. North America is depicted by the two small islands where Columbus originally landed above South America. The west coast of Africa is visible at the right edge of the photograph. Note the line near the equator, where the two halves or two eggs were glued together to make the globe round.

The actual ostrich egg globe.
Used with permission of **The Portolan** magazine.
© Washington Map Society
(Leigh@washmapsociety.org)

The copper **Hunt-Lenox Globe**, which many historians believe is a copy of the ostrich egg globe, also exists and is currently housed in the New York City Public Library. I've learned that some historians believe the Hunt-Lenox Globe is the older globe.

I purchased an ostrich egg on Amazon to determine the dimensions of the ostrich egg globe. I asked friend and local artist, Gail Sanderson, to recreate the globe using the pictures in *The Portolan* magazine.

Gail's finished product gave me a good visual of the globe and an understanding of what the characters in the book experienced when they saw and touched it. It is more egg-shaped than the actual globe because I did not buy two eggs and match up the rounder portions, as the original artist did.

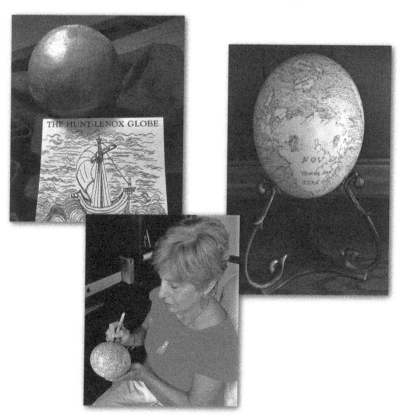

The LaLa Art Gallery & Garden Café
is located in Roatan, Honduras.

Layle Stanton and Charlie
at the LaLa Art Gallery and Café in Roatan

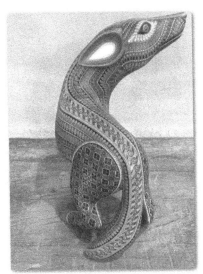

Alebrijes art at LaLa. Layle Stanton photo
Jacobo and Maria Angeles artists

The Wreck of the Aguila in Roatan is an easy wreck dive, resting at about 100 feet.

Chankanaab lagoon and dive site is located within the Natural Marine Park. You can dive through the caves leading from the sea into the lagoon.

Tetrodotoxin, the neurotoxin found in the blue-ringed octopus, is lethal and works as described in the story.

"Blue-ringed octopus Hapalochlaena fasciata"
by OpenCage.info is licensed under CC BY 2.0

Laura Wilkinson's *Cozumel 4 You* newsletter is a great way to keep up on Cozumel developments, just as Dayle found out in the story. You can subscribe at www.cozumel4you.com

Interaction between European explorers, including Columbus, and the Mayans did occur on several occasions. Columbus encountered a Mayan trading canoe near the Bay Islands in Honduras during his fourth voyage to the New World in 1502.

Real-Life Characters

Killer in Paradise is a fictional story, as are many of the characters. However, some characters are based on real-life Caribbean buddies, whom I have been lucky to meet and dive with, and who appear with their kind permission.

Michael Handy is very loosely (I hope!) based on Michael Handy, who really is a lawyer from Fort Worth, TX, and is also a fellow condo owner at the Residencias Reef. Mike has been begging me for a long time to make him, in his words, "a very bad guy" in one of my stories. *Hope I succeeded, Mike.*

Jeff "Scooby" Margolies and his wife, Jamie, dive together around the world. I have had the pleasure of diving with them and their three boys, Michael, Steven and Jason, in Bonaire and Cozumel, along with their friends Billy and Byng, and the rest of their *Diversified Divers* gang.

Jamie really is a mortician, and she provided the inspiration for how I would save Greg Dietrich's life in the story. Jeff, like Mike Handy, is also a lawyer.

Greg Dietrich is an accomplished artist and owns the Galería Azul Art Gallery in San Miguel, Cozumel, located at #449, 15th Avenue North, between 8th and 10th St. If you are ever in Cozumel, stop in and say "Hello." I am fortunate to own some of Greg's beautifully engraved glass pieces. You can view Greg's art at www.cozumelglassart.com

Greg Dietrich, completing another original masterpiece

Mike (Micko) Monahan is a retired NYPD officer and former private investigator. In addition to appearing in the book, Mike helped review police procedures for accuracy.

Mike is also a fiction author, having published his entertaining *Barracuda* series and most recently, *The Treasure of Hart Island.*

Visit Mike's Amazon Author Page: http://t.co/fxz3dEBdOZ

Fulvio Cuccurrulo (aka *Fulvio of the Deep*) is a Cozumel dive buddy. Fulvio also manages my Residencias Reef condo (where Dayle stays in the story) when he's not diving or hanging out with his glassy sweeper friends in a tiny cave on Punta Tunich Reef. This is Fulvio's

Fulvio inside the cave on Punta Tunich where thousands of glassy sweepers reside.

second appearance in one of my dive adventures, having also appeared in *Near Miss*.

Fiction

There is no Ghost of Chankanaab, as far as I know.

Only one ostrich egg globe was made, not two, and it was not destroyed in a fire as written in Chapter 9.

Fictional Characters

Most writers rely on their experiences and the people in their lives for inspiration and so do I. These fictional characters are based on friends and dive buddies:

- **Terry Hunter-Manetta** is based very loosely (more loosely with each book) on my friend Alison Dennis, owner/operator of *Scuba with Alison,* www.scubawithalison.com

- **Manuel** is based on Alison's boat captain, Carlos.

- **Joe Manetta** is loosely based on my friend and occasional dive buddy, Joe Troiano, whose legendary appetite for Italian food does rival Joe Manetta's.

- **Dayle Standish** is based on real-life Aussie, Layle Stanton, whom I met and dived with in Cozumel on Alison's boat. Layle currently resides in Roatan, Honduras. She owns LaLa Art Gallery and Garden Café in Roatan. Layle also appeared as Dayle in *Near Miss*. Visit her on Facebook at https://facebook.com/LALAGalleryandGardenCafe

ACKNOWLEDGMENTS

A heartfelt "thank you" to my test readers for patiently reading various versions of the manuscript. All of you made wonderful suggestions, which greatly improved the book:

> Michelle Beck, Alison Dennis, Terry Gallogly, Mike Handy, Thomas Hoover, Jamie and Jeff Margolies, Carol Mila, Mike Monahan, Karen Sunde, and Joe Troiano

Lorraine, Naomi, and Lorie. A special thank you to my editorial and design team for another incredible job of developmental editing and copyediting, creating a compelling and attractive cover layout, and designing a professional interior layout of the book.

The Portolan **magazine**, for permission to show the original ostrich egg globe.

New York Public Library Rare Books Division, for granting me access to study a copy of the Hunt-Lenox Globe.

The Wine Bar at Hartsfield Airport, Atlanta, Georgia. Thank you to the staff—Donna Woods, Natasha (Tasha) Bailey, Kathy Beers, and Michael Boggioni—for agreeing to appear in the book, and for making my lengthy layovers between Cozumel and New York not only bearable but enjoyable. The wine bar, located in International Terminal E, is truly an oasis in the desert.

Travelers enjoying a respite at the wine bar during their journey.